THE MYSTERIOUS DISAPPEARANCE OF MARSHA BODEN

ROSY GEE

ROMAREADS PUBLISHING

RomaReads Publishing

www.romareadspublishing.com

ROMAREADS
PUBLISHING

Paperback Edition 2024

ISBN 978-1-7384733-0-4

Cover Design by Ashley Santoro

Printed and Bound in Great Britain by Clays

For my beautiful daughter, Rachel,
who has been my inspiration,
not only with writing this book.
Diolch, cariad.

The Mysterious Disappearance of Marsha Boden

By

Rosy Gee

CHAPTER 1

MARSHA BODEN

L ittle Twichen is the kind of place where nothing much happens. A sleepy hamlet in Shropshire with an eclectic mix of residents. Some were born there, others migrated there, and some left, never to return. Others knew nothing else. Mary Flosworth had never been further than Greater Twichen, a few miles down the valley. She saw no need. Little Twichen had everything she could ever want from life.

Laburnum Lane is in the heart of the village and is as pretty as a picture in May. A magnificent specimen of the vibrant tree, after which it was named, laden with dripping golden chains, tops off the corner at Mill Street, where an equally stunning wisteria lights up the pretty junction. The lilac blooms regally adorn an ancient, picture-box house, aptly named Wisteria Cottage, its golden thatch settling over the black-and-white building like a thick, heavy, pie crust.

The village is a riot of colour at this time of the year. Copper Beeches are loud and proud sopranos, in sharp contrast to the altos and tenors of the yellows, vibrant limes, and velvety, rich dark greens. The baritones of the orchestrated colours of nature that the residents nurture and lovingly tend blast out, loud and proud. Snipped, primped, and pruned year in, year out, the competition is fierce with each villager jostling to become the proud owner of the prize of Best Gardener of the Year. It was an honourable title and the envy of most of the villagers, including Marsha Boden, a keen horticulturalist.

Marsha had slipped out to see Lloyd Peterson as soon as the coast was clear. Her husband had left for the day to attend to a funeral. Lloyd lived at Dovecote Manor and ran the Fletchingley Estate. He was known as Lloyd of the Manor, and even though an extremely wealthy tax exile living in Switzerland owned the estate, he was happy to leave Lloyd at the helm.

Walking her dog was a perfect cover and Marsha was careful to take a different route each time. She would slip in through the back door of the grand house, which was tucked away behind a group of straggly trees that acted as a perfect canopy for her deceit. Whenever she put on her walking shoes and reached for Jasper's lead, the Golden Retriever would magically appear, wagging his tail furiously, prancing around like a dressage horse practicing a complicated routine.

Lloyd was a gentle man and had been single for most of his adult life, having never found the right woman to settle down with. Marsha loved the way he would prepare for their liaisons by putting on her favourite music, surprising her by playing something from his Spotify playlist, after she had introduced him to the wonders of streaming music. She felt like a schoolgirl falling for one of the older, more mature boys, and her stomach had dozens of tiny butterflies fluttering around, making her feel giddy with excitement. Lloyd made her feel special. She felt safe with him and when they were together, it was as if nobody else existed. It was just the two of them in their own magical world.

Something else that she loved about him was his willingness to learn and adapt, even though one might have assumed that he would be fairly set in his ways. Perhaps the love of a good woman had brought out the best in him. She often used to wonder what else he would spend his vast wealth on. It was well known in the village that he was a rich bachelor, but because he kept himself to himself, most people had stopped speculating about how he enjoyed his wealth. Being an only child, he had no nephews or nieces, and although he occasionally kept in touch with his numerous cousins, they were hardly regular visitors to Dovecote Manor. In fact, Marsha couldn't remember the last time he had had a visitor, but she knew that he would have given them the shirt off his back if they had asked for it. Just as he would have given her anything she wanted. Absolutely anything.

'Hello!' she called out as she slipped Jasper's leash from his collar and hung it on the coat hook by the inner back door. She didn't wait for an answer but turned the ancient doorknob and pushed the heavy wooden door open, leaving Jasper to curl up on a comfy new bed on the porch, courtesy of Lloyd.

A Gregory Porter song was playing: 'Tell Laura It's Me.' Lloyd came through singing, 'Tell Marsha it's me.' He had a wicked glint in his eye and a broad smile lit up his handsome face as soon as he saw her. He cocooned her gently in his arms and they kissed in a long, passionate embrace.

'It's so good to see you' he whispered, 'I miss you.'

Marsha felt her body melt against his and had not felt this frisson of excitement in years. It was as if a burning desire had been rekindled and powerfully ignited deep within her.

'When are you going to tell that husband of yours that you're leaving him?' Lloyd asked, leading Marsha upstairs.

'I will tell him, I will.'

***

The thing about villages is that everybody knows everybody, and everything about them. When she had been a newcomer to Little Twichen, all those years ago, Marsha had learnt how to adapt. Or so she had thought. Once the round of dinner party invitations had dried up, locals wanting to get to know the newcomers, gleaning as much information about them as they possibly could, she sensed she was still an outsider, and probably always would be.

Being the wife of a Funeral Director came with its fair share of raised eyebrows. Guy was good at his job. Serious and compassionate, he dealt with bereaved people calmly and sympathetically, almost in a detached way, which Marsha thought he got just right.

A bookkeeper by trade, she had never really had to work, choosing to stay at home and raise their two children, but once the boys had left home, she took it up again, part-time, fitting in with what suited her. She had taken it up again out of boredom more than anything else. Apart from her love of gardening and the odd bit of volunteering work at the Village Hall, she had little else to fill her time. That's how she had first met Lloyd. He had been giving a talk about the history of Dovecote Manor, and then she had bumped into him again at one of the Open Garden events that the village held each summer. Another villager, Bert Humble, had introduced them, and Lloyd invited her to Dovecote Manor to show her around his walled garden. Each time she had visited, she learnt a little bit more about him. He was very erudite and kept the Manor in good order, and was always immaculately turned out. She felt herself being drawn to him.

Things at home hadn't been good for years but she carried on, thinking things would improve. But they never did. She recalled back in the early days how she resented having to go without holidays because Guy would never leave the business unattended. 'I told you before. Why would I want to spend my time with a bunch of dead people next door?" she remembered snapping at him, irritated by the repetitiveness of his questions about why she wouldn't help out more. 'You might feel comfortable surrounded by dead bodies but I am not!' Eventually, she and Guy had reached a point where they merely tolerated each other.

So, when Lloyd showed an interest in her, she felt as though she had been re-awakened. The sexual chemistry between them was incredible, and when she returned home from one of her trysts, it was difficult to disguise her sparkly eyes and lightness of step. She had to really concentrate on acting as though nothing out of the ordinary had happened, all the while re-living the amazing physical union she had just enjoyed. Guilt trickled through her at times and at others, it ran off her like droplets of rain from a waxed jacket. She had reached a time in her life when it was about time that she started putting herself first.

Nothing much did happen in Little Twichen, until the day Marsha Boden mysteriously disappeared.

CHAPTER 2

BERT HUMBLE

Bert Humble loved to chat with whoever would listen and rather fancied himself as a bit of a Monty Don, who, rumour had it, lived not far away. He would offer gardening advice to anyone who was happy to take it, usually when he was sitting on the wooden seat at the base of the old oak tree on the green. But even he was shocked into silence when he went into the village shop, one quiet morning in May.

'Sixty-five houses. It's all going ahead. No doubt about it,' Mr Tidmarsh announced from behind the old wooden counter.

'What?' A pint of milk in one hand and Gardeners' World tucked under his arm, Bert raised his other work-worn hand to his cloth cap and tipped it back, scratching his forehead in a distracted manner before dropping it gently back into place.

'I don't want no 'ousing estate in my back garden,' he said, gruffly, jerking his thumb up and over his shoulder in the general direction of Laburnum Lane. 'Your Billie's got a lot to answer for,' he told the shopkeeper tersely.

Mrs Tidmarsh came scuttling through, her beaky little bird-like face peeking around the corner. The passageway joined the house where she and Mr Tidmarsh had lived for over forty years.

'What's up?' she asked, her beady eyes darting back and forth. She wiped her tiny hands on her frilly, rose-patterned apron, the wonderful aroma of freshly baked cakes following her through into the main body of the shop.

'Bert's just 'eard that the development is definitely going ahead,' Mr. Tidmarsh told her in his lilting Shropshire accent. His large frame stood squarely behind the counter.

Mildred Tidmarsh went to stand next to her husband, as if in a show of solidarity. She knew that everybody was against the development. And their son, who was behind it.

The funereal silence was broken by the jolly tinkling of the shop doorbell when Guy Boden, the local Funeral Director, burst in.

'Has someone died?' he asked, looking around expectantly.

'No, but this village is gonna bloody die, that's for sure,' Bert announced. 'Another sixty-five 'ouses are going up there off Laburnum Lane. Bloody ridiculous. We don't need no more 'ouses in this village. Bloody ridiculous' he repeated, as if by saying it again made things any better.

'Oh. I am sorry to hear that,' Guy responded in his clipped Surrey accent, walking briskly the few steps to the counter. 'Can I have my paper, please?'

While Mr Tidmarsh rummaged around behind the counter, Guy pulled a handful of coins out of his corduroy trouser pocket.

'I know that my wife is dead against it, but people have got to live some-where,' he said, peering over the top of his silver-framed glasses. His voice was upbeat and neither Mr or Mrs Tidmarsh responded, but remained silent. You could have cut the atmosphere with a knife.

'That'll be seven pounds fifty, please.'

Mr Boden, after examining a raft of coins in his hand, decided he would pay by card instead and tapped the machine on Mr Tidmarsh's counter. 'Can I have a receipt please?'

After what seemed like an eternity, during which the glum silence hung in the air like a bad smell, the Funeral Director left with The Times gripped firmly under his arm, tucking the receipt into his wallet as he went.

Bert shook his head and tut-tutted under his breath, following Mr Boden out. Mr and Mrs Tidmarsh looked at each other. Their son, Billie, had done it again.

CHAPTER 3

MISS MOORCRAFT

Helena Moorcroft was the village gossip and a dried-up, shabby old spinster. She had cruelly been nick-named Whiskas by the school kids because of a thick growth of white hairs on her chin, and her habit of luring stray cats into her smelly house. She spotted Marsha walking her dog and made a beeline for her. She had nothing better to do and found that gossiping helped to pass the time.

'Hello, Marsha. Nice day.' Her walnut face stared at Marsha expectantly, her piercing blue eyes boring into her friend as if trying to extract some information.

'Yes, Helena,' Marsha responded, careful to pronounce it Hell-ay-nah after being admonished for the wrong pronunciation early on. 'It certainly is.' It was clear from Marsha's body language that she liked Miss Moorcroft, although sometimes, she found her rather trying.

Miss Moorcroft thought Marsha was one of the nicest people she had ever met and had a lot of time for her.

'Have you heard the latest gossip about the doctor and his wife?' Miss Moorcroft pressed on.

'No, but if you'll excuse me, I really must be getting on. I have a stack of things I need to do,' she said curtly, cutting Miss Moorcroft off in her prime, leaving the crestfallen spinster standing alone in the middle of the pavement, a disappointed look on her face.

Miss Moorcroft had never understood why Marsha never had time for village tittle-tattle. Perhaps it was because she was an outsider and generally gave the impression that she wasn't that bothered about what her neighbours got up to. But Miss Moorcroft recalled with glee that even Marsha Boden had enjoyed hearing about the wife-swapping episode in Upper Markle, although even Miss Moorcroft had her doubts about its authenticity. It seemed rather far-fetched to have a vicar's wife cavorting with a car salesman who then got involved in a threesome with the local barmaid. Apparently, the vicar was oblivious to his wife's antics and Miss Moorcroft often wondered why the person closest to the deviator, was the last to know. Continuing her journey down to Tidder's, she wondered why Marsha had been a little offhand with her today. It wasn't like her at all.

Bert Humble buttonholed Marsha almost as soon as she had escaped the clutches of Miss Moorcroft. He was bemoaning the proposed new housing development yet again, which he had just heard was definitely going ahead.

'We don't need no more 'ouses,' he grumbled loudly.

'None of us want another influx of outsiders, Bert, but people have got to live somewhere. Nobody likes change, me included. We did everything that we could to stop it. We did our best,' she said with a sigh. 'It just irks me that bloody Billie Tidmarsh is behind it all. He has no conscience that man.'

'Aye. He's a rum 'un. You've been great, though,' Bert told her, sincerely.

Marsha shrugged. 'Well, I'm sorry we couldn't stop the development going ahead, but we had a bloody good try, didn't we?'

'Aye. We did. All thanks to you and those meetings you arranged. All them letters you wrote to the Council. And that petition! Didn't do any good in the end though, but, like you said, we did our best.' Bert looked deflated, as if all the fight had gone out of him.

'Well, let's look on the bright side,' she said, trying to cheer Bert up.

'What side's that then?'

'We could have a lot more recruits for the gardening club.'

Bert gave a weak nod of his head and even managed half a smile. 'Aye. There is that, I suppose.'

CHAPTER 4

DR. AND MRS BURSFORD

Nigel and Kate Bursford's two boys, Robbie and Chase, were like two feral cats. Neighbours could hear them squabbling loudly in their back garden all the time. When the boys were arguing, Nigel or Kate's raised voices could be heard berating them.

'Robbie! What have we told you about hitting Chase? He's younger than you and not as strong as you, so be careful!' Their feeble attempts at parenting fell on deaf ears and it seemed that the more Robbie was admonished, the less he listened. Everybody knew that things were strained between the young couple. He was a busy GP and she was the Headteacher of the village school. Having two unruly boys was just another added pressure.

The thing with gossip is that it starts as an inane comment, and, a bit like Chinese whispers, eventually turns into a tale blown out of all proportion. In Nigel and Kate's case, the rumour that was flying around turned out to be true. Even Miss Moorcroft was flabbergasted when she heard the juicy tidbit.

When Kate turned up at the school, the young mums at the school gates were clustered closer together and tighter-knit than usual. They were a mix of mothers stuck in the benefits cycle from the small council estate off High Street, and the upper-class yummy mummies, who had their own little clique off to one side. Kate was walking stoically with her head held high, her boys clasping tightly, one onto each hand, a slightly flushed look on her face. The women stopped when they saw her and turned, one by one, as if daring her to do a walk of shame between them. They were whispering and nudging each other as she approached.

Kate was worried that Robbie and Chase sensed something was going on. Children could be very perceptive. A preamble to a playground fist-fight perhaps or a slanging match between the mums from the Council estate. She knew that Robbie had seen an argument once when he told her he had crouched behind the bike shed when hiding from Chase. She remembered having to get involved, separating the women, who were involved in a terrible catfight. It had all been very uncouth. She held her head high, looked straight ahead of her, and walked with her boys between the two groups of women.

Later that day, after school had finished, Kate received the same icy reception at Coppice Lane Surgery. She dropped the boys off leaving them in the capable hands of the Practice Manager. It was just until the end of afternoon surgery, when their father would take them home as they had agreed over breakfast that morning.

As soon as Kate got back in her car in the surgery car park, she called her Mum.

'Darling, what is it? You sound dreadful.'

'I don't know where to start'.

'Try at the beginning,' her mother encouraged, gently.

Kate told her mother that she was on her way to see them and would tell them everything when she got there.

Twenty minutes later, as she pulled into the driveway of Churchdene House in Ludlow, it felt like a different world. When she entered the grand house, a stunning flower arrangement in the hallway gave it an air of calm and serenity.

Her parents greeted her in the drawing room and looked at one another before looking expectantly back at their daughter. Kate laid her jacket on the arm of the sofa and sat down, her bag at her feet.

'What is it, Kate?' her father urged.

'Things between me and Nigel haven't been good for some time. You know about his...' Kate wasn't sure if her parents knew, but said it anyway. 'Drinking. He's hardly ever at home and when he is, he's usually drunk. It's not nice for the boys to see their father like that. Anyway. I met someone. We're very fond of each other,' she reflected.

Her parents looked at each other, worried looks etched on their faces. 'Well, as long as you're happy, that's all that matters,' her father said gently. 'I suspected things hadn't been good between you and Nigel for some time. I could see it in your eyes.'

'Would you like a cup of tea, dear?' her mother asked.

'I'd love one, thanks, Mum.'

Kate looked down into her lap where her hands were clasped firmly together. 'Things between me and Nigel have been awful, to be honest. His mood swings are getting worse and he's drinking more than ever. Zelda and I hit it off when we met at one of the quiz nights at The Sun, we became friends and one thing led to another. She's a very kind person.' Her voice softened the instant she spoke of the other woman.

Eventually, wringing her hands together, Kate's mother said in a small voice, 'What's going to happen to the boys?'

Kate sighed. 'I have no idea,' she said wearily. 'Nigel and I have got to sort something out between us. I don't know if I will be able to keep my job. The villagers might try to oust me out of the school when they hear about this. You know how small-minded people can be sometimes.'

Mrs. Bevan blanched at her daughter's words and Kate knew her Mum would never be able to look her W.I. friends in the face again. It was unthinkable. Her daughter was a lesbian and then possibly was being fired from her job as Headteacher of the village school. Kate knew that it was probably her mother's worst nightmare.

After they had all had tea and some of Mrs Bevan's homemade lemon drizzle cake, Kate got up, reluctant to leave. 'I'd best be off but I wanted to tell you in person. You know. Before the rumours hit town.' She shrugged herself into her jacket.

'Well, if there's anything you need. Or anything we can do to help. You know where we are. You only have to ask.'

Kate thanked her parents and hugged them both. On her drive back along the A49 to Little Twichen, she felt relief at having told them, and thought they had taken the news well. Craving a distraction, she clicked the radio on. The upbeat song of Whitney Houston's, 'I Wanna Dance with Somebody' blared out. She felt better for hearing the song and a fleeting frisson of excitement shot through her at the thought of starting a new life with Zelda. Even though she knew that there was a long, bumpy road ahead during which time she would have to shoehorn herself out from Nigel's melancholic lifestyle. She smiled when she remembered how she and Zelda had first met. It was in The Sun on a Tuesday, quiz night. She had gone along with Marsha, and Zelda had been on her own. They had asked her to join them and then Marsha had had to leave because she wasn't feeling well. As she thought back to that evening, Kate wondered if Marsha had sensed something and left on purpose. It was the kind of thing she would do.

Kate recalled the way Zelda brushed her arm against hers, or touched her hand when she whispered one of the answers in her ear. And how they had giggled. Like two schoolgirls. And how Kate felt as though she had known Zelda all her life, instead of just a few minutes. She was gentle and kind. Instead of being cross that her friend had let her down, jettisoning her in favour of a hot date with some guy on Tinder, she was philosophical. Pleased that her friend had a date. Her beautiful smile drew Kate in. Like a magnet. A burst of sunlight that warmed her through and through. She felt safe when she was with her, and sensed that Zelda would be there for her, no matter what. Her stomach flipped a quick somersault at the thought of being with her, and she couldn't wait to feel her softness against her. She got goosebumps at the very thought of it.

Jolting back to the present, she knew that Nigel would make things difficult for her. She knew he loathed not being in control, and felt a sense of relief at the thought of not having to put up with his heavy drinking, and terrible mood swings. When she told him about her relationship with Zelda, he had reacted very badly.

'Since when have I not been enough for you?' he had screamed. 'Well? And when did you decide you were a lesbian?' She recalled how she could smell his sour breath and feel his spittle on her face and turned away, disgusted.

He had shouted even louder. 'Don't you walk away from me when I'm talking to you! Do you hear me?'

'I'm not having this conversation, Nigel. Would you prefer it if I left you for another man? Is that it? Is it because your manhood is in question?' She knew she had touched a raw nerve and shuddered when she remembered the way Nigel's eyes had bulged in his head. She thought he was going to lunge at her. Kick her, or punch her, but instead, he turned away. Burying his head in the sand, just as he always did. Another drink would solve the problem.

Pulling her VW Golf into the driveway of The Granary, she wondered which husband would greet her. An angry drunk one or a sober, pleasant man. She felt bad about breaking up the family; the boys didn't deserve it, but she didn't deserve a life of misery as Nigel battled his demons.

Living with the roller coaster of emotions that she had to cope with, never knowing who was going to greet her at the start and end of each day, was extremely wearing. The long working hours and on-call rotas that Nigel constantly worked, meant that they hardly spent any time together anymore. Kate knew her husband was a good doctor, but they had had so many rows about his long hours. She used to beg him to put his family first, but he never did. Consequently, she felt as if the burden of parenting had fallen heavily on her shoulders. That's where Marsha had been a godsend. Picking up the boys from school and keeping an eye on them. She was wonderful and they had become good friends. Marsha was also a good listener.

When Nigel was at home, he preferred to find solace in a bottle rather than spending time with his wife. Kate was affronted by that and found it incredibly draining. The endless arguments. It was an emotional roller coaster that she was desperate to get off.

Locking her car with her key fob, she walked along the path to the side door passing the neatly tended borders along the way. They were full of vibrant plants and flowers that she had lovingly chosen and nurtured. A waft of scent floated up from the Nicotiana as she passed by. Opening the door into their smart new kitchen, she noticed an empty bottle of vodka on the granite worktop.

'Shit,' she thought wearily. 'The angry, feisty Nigel was at home tonight.'

CHAPTER 5

GUY BODEN

Boden's Funeral Directors is located at the end of High Street and strangely, is one of the first things you see when entering the village of Little Twichen. The frontage has changed several times over the years, with the most recent upgrade being in keeping with the ecologically friendly funerals that everybody seems to want these days. The gated entrance led into a golden pea gravel courtyard. A modern oak-framed timber house and matching buildings draws you into the tranquil setting. From wicker caskets to woodland burials, Guy Boden and his small team of staff were on hand to help guide families of those recently bereaved, through the maze of various funeral packages. Arranging a dignified send-off could be very expensive.

Coppice Lane Surgery was down and across from Boden's. When relatives called into the GP's Surgery for a death certificate, they had a short drive into Ludlow to register the death and then, in due course, they would meet with Guy or one of his team back at Boden's to go through the funeral packages. The wheels of local commerce were well-oiled. In turn, Boden's recommended the small and friendly firm of Barnett Walters Solicitors to deal with the estate of the deceased. Just as they, in turn, recommended Ashcroft Estate Agents to their clients for clearing out a property and putting it on the market for sale. That's how it worked in small communities; back-scratching at its best. A small but tight band of brothers ready and willing to help each other out whenever they were needed.

Today, Guy was attending a funeral in Upper Markle, a couple of villages away, for a twenty-two-year-old lad who had been killed in a hit-and-run accident. It was expected to be one of the biggest funerals in the area for some time. It was going to be a long afternoon. He always kept his mobile on silent when he was working and if Marsha needed to contact him, she would send him a WhatsApp, but there were no messages from her today. Just a couple of other messages that he would deal with later.

After the funeral, driving back along the narrow country lanes with his young side-kick, Bryan Jamison, he pulled over to let a gigantic tractor pass, but as he did so, a sprig of cow parsley got stuck in his nearside wing mirror. 'Bloody tractors,' he muttered.

Bryan was tapping away on his mobile with both thumbs. Guy Boden couldn't resist asking, 'Arranging a hot date, Bryan?' He was a good-looking young man and the type of lad that Guy would call a player. He had heard a couple of the ladies in the office talking about how he often had two or three girls on the go at the same time.

Bryan smiled and his handsome face lit up. 'You could say that, Mr Boden,' he said cheerily, and he continued texting.

'I might as well drop you off home now. We go right past your house, don't we? Pointless coming back to the office now.' He pulled over to let another tractor pass. 'Bloody tractors,' he muttered again.

'Er, yeah but what about my car?'

'Ah. Right. You'd better come back with me now then.'

Keen to have an early finish, Bryan said he would ride over on his bike and pick it up in the morning, being as it was a Saturday.

'Okay. Whatever suits you,' Guy said absent-mindedly, carefully nego-tiating a staggered junction. 'I'm off and out early tomorrow. I'm going fishing for the day in West Wales. But Marsha will be at home.'

'I didn't know you were a fisherman,' Bryan said, finally stowing his phone away in his inside jacket pocket.

'I find the peace and quiet very therapeutic. A friend of mine invited me ages ago but I've just never got round to taking him up on his offer. I thought it was about time that I had a day off.'

Guy liked Bryan and thought he had fitted in very well at Boden's. He seemed like a decent young man.

'Everything alright, Bryan? he asked. 'You've gone very quiet.'

'Yeah. Just thinkin' that's all,' Bryan said, chewing his thumbnail.

CHAPTER 6

MARSHA BODEN

Marsha noticed Lloyd's brand-new Range Rover parked outside Wisteria Cottage as she made her way along Laburnum Lane. She was a little preoccupied and thought nothing of it.

Mindful not to take the same route to Lloyd's each time she called in, she took detours for Jasper's walk. Sometimes, she took the circuitous route down High Street and up Laburnum Lane before turning off towards Dovecote Manor. Other times, she cut across the fields. On other occasions, she would cut through the woodland, which at this time of the year, was covered with a thick carpet of bluebells. Whichever route she took was just as beautiful. Jasper loved a good, long walk.

When Marsha reached Dovecote Manor, she was surprised to find the house empty and then remembered she had seen Lloyd's car in the village earlier, but hoped he would be back soon for their rendezvous. He must have some business to attend to, she thought. Running an estate was a tough job and no two days were the same, as she had learnt from listening to him. He told her that most people think it's an idyllic lifestyle, living in the countryside, surrounded by fluffy little animals with game birds running around everywhere. The reality was very different: long hours, physical hard work, lots of forward planning, and an unpredictable income that could fluctuate drastically from one year to the next. Whether it be due to the after-effects of the pandemic, or the war in Ukraine, which had impacted the price of stock and poultry feed, not to mention the skyrocketing of oil and diesel prices. Organising shoots in the shooting season and overseeing a clutch of farms, ensuring their profitability, wasn't easy, but Lloyd seemed to take it all in his stride and was, to her eyes, a very capable Estate Manager.

In Little Twichen hardly anybody locked their doors and so Marsha entered the manor through the back door, as she always did. She removed a coffee and walnut cake that she had made especially from her rucksack, and fished around for some plates in the bespoke kitchen cabinets, before popping the kettle on. She couldn't stay long; she wanted to get back before Guy returned from the young lad's funeral in Upper Markle. When she heard Lloyd's Range Rover pull up outside, her heart skipped a beat.

'Sorry I'm late darling. I had something I needed to do.' He placed his Fedora hat neatly on the peg next to the Aga and gave Marsha an enveloping bear hug, holding her close to him. She caught a waft of his expensive eau de cologne and relaxed into his warm embrace, revelling in his closeness.

'Is everything alright?' she asked, looking up into his rugged face.

Releasing her, Lloyd walked over to the window seat and shifted a stack of Country Life magazines, before lowering himself down onto the padded seat. Looking out across the beautiful Shropshire hills beyond he said, 'It was five years ago today that those two young girls died.'

Marsha remembered hearing the news in the village which went around like wildfire. Two teenage girls had been found dead in their tent on the hillside near Dovecote Manor. The girls had turned in for the night, taking the tray of barbecue coals inside the tent for the residual heat. The Coroner's Report recorded a verdict of accidental death. It confirmed that they had died from carbon monoxide poisoning. Marsha recalled thinking that she would have done the exact same thing, without realising that the consequences could be fatal.

'I have always let the odd passerby camp on the hillside but after that, I send people to the campsite on the edge of the village. The girls were local and I thought I was doing them a favour. When there was no sign of them by late morning, I went to investigate and that's when I found their bodies. It was terrible.'

Marsha's heart went out to him as he was clearly still deeply affected by the incident. She poured him a mug of tea and handed it to him with a slice of cake.

'I saw your car earlier, outside Wisteria Cottage.'

'Yes, one of the girls lived there and I call in occasionally to see how the family are doing. They don't blame me but the guilt is terrible. I still can't believe that it happened.'

'It wasn't your fault, Lloyd. You mustn't blame yourself.'

'I know, but...' He ate the cake and drank his tea in silence.

'Wasn't it tragic about that young lad over in Upper Markle?' she said, and then realised as soon as she had said it that it probably wasn't the best thing to say in the circumstances.

'Yes. I heard about that. I heard that it was a hit-and-run. Who would do such a thing?'

'Well, whoever it was doesn't have a conscience.'

Lloyd was deep in thought and continued to drink his tea in distracted silence, staring out of the window. Then he nodded. 'Whoever hit him must have known about it.'

'Yes, that's what I thought,' Marsha responded, sliding the remainder of the cake into a large plastic container she had found in the Welsh dresser.

'Listen. I wanted to talk to you about something.'

'What's up, love?' he asked.

'Well, I heard something in Ludlow recently. Did you know that Billie Tidmarsh is behind the new housing development? The company fronting it belongs to him.'

'No. I haven't heard anything. Isn't he a successful businessman? I'm not sure what your point is.'

Lloyd could see Marsha struggling with her inner self. 'Well, 'businessman' is rather stretching it. I heard that he's involved in all sorts of things.'

'Such as?'

'He has his fingers in a lot of different pies, if you get my drift. Everybody knows he's a wheeler dealer but what I heard was that he's recently got involved with something a lot more sinister.'

Lloyd stood up and placed his mug on the wooden farmhouse table. He took Marsha's hands in his. 'What do you mean?'

Marsha looked up at him. 'I don't want to say too much. Not yet, anyway. But he's up to no good, that's for sure.'

Lloyd looked concerned. 'Listen, when are you going to tell that husband of yours that you no longer want to be with him? I want you to move in here so that we can be together. All the time. I want to look after you, Marsha.'

'I will tell him. I promise. I just need to find the right time, that's all.'

Lloyd let her hands go and moved away. He leaned against the Aga. 'Don't you want to be with me?' he asked sternly, a furrow in his brow.

Marsha blanched. 'Of course I do! Don't get cross with me,' she pleaded, 'It's not that simple. What will people say? Don't you think it would be rather awkward if I moved out of Boden's Funeral Directors and straight into here? With you. The gossips would have a field day.'

'Who cares what people think? I don't. And you shouldn't either. Two people fell out of love and two people fell in love. It's as simple as that. I want to be with you, Marsha.'

'And what would I tell the boys? What will they think of me?

'You'll find a way. All I know is that I can't live without you, my darling. I want to spend every waking moment with you. Is that so terribly wrong?'

Marsha stepped away and picked up her bag. Then she turned to him, smiled, and said, 'Alright. I'll speak to Guy tonight. I promise.'

Lloyd's face lit up like a child on Christmas morning. 'Thank you.'

When she got home, Marsha felt heavy-hearted at the prospect of telling her husband of thirty-three years that she was leaving him. She knew it would be tough, and poured herself a large glass of wine, before making her way out into the back garden. As she curled up on the comfortable wicker furniture, she relished the peace and solitude. A blackbird, sitting on the branch of a nearby tree, broke into a beautiful, melodious song. A cacophony of chirping, warbling, and chirruping from other smaller garden birds suddenly joined in. Marsha realised that one of the things that she loved the most about living in Little Twichen, was the constant chatter of birdsong. Her friend Kate, who lived on High Street, often told her that as soon as she settled down for some quiet time in her garden, somebody would start mowing their lawn or begin strimming, and then as soon as they had finished, somebody else would start up a chainsaw.

Another sound that Marsha loved was the chiming of the church clock on the hour, every hour. Sometimes, she would count the chimes in the small hours when she lay awake if sleep eluded her. Sipping her wine distractedly, she was deep in thought. Finally, clicking her Paperwhite into life, she settled down with the next book in the Grace series by Peter James.

Although the last of the day's sun was pleasant and warmed her through, a shiver ran down her spine, and she just couldn't seem to settle.

CHAPTER 7

THE NEW HOUSING DEVELOPMENT

The Green Circle Housing Group had convened a meeting in the village hall to give the residents one last chance to get them on the side of the new estate. The young man who had been sent along held his own, and spoke with decorum. Considering he was on a hiding to nothing right from the start, he did well.

Marsha stood up to speak first. 'Is the attenuation pond big enough to cope with the run-off of water from the sloping site?' she asked, adding, authoritatively, 'The field where the proposed development is planned, floods every year, without fail.' She spoke eloquently and had obviously done her homework beforehand. But she had been doing this for a long time. Fighting on behalf of the villagers. She repeated what she had often told Parish Council members in the past. Little Twichen doesn't need another housing development. She was adamant that the site was unsuitable and that if the Council insisted on building more houses, they should find a site on the periphery of the village. Not slap bang in the middle, ruining a beauty spot, not to mention the irreversible damage to the ecology on the proposed site. As a keen botanist, she had been concerned that the destruction of the grassland habitat could restrict and isolate colonies of species, especially the endangered bee orchid.

The young man fielding the questions fired at him from the crowd assured her that the Engineering Contractors had carried out their calculations and the plans had been passed by Shropshire Council, so, in other words, it was a done deal. Despite all the questions raised by members of the public, and the Parish Council, it was a fait accompli.

Most of those present accepted the inevitable because the arguments for and against the development had been rumbling on for five long years, but Bert Humble was having none of it. He was angry that Billie Tidmarsh could build a housing estate right in the heart of Little Twichen, all in the name of money making. He leapt up and began waving his arms around in a windmill fashion, animatedly shouting, 'We don't want you here! Do you hear us? Take your bloody 'ouses and build them somewhere else because we're not going to let you spoil our village!' He was jerking around like a child's puppet on a string, his arms flailing around wildly. Eventually, he managed to calm down as he felt dozens of pairs of eyes staring at him.

The ballsy young official, seated at the table at the head of the hall, stood up and directed his reply at Bert, 'As Shropshire Council have already passed the plans, building work will begin in the next two weeks.'

'Well, we'll bloody well see about that!' Bert shouted, waving his fists around, before plonking himself down into his chair with a thud, like a petulant child.

The seated crowd was shaking their heads in disbelief. There were ways of getting your point across and the outburst by Bert Humble was not the way to go about it. Tim, a young engineer on the Parish Council, had spoken clearly and calmly and asked for reassurances on certain issues, like street lighting, and whether the houses would have chimneys. His intelligent and well-rehearsed cross-examination of the developer's fall guy had far more of an impact than any outburst from a disgruntled villager.

The residents of Little Twichen had every right to be opposed to the development. Not only were they getting sixty-five more houses, along with all the associated mess, noise, and disruption related to their construction, such as heavy lorries thundering back and forth in a constant stream, but the infrastructure of the village was also expected to absorb all the extra people and the extra vehicles. The developers wanted to build a housing estate in the heart of their village, and that's what they were going to do.

After the meeting, everybody peeled off in different directions, and Bert was left to lick his wounds as he found himself walking home alone, Marsha having beetled off ahead.

'That was very brave of you, Bert,' Miss Moorcroft remarked, having been at the meeting and witnessed his outburst. She had made a beeline for him when she saw him leave, catching him up. She linked her arm through his and suddenly, he didn't feel quite so bad.

CHAPTER 8

KATE BURSFORD

When Nigel and Kate converted the cavernous old barn into a tasteful family home, they created a cosy snug off the lounge-kitchen-diner, which was over thirty meters in length. It had floor-to-ceiling bi-folding doors along its entire length. Overlooking the field where the proposed development was planned, the luxurious room made a big statement, but it was not in the least bit cosy.

Kate dropped her expensive handbag on one of the smart bar stools around the island in the snazzy kitchen at the top end of the enormous room.

'Nigel. Where are you?'

'Through here. In the snug.'

'Are the boys in bed?' she asked when she reached the small sitting room, where Nigel was slumped in his usual chair by the window, looking particularly glum.

'No, I took them to Mum and Dad's. We need to talk.'

Kate sat down opposite him on their navy blue velvet settee and kicked off her shoes. 'Yes, we need to talk,' she responded wearily. 'We've been through this so many times. Your drinking and mood swings have affected how I feel about you. You must know that.' She tried to keep her voice calm but the hysteria was building inside her.

Nigel looked as though he had been punched in the stomach. 'Is that why you're leaving me or is it because you want to be with that woman?' He spat the last few words out with disdain. 'Be honest, Kate.' He glared at her, leaning forward, resting his forearms on his knees, clutching a drink in his right hand.

'It hasn't been easy. I thought when we moved here things would get better, but you seem to be working longer hours than ever. Your drinking is getting worse. We drifted apart a long time ago. I guess I was open to another relationship forming and it just happened.' Kate looked down in a resigned fashion.

'Well how else do you think we could afford to do this place up?' he asked. 'Not to mention when you decided that the kitchen wasn't to your liking and insisted on having it ripped out and replaced with another one, which looks exactly the bloody same to me. Have you any idea how much everything costs? No, I don't suppose you do, because you only think about you and what you want.'

'That's not fair!' Kate retaliated. 'I work hard too. And who do you think looks after the boys? Not you because you're never here and when you are, you're in here drinking yourself into a bloody stupor.'

Nigel didn't respond but glugged down a couple of large mouthfuls from his glass, which Kate knew contained a potent cocktail of vodka with a splash of tonic. The ice cubes tinkled as he placed it back on the side table next to him.

'Look, we've reached the end of the road. I don't love you anymore,' Kate said, letting out a huge sigh. 'I'm sorry.' She could see the impact that her words were having on her husband and watched as his shoulders drooped even further.

'Kick a man while he's down, why don't you?' he spat back angrily.

'You're always down, Nigel! It's the bloody booze. When are you going to realise that it's the root of all our problems? It's destroyed us.'

Nigel's face crumpled in on itself as the realisation of what Kate was saying hit him like a sledgehammer. Tears began to well up in his eyes, then spilled over and ran down his cheeks. 'Don't leave me, Kate,' he begged. 'Please. Don't go' he pleaded between great, heaving sobs.

'I can't keep doing this Nigel.' She placed her head in her hands in a resigned manner. Then she looked up and said, 'I've made up my mind. How many times have we had this conversation before? And each time you promise to change. But you never do. I'm going to stay with my parents for a few days. I'll take the boys with me.' She stood up to leave the room. Nigel looked bereft and was staring at her as she left with a sad, puppy dog expression on his face.

Kate went upstairs and ran a hot bath, relieved to get the talk out of the way. Tomorrow, she would ring her solicitor to make an appointment. The call that would begin the process of ending her marriage.

Following a fitful night, Kate wasn't in the least surprised to discover that the space next to her was empty. Nigel had probably passed out in the snug. It wouldn't be the first time he had spent the night asleep in his chair. She had a heavy heart, but a positive outlook. At least Nigel hadn't lashed out at her, which he had done in the past. She wouldn't be sorry not to have to keep living a lie and could start to move on with her life. She knew there was a lot to sort out and that it wouldn't be easy, but she had her parents and friends around her for support. Marsha was her biggest advocate and promised that she would do everything she could to help. She had been wonderful, listening to Kate rambling on, airing her worries and concerns.

Raising Roman blinds and drawing curtains on her way downstairs, letting the glorious spring sunshine flood into their beautiful home, she hoped that she and Nigel could come to an arrangement about the house.

She loved The Granary and had it just the way she wanted it. It would be a shame to leave it and she would do her best to stay, not only for her own sake, but it would be consistency for the boys. It would give them stability, which was what they would need during the period of separation.

When Kate saw Nigel slumped in the chair in the snug, she thought how sad it was. That he preferred to sleep in a chair rather than next to her. When she saw an empty container of pills by his side and a half-empty bottle of vodka on the floor next to him, she panicked.

'Nigel! Wake up! Nigel!' She shook him really hard but he didn't respond.

'Nigel! Wake up!' she shouted, pinching his face.

'God, no. Nigel! What have you done?' She felt for a pulse. Nothing. Then she instinctively knew by the pallor of his skin that he was dead. Her first thought was for the boys. Even though she had fallen out of love with her husband, she felt terrible that the man she had once loved so deeply, had decided to end his life.

'Christ', she thought, 'What have I done?' The boys could come back any minute and she didn't know who to call first, her parents-in-law, the surgery, or the emergency services.

Frozen to the spot, she couldn't take her eyes off her dead husband slumped in the chair in front of her.

Chapter 9

Marsha and Guy

As soon as Marsha heard her husband's car pull up outside, she switched off her Kindle and went indoors. She had been distracted and wasn't able to concentrate on 'Want You Dead', despite normally devouring the books with intense pleasure. She had had to re-read several pages before the words had sunk in.

She had promised Lloyd that she would speak to her husband tonight, and that was what she was going to do, even though she was dreading it.

She could see Guy busy out in the garden. His fishing rod was leaning up against the shed, near the door. He would probably be out there for ages, she thought despondently, and so decided to pour herself another glass of wine for some Dutch courage. She had made a salmon and asparagus filo pastry pie which they would have with a salad she had prepared earlier. She wasn't hungry but knew that Guy would want to eat. He was a stickler for having 'proper meals' as he called them, homemade from scratch, and he insisted on eating at the dining table, although she much preferred to eat at the small table in the kitchen. Everything he seemed to say or do lately, irritated her. Tonight, she decided, they would eat in the kitchen whether he liked it or not, and as she set about laying the table, she couldn't help thinking that tonight might be their last supper.

She knew that Guy would take the news of her leaving him badly. He would miss having her around. She had been a good wife. Always on hand to cook, clean, wash, and iron his clothes, and she was a good homemaker. It wasn't until she had met Lloyd, that she realised her marriage was in pretty bad shape. The lust and excitement of their former years had long fizzled, like a damp firework, and they had grown apart, merely going through the motions of being husband and wife.

Eventually, when Guy had finished faffing about collecting all his fishing gear together and loading it into the back of his car, he came in, washed his hands, and immediately asked what was for supper. 'I'm starving,' he said, rinsing his hands under the hot tap and then drying them on the hand towel hanging over the rail on the Aga.

Marsha was very quiet and decided to tackle the tricky subject after their meal.

'How was the funeral?' she asked, genuinely concerned for the young lad's family.

'Oh, you know. Sudden deaths are always more difficult for families to come to terms with'.

Marsha nodded in agreement as she put the pie and salad on the table. They both helped themselves. Guy piled his plate high but she only took a miniscule portion.

'There was a huge crowd there from the Young Farmers,' Guy said, pouring himself a glass of wine, not offering any to Marsha. 'I overheard some of them talking and apparently some of the lads were discussing forming a group to try and find out who the driver of the car was. I just hope they don't turn into vigilantes and take the law into their own hands.'

'Oh, that would be awful. But whoever did it must have known that they hit somebody.'

'You would have thought so,' Guy said, shovelling some salad into his mouth. 'I mean, you would know all about it. Remember when I hit that pheasant and had to have the whole front grille of my car replaced?'

Marsha nodded. 'Yes, I remember it well. I dealt with the insurance company. It was a nightmare.'

As soon as the plates were cleared away, she broached the subject, having tried to formulate some words in her head while eating, but couldn't seem to find the right ones.

'We need to talk,' she said finally, putting both hands on the table and looking directly at her husband sitting opposite.

'Oh, don't go on at me, just because I'm taking a day off to go fishing.'

'No,' she said wearily, 'It's not that.' She could see that he was blissfully unaware of the bombshell she was about to drop.

'Well, what is it then?'

'I can't do this anymore.'

'Do what?' he asked quizzically.

Marsha stood up. 'I'm leaving you. I can't do this anymore,' she said waving her arms about. 'Cooking, cleaning, washing, ironing. Being Mrs. Invisible while you go about running your thriving business without a care in the world. When was the last time you noticed me, Guy, I mean actually noticed me?'

Guy was looking at her in utter disbelief. He adjusted his glasses on his face and was about to speak but Marsha carried on ranting.

'And when was the last time we had a holiday? A breakaway, together? Probably not since the boys came with us and that was bloody years ago.' Suddenly, all the pent-up anger and frustration that Marsha had been feeling for the last few years surfaced. She was babbling, as if she couldn't get the words out quick enough. 'I'm going to pack my things and go away for a few days.'

'What do you mean, go away? Where to?'

'I'm going away. From here. From you. Walking out of this marriage. There, I've said it.' She took a slug of her wine and cradled the glass in both hands.

'Well, you might want to end this marriage. But I don't,' he said gloomily. His voice softened. 'I don't want you to leave. Please don't go. Sit down. Let's talk about this.'

'It's too late for that. My mind is made up. I'm leaving in the morning. When you come back, I'll be gone.'

'Just like that? I don't get a second chance? For Chrissakes, Marsha!'

Marsha placed her glass on the table and wanted the ground to swallow her up. She wished she could time-travel forward and be with Lloyd in his kitchen at Dovecote Manor, instead of here with Guy. But life wasn't that simple.

'I've met somebody,' she said bravely. There. It was out now. And she didn't care what he thought or what anybody else thought for that matter. She recalled her conversation earlier with Lloyd and realised that he was right. It really didn't matter what people thought. What mattered was her happiness. She had to start thinking about herself and stop putting other people first.

'What? You've been having an affair? Behind my back? Who is it? Tell me, who is it? I'll bloody well kill him!' He was shouting. Marsha flinched. She had never seen him so angry.

'I'm not going to tell you. It's none of your business.'

'It bloody well is my business! If another man has been sleeping with my wife, then it is well and truly my business!' Guy's face was getting redder and blotchier. Suddenly, he picked up his wine glass and hurled it across the room. It shattered loudly against the wall sending shards of glass in every direction.

Marsha ducked, then flinched before scuttling through to the sitting room, sidestepping pieces of glass.

'Don't you walk away from me when I'm talking to you!' Guy shouted, and he ran after her, grabbing her by the wrist as she tried to go upstairs.

'Ow! You're hurting me. Let go!'

'Not until you tell me who it is.' He tried to force her to sit at the bureau. 'Now you're going to write a letter to whoever it is. Tell him that it's over and you have decided to stay with me.'

'I'll do no such thing!'

Suddenly, Guy grabbed Marsha around the throat with both hands and started to throttle her.

She couldn't breathe and fought desperately as his grip tightened. She was gasping for air and shot an elbow back sharply into his ribs, forcing him to let go.

'I'm warning you. If you don't stay with me, your life won't be worth living,' he growled, glaring at her.

Marsha didn't recognise the man in front of her. He had turned into a monster, so she pulled out the chair from underneath the bureau, sat down, and began to write. Her hands were shaking as he stood menacingly over her.

'Now, put it in an envelope, write the name and address on it, lock it in the drawer and we won't talk about this ever again. Do you hear me?' Guy was unsure why he made his wife do this, but in the heat of the moment, he wanted her to feel remorse.

Marsha nodded and did exactly as he said.

'Now, give me the key and that's the last we'll say about the matter. You're clearly not yourself. You need to make an appointment to see the doctor tomorrow, do you hear me?'

Marsha nodded, thinking how patronising he sounded, but fearing for her safety and not wanting to set him off again, she tried to speak. 'Can I...can I,' her throat still felt constricted. 'Go to bed. Please?' she croaked, holding both hands to her throat trying to soothe it. She desperately wanted to get away from him.

'There's no need to be scared, love. Give me your phone and we can talk about this in the morning. Sort it all out. You're not yourself. Now, go on up to bed and I'll sleep down here. Just in case you were thinking of sneaking off in the middle of the night.' His eyes were glinting and his jaw was still pulsating with anger. He smiled at her. An evil smile.

Reluctantly, Marsha handed over her phone and went upstairs, immediately grabbing the handset out of the cradle on the bedside table, but the phone was dead.

'Shit,' she thought. Guy must have unplugged the phone downstairs so that she couldn't use it. She sat on the edge of the bed feeling alone. And very frightened. She wondered how things could ever have come to this.

Chapter 10

Bryan Jamison

Young and impressionable, Bryan Jamison had fancied Marsha Boden since his first day at work, when he had watched her playing with her dog. Her long, silvery blonde hair was tousled and slightly unkempt, but that added to her charm. She had a sylph-like figure, but with curves in all the right places, and was always well turned out. She usually wore jeans or corduroy trousers and what his mother would call 'sensible' shoes. Funky trainers or smart Skechers. She looked great in a checked shirt, which she usually left open and wore over a white tee shirt. She had beautiful teeth and lovely sparkly eyes, bluey-grey-green in colour. Not that he had ever looked into them, but he saw her laughing once with Lloyd of the Manor and thought she looked so carefree and happy. She was a beautiful woman in every sense of the word. He couldn't help thinking how lucky Mr Boden was, sleeping next to her every night. He used to fantasise about what it would be like to fuck her.

Bryan had never had a problem with finding women, in fact, quite the opposite. Women seemed to throw themselves at him. He was quite fond of his current girlfriend, Lucy, who was very keen on him. She worked in Boots in Ludlow as an assistant on the till, but had told him that she wanted to become an estate agent. One day, she assured him, she would run her own estate agency business. He liked her ballsy attitude. She was also great in the sack.

Cycling along the back roads from Lower Markle to Boden's the following Saturday morning, wearing jeans and a dark hoodie, he was hoping to find Marsha alone. He knew Mr Boden had gone fishing for the day. Swerving to avoid a particularly deep pot-hole in the road, he thought about the offer that Billie had made to him over a pint recently. He'd said it was driving goods around and the pay was three times his salary at Boden's. And Billie had told him that there would be a few bungs, or cash in hand if he did the job well because the hours were long and unsociable. Bryan had always admired Billie. Ever since they had been at school together. Billie was a lot older than him, but had always been the cool guy that the younger kids looked up to. Bryan was excited at the prospect of finally getting to work for him, having pestered him in the past. But Billie had always told him that he wasn't ready. The job offer felt like validation that he was now worthy of being in the same league as him. He felt bad about leaving Boden's but would tell Mr Boden next week. There was no rush. Billie had told him that the driving job wasn't regular hours, so with any luck, he could do a bit of moonlighting before he handed in his notice.

When he reached Boden's, he was relieved to see how quiet it was. Dismounting from his bike, he wheeled it across the gravel courtyard to his car and clicked it open. He fed the bike into the back of the small hatchback, but it wouldn't go all the way in, even with the back seats down. He went in search of some string and found some in the back room behind the office. The shelves were littered with paraphernalia associated with burying the dead: embalming fluid, drainage tubes, hairbrushes, lowering straps, sheets of tarpaulin, blocks of oasis, a top hat, and a myriad of other odds and ends, including the ball of green twine. He cut a length off with a penknife that he always carried.

After he had finished tying the back of his car down to secure it, he looked up and saw Mrs Boden in an upstairs window of the house.

'Hi Mrs B,' he called out as he entered the kitchen, 'It's only me!'

'Oh, come in Bryan! I'll be down in a minute,' Marsha called out.

Bryan was tempted to go up and find her, but he noticed a small white envelope propped up against a vase of pink tiger lilies on the table. It had Marsha's name on it. It wasn't sealed. He picked it up, slid the flap open, pulled out the note inside, and started to read.

My darling, Marsha. Please forgive me. My outburst last night was completely out of character, as you well know. Let's go away somewhere, anywhere, you choose. Spend some time together. It's what we need. I will do anything to get our marriage back on track. Please my darling, give me a chance. G x

'Well, well,' he thought. 'So Mr and Mrs Boden were having marital problems. Interesting.' Naughty thoughts started formulating inside his head and he felt his manhood hardening at the thought of fucking her.

Quickly, he shoved the note back where he had found it when he heard Mrs B approaching.

'Morning Bryan. How are you today?' Marsha appeared looking distracted. Bryan thought she looked pale and seemed to have lost her sparkle. He noticed she was wearing a scarf wrapped tightly around her neck, despite the warm weather.

'Morning, Mrs. B. How are we today?' He quipped, giving her a long, lascivious look, undressing her with his eyes.

Marsha smiled wanly and looked as though she had something on her mind. 'I'm okay, thanks. Time for a quick coffee?' she asked.

'Yeah, thanks. Did Mr B get away alright on his fishing trip?' he asked, looking around furtively.

'Yes. Yes, he did. He was up at the crack of dawn and away. I don't suppose I'll see him again today. He loves his fishing. It does him good to get away.' She put the kettle on. 'Did you see Jasper outside?'

'No.'

'Oh, that's odd. I could have sworn I let him out earlier. How did that young lad's funeral go yesterday?' she asked, busying herself with making the drinks.

'It was really sad,' he replied, his handsome face taking on a serious look.

A delicious aroma of freshly brewed coffee suddenly filled the homely kitchen.

'The church was packed out. His parents put on a brave face but his three sisters were in a terrible state.'

Marsha stopped what she was doing to listen to Bryan, who was leaning nonchalantly against a small bookcase.

'I can't imagine what it must be like to lose a child. In such tragic circumstances. Did you hear anything more about how it happened?'

'All I heard was that he was walking home from the pub, after a few pints too many, and was found in the ditch the next day by a dog walker. There are no lights along that stretch of road. Whoever ran into him must have realised what they'd done, but they just left him for dead.'

'Oh, that's terrible,' Marsha said, her face contorted with anguish. She turned away and carried on preparing the drinks.

Bryan shifted his weight from one foot to the other as he looked across at Marsha, admiring every contour of her body as she reached up into the cupboard for some mugs. While she was waiting for the coffee to percolate, Marsha excused herself and went into the sitting room next door, which Bryan thought was a bit odd. He could hear drawers opening and closing.

'Everything alright, Mrs B?' he called.

'Yes. Yes. I'm just looking for something.' She reappeared looking preoccupied and carried on preparing the drinks. 'Milk, two sugars?'

'Yeah, thanks.'

Eventually, she placed two steaming mugs of coffee on the table. Marsha's head suddenly snapped to the letter, clearly noticing that it had been moved.

'Do sit down, Bryan,' she said uneasily. 'You're making me feel uncomfortable.'

CHAPTER 11

LLOYD PETERSON

Lloyd Peterson wasn't unduly concerned at first. It was early afternoon and Marsha still hadn't answered any of his calls. She had sent him an e-mail first thing that morning. She had said that Guy had taken the news of her leaving him very badly. He had confiscated her phone and had gone out for the day fishing. She had also mentioned that he had grabbed her by the throat. She told him she would pack a few things and would be over as soon as she could.

Instinctively, Lloyd wanted to go and collect her and had immediately responded, saying just that, but she was having none of it. She didn't want any trouble and asked him to stay away.

Reluctantly, Lloyd decided to drive into Ludlow to do some shopping. He wanted to cook them both a special meal that evening to celebrate moving in together. Besides, he needed the distraction. By late afternoon, with still no sign of Marsha, he could stand it no longer. He jumped into his Range Rover and headed straight to Boden's. There was nobody around. He could see Marsha's car parked next to the house. He went to the back door and knocked but there was no reply. He tried the door. It was open.

'Marsha!' he called. Feeling very uncomfortable being in the home that his lover shared with her husband, he was conscious of the fact that Guy could return at any minute. He noticed Jasper's bed in the corner of the kitchen, but there was no sign of the dog. He went from room to room downstairs but there was no sign of anybody. Everything seemed normal. He called out for her upstairs, 'Marsha?' Apprehensively, he decided to venture up the stairs, feeling uneasy. On the landing, he was unsure which room to go into first. The bathroom door was open so he started there. Nothing. He looked in all of the bedrooms, one at a time, and a whistle-stop tour revealed nothing out of the ordinary, and no Marsha. He had a thought that he might have missed her on his way over. He had driven through the village but Marsha might have taken the back roads to his place. That's it, he thought. Their paths must have crossed and she was probably sitting up at the manor wondering where he was. But then he remembered that he had seen her car outside, so she must be close by. Then he realized. She had probably taken Jasper for a walk. He couldn't see the dog anywhere. That was it. She must be out walking the dog.

He had one last look around outside and then decided to head back home. He was completely puzzled. He tried her mobile again, but it went straight to voicemail.

CHAPTER 12

GUY BODEN

Two days later

'When was the last time you saw your wife, Mr. Boden?' the police officer asked in a clipped, official-sounding tone of voice. Sitting at the kitchen table of his home, opposite the policeman, Guy Boden had his head in his hands.

'I've already told you, officer' he replied impatiently. 'Friday evening. We had had words but everything was fine and then I left early on the Saturday morning for my fishing trip.'

'And you didn't see her before you left?

'No. I didn't want to disturb her.'

'And what time did you return?'

Blowing air out from his puffed-up cheeks and rubbing his hair, Guy Boden said, 'About eight-thirty, I think. Marsha wasn't here so I assumed she was out for the evening. I watched TV and must have dozed off in the chair. Things weren't great between us,' he said wearily. She often gets talking to folk in the village. She's always helping somebody or other out. She's a very kind person.'

'Such as?' the officer interjected.

'Oh, I don't know. Erm, Kate. The doctor's wife'. He stopped to think for a moment. 'She and Kate are good friends. Sometimes she babysits her two boys or picks them up from school, if Kate's working on. They like going to quiz nights at The Sun. Or sometimes, she'll call round for a drink. You know. Girlie nights in.' He mimicked the last few words as if he could never understand the concept of two women chatting over a glass of wine. 'I think Kate was going through a difficult time at home, because Marsha was spending more and more time round there.'

'Where is "there"?' the officer asked.

'The Granary. On High Street.'

The policeman jotted something down in his notebook.

'Anyone else she helps out?'

'Yes, she does some volunteer work at the village hall. Serves lunches to the elderly folk who meet there once a week. She also helps anybody who can get some of her time to help out in their gardens. She's a keen horticulturist.'

'And does she work, Mr Boden?'

'Yes, but only part-time. She's a bookkeeper. Self-employed. She works for several businesses in Ludlow. She mentioned something about some antiques business, and seemed concerned about something, but wouldn't talk about it.'

'Do you have a name?'

He hesitated before saying, 'Billie Tidmarsh.'

Again, the officer jotted something down. 'So, where do you think she is?'

Guy Boden looked vague. 'I don't know. I already told you. We'd had words and I thought she might have gone to stay with her sister for a few days without telling me.'

'Has she done that before, sir?'

'Yes. She sometimes takes off for a few days. Says she 'needs some space.' She was behaving a bit odd lately, come to think of it. She was very distant towards me.'

'And you telephoned your sister-in-law, did you sir?'

'Of course, I bloody well did,' Guy half-shouted, exasperated.

'What did she say?' the officer interjected. 'And I'll need her number.'

'She hasn't seen her. They last spoke a couple of weeks ago and she said Marsha sounded fine.'

The officer made more notes in his notebook.

'What was your wife wearing the last time you saw her, sir?'

Guy Boden looked completely blank. 'I can't remember,' he said flatly. 'Anyway. I told you. I left early on Saturday morning and I didn't see her when I left. She was still in bed as far as I know. I slept downstairs because I had an early start. I didn't want to disturb her.'

'Is there anything else you can tell me, anything out of the ordinary, any clue as to where your wife might be?'

Guy thought for a moment. 'Yes,' he said slowly, his brow furrowed. 'There were some dog treats on the floor near Jasper's basket. Marsha bought them ages ago but he didn't like them. I put them in the bin.'

'Could you fish one out for me, sir? I would like to get it analysed. Just in case somebody tried to poison your dog.'

Guy got up slowly as he was trying to process what the officer had just told him. Rummaging around in the bin he eventually found what he was looking for. He handed an innocent-looking dog biscuit to the police officer, who asked him to drop it into a plastic evidence bag he was holding out in front of him.

'And your dog, Mr Boden. He was here when you got back?'

'Yes, he was in his basket. He was very quiet and subdued though. Not his usual self. He looked very dirty as well.'

'One last question. Do you have CCTV?'

Guy looked at him wide-eyed. 'No. There's no need. Nothing much ever happens around here.'

'Well, not until your wife goes missing,' the officer said sardonically. 'You will let me know if you remember anything else, won't you?' he said, handing him a card with his contact details on it. He closed his notebook. As he did so, he had a look on his face that clearly conveyed the fact that he did not completely believe the man who was sitting in front of him.

CHAPTER 13

THE INVESTIGATION

'Right. Listen up, everyone! Here's what we've got so far.' Detective Inspector Clive Daniels was heading up the team to investigate the disappearance of a fifty-six-year-old woman from Little Twichen.

'We believe Guy Boden might have been one of the last people to see his wife.' He pointed to a photograph on a whiteboard next to Marsha's. 'He didn't report her missing until two days later, on Monday 30th May. We received a call two days before from a very anxious Lloyd Peterson. We also have a witness who saw the couple's dog, a Golden Retriever, up at Dovecote Manor, which is where Lloyd Peterson lives, on Saturday, around midday. Also, the young lad who works at Boden's, Bryan Jamison, told us that he called in to have a coffee with Mrs Boden when he collected his bike on Saturday morning.'

A ripple of murmurs went around the room of the small team of officers deployed to work on the investigation team.

'When questioned, Guy Boden said he and his wife had had a row and he thought she had gone away for a few days because...' He referred to his notebook. '...she needed some space.' DI Daniels looked around the room expectantly. 'He wouldn't say what they argued about but I think it's fair to say that they were going through a rough patch in their marriage. We have it on good authority, in fact, straight from the horse's mouth, that Marsha Boden and Lloyd Peterson, the Estate Manager at Dovecote Manor, were having an affair. They were planning on setting up home together. They had managed to keep a lid on things by all accounts, as it wasn't common knowledge around the village. Mr Boden did not divulge this information to us, but I think that he and his wife may have argued about the affair, and the fact that she was going to leave him. We don't know if he was aware of the identity of his wife's lover. Anyway, he mentioned a note he said he had written and left on the kitchen table. Nothing was found when we searched the property. He told us that he had begged her to stay, to try and rekindle their marriage.'

A few nodding heads accompanied another ripple of murmurs around the room. 'Guy Boden also mentioned that his wife was very distant towards him and had been behaving oddly. Damien, I want you to speak to her GP. See if she was taking any medication. Or had any health issues.'

'Right, OK sir,' Damien replied. He was sitting with one leg crossed over his other knee.

'Della, I want you to visit Mrs Boden's family. Take Leila with you. Find out what you can about Marsha Boden. Talk to her sons and see what you can piece together about why she would just up and leave without telling anybody.'

'Sir.' Della was never one to waste words.

'Everybody else, I want you to carry out a door-to-door in Little Twichen.' Another ripple of mutterings. 'Mrs Boden was a bookkeeper and her husband mentioned something about a business in Ludlow, and he gave us a name. Billie Tidmarsh. Follow up any leads. Go with your gut instincts.' DI Daniels patrolled the room. 'I'm going to organise a search of the village and surrounding areas, but that could take some time.'

'Sir?' Damien volunteered. 'What about Mrs Boden's mobile phone? Does that give us any clues as to her whereabouts?'

'Lloyd Peterson said he received an e-mail from her at 07.33 on Saturday morning. She told him that her husband had confiscated her phone the night before, following their argument. The landlines weren't working in the house or the office. She must have one of those gadgets you can get to connect to the internet. My wife has one because sometimes, in remote places, the internet isn't great. Always needs to be in touch with the kids.' He paused and then went on. 'Anyway, Mrs Boden intimated that her husband had disconnected the landline. Let's get her phone records and see what we can find out. Also, check her laptop, and let's get that e-mail to see exactly what she said.'

DI Daniels continued. 'She also mentioned that her husband had taken the news of her leaving him very badly, and had grabbed her by the throat. Of course, she could have just jumped in her car and headed over to Dovecote Manor first thing, but apparently, she told Mr Peterson that she was packing a few of her things together first.' He looked around the room at his team and then went on. 'We questioned all the staff at Boden's. Mrs Ann Jones, the Office Manager, told us that she saw Bryan's car on the drive on Saturday morning when she was on her way into Ludlow, which ties in with his story of him collecting his bike. When we questioned staff in her husband's butcher's shop, they corroborated her statement. Apparently, her husband was away for the weekend. Visiting family in Wales. So she had to man the business. It seems she's a bit of a stickler for detail. We also discovered that she and the cleaning lady at Boden's don't get on at all. In fact, we think they hate each other's guts. According to what the other staff members have told us, they are often heard coming to blows or having a slanging match.

DI Daniels' face clouded over and he carried on briefing his team. 'Now, it could be that everything got a bit too much and Marsha Boden decided to take her own life. Let's keep an open mind on her disappearance. I think we should also get a search of the stretch of river organised where Guy Boden went on his fishing trip. Or,' and his demeanor lightened, 'It could be that she went for a walk and fell and hurt herself. Or has gone away for a few days to think things over. Those last two scenarios are not very likely as we know that she didn't have her mobile phone with her, but if she was suffering from any health issues, that could have a bearing on things. Also, let's get somebody looking at all of her social media accounts, her bank accounts, etc, and see if we can piece together her last movements. From what we know so far, she was a very kind person who gave her time freely, always happy to help people in whatever way she could. It seems that she was very popular in the village. So let's try and find out what happened to her.'

CHAPTER 14

PLATINUM JUBILEE CELEBRATIONS

Red, white, and blue bunting fluttered in the breeze across the narrow lanes and streets around the hamlet of Little Twichen, giving it a wonderful patriotic feel. The Queen's Platinum Jubilee weekend promised to be a community extravaganza. There was a treasure hunt, a film show in the Village Hall, and a special service in the church. Street parties had been organised on Laburnum Lane and Mill Street. The Swan was hosting a garden party. Some villagers had formed their own satellite committee to organise a river party, which promised to be both fun and a health and safety nightmare.

Royalists through and through, Mr. and Mrs. Tidmarsh spear-headed the organisation of the street parties. Their shop was on High Street and juggernauts regularly thundered past at an alarming rate. There was no way they could even think about closing off the main artery through Little Twichen. Instead, they would join the Laburnum Lane party as they once owned a cute little terraced cottage there, Chestnut Bough. All in all, the celebrations promised to be a right royal affair. They were going to do Her Majesty proud.

Events kicked off with a tug-o-war on the village green, with crowds of young farmers descending from the villages all around. They were keen to show off their prowess to the crowd, including a group of pretty young girls who had gathered especially to watch.

The Treasure Hunt, organised by The History Society, proved to be challenging for some, with some people complaining about the difficulty of some of the clues. Overall, though, it was a good turnout and a good community spirit prevailed.

A live band set up on a small stage in the beer garden of The Sun Inn on Saturday afternoon. There was a hog roast, which smelt divine. It went down a treat with the revellers, who tucked into the soft white baps stuffed with warm, melt-in-the-mouth pork and a dollop of apple sauce. The large, sprawling garden was full of a cross-section of the community, ranging from toddlers to octogenarians. Several dogs, some on leads and others roaming around mainly sniffing out leftover scraps of meat or bread, basked in all the adulation they received. The sun came out, adding to the party atmosphere, with most of the crowd singing along to the words of the songs that the band belted out. Eventually, Caz, a spirited older hippy lady, got up and led the swaying, rhythmic dancing late into the night, others joining in enthusiastically the longer the beer flowed.

The televised party at Buckingham Palace was well received. A big screen was erected on the village green at the last minute, due to the fine weather. It was a wonderful opportunity for the village to come together and watch, as the fantastic array of acts performing along the Mall, kicked off the Jubilee celebrations. The patriotism was palpable and as the evening wore on, many of the older folk raised their glasses to Her Majesty, Queen Elizabeth II, who had dedicated her life to her country, the commonwealth, and its collective citizens. The younger members of the community were only interested in enjoying the party atmosphere. The general consensus among them being that there was no point to the Royal family. They thought the money could be better spent elsewhere. Their cynicism saddened the older generation, whose deep respect and admiration of Her Majesty, spanned many decades.

Two days of celebrations were rounded off on Sunday 5th June, by a jubilant peal of the church bells, which could be heard right around the village.

It was just over a week since Marsha Boden had gone missing.

CHAPTER 15

MISS MOORCRAFT

Miss Moorcroft was driving back from her weekly trip to Ludlow library and was deep in thought. She was shocked when she overheard some patients gossiping in the waiting room at Coppice Lane surgery while collecting her medication. The place was buzzing with the devastating news of the doctor's suicide. She wondered what was so bad that he had decided to take his own life.

As she headed up High Street in her Morris Minor Traveller, she spotted several police vans parked outside The Swan. Without checking her rear-view mirror or indicating, she swung a right into Mill Street so that she could try and see what was going on. Weaving her way precariously around parked cars, as if negotiating a giant obstacle course, she became so engrossed in not hitting anything, peering studiously over the top of the thin, black steering wheel, that she forgot all about why she had come this way in the first place. Turning left up Laburnum Lane and nearing the top of the street, she indicated to take the sharp left onto Snickets Lane and back down onto High Street. Her detour had gained her nothing but sweaty armpits and the need for a strong cup of tea. Miss Moorcroft had never enjoyed the pleasures of power steering or power-assisted anything on her car. She couldn't be doing with all those fandango, modern gizmos, and lurched into a conveniently large space just down from her cottage. She was very territorial about the parking outside 15 High Street. Spotting

Mrs Jones, the butcher's wife, who was walking down the street talking to a policewoman, she quickly clambered out of her pride and joy, almost forgetting to put the handbrake on in her haste.

'Mrs Jones!' she called out in her thin, reedy voice, striding away from her car. She was wearing a tweed skirt, a tatty old green cardigan buttoned up to the top, stout walking shoes, thick brown stockings, and a headscarf, much like the Queen wore.

'Mrs Jones!' she called out again, still with no response. The butcher's wife was deep in conversation with a policewoman and carried on walking away from her. Miss Moorcroft practically broke into a sprint to catch them up, but they were fast fading out of view as they neared the end of the street. Miffed that she had been ignored, because she was convinced that Mrs Jones must have heard her, she decided against catching them up and reluctantly turned back. She would see if she could rendezvous with them on Snickets Lane instead. Then she had a horrible feeling. She realised that she hadn't seen Marsha for a few days, which was odd because she invariably walked her dog every day. If she had gone away, her friend would have told her. She grabbed her purse and carefully picked up the large, lidded wicker basket from the front seat of her car. She headed off briskly, making sure to keep the basket steady. The first person she bumped into was Bert Humble, which was a very pleasant surprise.

'Hello, Bert,' she said jovially. 'How are things?'

'It's bloody ridiculous,' he said, ignoring her greeting. 'Have you seen the size of the pot-holes on Laburnum Lane?' he exclaimed indignantly, making an imaginary gap between his arthritic hands, like a fisherman describing the size of his catch. 'Bloody enormous! But this tiny lane is perfectly smooth. I wonder if it's because a certain Councillor lives here?' he said sarcastically.

They had both stopped in the middle of the narrow, newly tarmacadamed road, which Bert used as a cut-through from Laburnum Lane to High Street on his way to Tidder's. The Lane was lined with pretty thatched cottages and a converted Wesleyan Chapel, all with neatly tended gardens, which were a riot of beautiful summer blooms.

'You don't need to tell me, Miss Moorcroft responded in her posh, plummy voice, 'I thought my teeth were going to fall out the other day when I hit one, not to mention the damage it must have done to my car.' Kitty's head popped up comically from under one of the flaps of the wicker basket as if to say, 'You didn't tell me about that!' and then disappeared again.

'Have you seen the police vans outside The Swan?' Miss Moorcroft asked anxiously. 'And did you see Mrs Jones talking to a policeman?'

'No. No, I didn't. What do you think's going on?'

'I don't know, but I'm going to find out. Have you seen Marsha lately?

Bert twiddled his handlebar moustache between his thumb and forefinger, his brow furrowed. 'No. Come to think of it, I haven't,' he said, his face clouding over.

'Anyway, I'm glad I've bumped into you,' Miss Moorcroft said, forever the opportunist. 'I'm having trouble with my ride-on mower. Is there any chance you could pop round and have a look at it for me?' She knew she had put Bert on the spot, which was her wont to do with most people. A loud buzzing sound could be heard as several bees foraged around in some lavender nearby.

'Aye, go on then,' he said, mulling it over. 'I'll pop round tomorrow, if that suits ya,' he said in his thick Shropshire accent. He smiled at her warmly because after she had been his ally following the meeting at the village hall, Bert had warmed to Miss Moorcroft.

She was clearly delighted with his response. 'Oh, marvellous! I'll make sure I've got something nice for you. As a treat. A thank you. Oh, and before I forget.' She turned her attention to the basket she was carrying. 'Here are those library books you asked me to pick up for you.' She lifted one of the flaps on the basket and scooted Kitty over, who was curled up on the books, and handed them over to Bert. A cloud of cat hairs fluttered away on the breeze. 'You'll have to come with me the next time,' she said, smiling, feeling buoyed up by the way things were going between her and Bert. She turned on her heel with a spring in her step and headed back home, forgetting all about her quest to find out what the police were doing in Little Twichen. She was keen to make Bert feel welcome when he called round to fix her mower. She had a new mission now and was happy to have something to fill her long, solitary days.

As soon as she got back to her cottage, she went into the hallway and called Marsha but there was no reply. Then she called the doctor's wife. 'Kate, how are you?'

There was an awkward silence. 'Oh, you know, Miss Moorcroft. I'm still in shock, to be honest with you.'

'Yes, I'm sure you are. I'm sorry to bother you, but I was just wondering. Have you heard from Marsha recently? I haven't seen her walking the dog.'

'No. I haven't. I'm afraid I've been a little preoccupied...' Kate sounded tired.

'Yes. Of course. I'm sorry to have disturbed you. But if you hear anything, will you let me know?'

'Yes, of course I will.'

After she ended the call, Miss Moorcroft began rummaging around in her rickety old kitchen cabinets. She was sure that she had some flour somewhere and eventually, found a crumpled old bag of Homepride self-raising flour, in which she discovered some weevils had taken up residence. Undeterred, she hoisted them out with a teaspoon and continued to measure out the ingredients for scones. She was pushing the boat out. She knew that if she put a few custard creams out for Bert to have with his mug of builder's tea, he would probably charge her for fixing the mower. But if she put some homemade scones out on a doily with some strawberry jam and clotted cream, he was more likely to do it as a favour. If it needed a new part though, she would have pushed the boat out for nothing, but she was prepared to take that risk. Her mother always used to say that the way to a man's heart is through his stomach. Having never married, Miss Moorcroft had admired Bert Humble from afar, since he had become a widower, but that's as far as it ever got. She was secretly hoping that things might change between them.

Vera Lynn's 'We'll Meet Again' was blaring out of the old transistor radio as Miss Moorcroft carefully lifted the golden, fluffy scones from the baking tray and left them to cool on a wire rack on the ancient worktop.

Putting the kettle on, she wondered where Marsha was. She would have enjoyed her company over a cup of tea and a freshly baked scone.

CHAPTER 16

A FUNERAL

As June rolled into July, the weather had turned a lot warmer and Little Twichen was awash with colour. Spindly white ox-eye daisies, papery thin lilac poppies, and pretty lemon and peach-coloured tea roses, jostled for the limelight in borders around the village. The perfumed roses were an absolute delight; typically English, just like the village.

There was a sombre mood in Little Twichen church, which was packed to capacity for the doctor's funeral. Coppice Lane Surgery had turned out in force. Kate led the entourage with her boys, one on either side of her, her parents close behind. Nigel's parents were behind them, followed by other family members. Zelda held back, mingling with the rest of the mourners.

Kate overheard Mrs Tidmarsh whispering to Tom Jones, the butcher, who was huddled up next to her in the pew, saying that she couldn't believe what had happened. She noticed Mr Tidmarsh deep in thought. Hushed whispers rippled around the nave as several members of the congregation shook their heads in disbelief. Kate could feel eyes boring into the back of her as she walked stoically past the mourners gathered to pay their respects.

Judging by the turnout, Dr Bursford had been a popular figure amongst the villagers. A large percentage of them had been his patients and heads nodded and bowed in unison out of respect.

When the service finished, Kate waited on the church porch, thanking the mourners as they filed past, each shaking her hand or pecking her perfunctorily on the cheek, offering their condolences. The line of people wishing to pay their respects seemed to go on forever, but eventually, her father appeared by her side and offered the crook of his arm, which she gratefully accepted. She felt uncomfortable under the microscopic gaze of all those present.

As she walked bravely with her father through the churchyard, the boys having been taken home by their grandmother, she overheard somebody say, 'I wonder if the doctor killed himself because his wife was leaving him for another woman.'

Kate's parents had organised the wake at The Swan, which was a very muted affair. Although the weather was warm enough to sit outside, Kate preferred to be indoors. It was all she could do to get through the day, smiling weakly and nodding as people paid their respects. It was awkward at times because nobody knew quite what to say. She hankered after getting back to her boys to tell them how much she loved them. Goodness knows what the effect of their father's tragic and untimely death would have on them, she reflected as she sipped her tea.

Her parents had invited her and the boys to stay at Churchdene House for as long as they wanted. Graciously accepting, she wasn't sure how she felt about going back to The Granary. Her beautiful home had been tainted by Nigel's suicide, but she drew strength from the fact that Zelda was waiting in the wings for her. She was grateful for the loving glances her lover had directed at her throughout the day. They would talk when the time was right but, for the time being, she would continue acting as the grieving widow.

CHAPTER 17

ANN AND TOM JONES

Ann and Tom Jones had been together for over thirty-five years. To say the sparkle had gone out of their marriage would be an understatement. Originally from South Wales, they had moved to Little Twichen in 1997.

Tom had branched out on his own after he became a master butcher under the watchful eye of Evans & Sons, Family Butchers, who had taught him everything he knew about butchery. He had hankered after a shop of his own for as long as he could remember. When the opportunity presented itself in Little Twichen, he and Ann had made the move to England. It had been good timing. Ann had been convicted of cruelty to animals and things had all got very unpleasant. It hadn't been easy, making the transition from a busy smallholding to a small shop, but the couple did their best to integrate into the village and get the business off the ground. Eventually, with a lot of hard work and several re-mortgages of their home, they scraped by, and when the children started school, their social circle expanded. Before long, they had acquired a close-knit group of friends in the shape of parents of their children's classmates.

The years sped by and Tom's business flourished with customers flocking from miles around to buy the best cuts of locally produced meat, dairy products, and, the latest string in his bow, a range of homemade sauces and chutneys. The long hours that he put into his business had paid off even though it had taken a toll on his marriage. He lived for the business. In the early days, things had been tough, and providing for his wife and two children was his sole aim. Ann's lack of empathy grated on him at times. She had no idea how close the business had come to folding completely. Sometimes, his wife's ambivalence towards the business irked him. He worked incredibly long hours and even after the shop had closed, he still had all the paperwork to sort out.

Ann worked hard in the business initially, but her interest soon waned and she would do the occasional shift behind the counter, but only if Tom couldn't manage on his own. She preferred to host long, chatty lunches with her friends. They would compare notes about their children's progress at school, or swap knitting patterns and while away entire afternoons.

Once the children had left school and a vacancy came up at Boden's for an Office Manager, she jumped at the chance. It was an opportunity to be free from the butcher's shop. And Tom. She needed a change and the idea of working at a funeral director's appealed to her. She was fond of Mr Boden and got the impression that he liked her too. He and Marsha were part of their wider circle of friends and they had known each other for some years before she went to work for him. He always had time for her. When their paths crossed at various gatherings in the village, Bonfire Night get-togethers, Christmas parties, or the annual Wassailing at the orchard up at Dovecote Manor, he gravitated towards her, seeking her out. They both shared the same wicked sense of humour. Invariably, they ended up telling each other very rude jokes, often with a double entendre, while Tom and Marsha mingled with the other guests.

CHAPTER 18

BRYAN AND BODEN'S

The atmosphere at Boden's was very downbeat. Nobody seemed to know what was going on. There had been a big police presence with dozens of officers searching the various buildings and in particular, the house, where Marsha was last seen. Each member of staff had been questioned, including Bryan, who seemed very distracted. He had been taken into a make-shift interview room, a small office where relatives could talk quietly among themselves about the various funeral packages on offer.

'So, Bryan,' Detective Inspector Clive Daniels began. 'When was the last time you saw Mrs Boden?'

The young man thought before speaking. 'It was Saturday morning. I rode over on my bike to collect my car. Me and Mr Boden had been at a funeral in Upper Markle the day before, which finished at around four-thirty. As we were passing my house on the way back, Mr. Boden said I could finish early and dropped me off.'

'That was very kind of him,' the DI said, making some notes in a small black notebook.

'Yeah. He's a good boss.'

'And. What happened then?'

'Well, I put the bike in the back of my car. It wouldn't fit so I had to get some string from the back room behind the office to tie the hatchback down.'

'Mr Boden always leaves his offices open, does he?'

Bryan shrugged. 'I dunno. I've never thought about it. We're like one big family here at Boden's.'

'So, you got in your car and drove off?'

'No.' Bryan kept eye contact with the officer. 'I went to the house to see Mrs B. We sometimes have a chat and she made me a coffee. Then I left.'

'And how did she seem?'

Bryan thought for a moment. 'A bit distracted but she was her usual chatty, friendly self. She's a very nice lady.' He had a faraway look on his face as if picturing Marsha in his mind's eye.

'Did you have a crush on Mrs Boden?'

Bryan's head snapped up. 'No!'

'Come on. She was a very attractive woman. Did you make a move on her? That day. Did she shun your advances?'

Bryan shook his head. 'No. I did not! Like I said. I drank my coffee. We chatted about the funeral of the guy who was killed in that hit-and-run accident. Then I left.'

DI Daniels studied him closely. 'And what did you hear about that accident?'

'That a bloke had had a few too many beers at the pub, walked home, wasn't wearing any high viz gear and somebody ran into him and left him for dead.'

'How do you know so much about the incident?' Suddenly, the DI's interest was shifting.

'I was involved with organising the funeral. It's surprising what you overhear. Mourners don't seem to realise that we're there. It's like we're invisible. But we're in the background. Listening.' He gave the DI a cocky half-smile.

'Where were you the night this incident happened?'

'Can't remember. Probably with my girlfriend, Lucy.'

'And she'll corroborate this will she?'

'Yeah. I can give you her number if you like.'

'Thanks. That would be very helpful.' The DI made a note of Lucy's mobile in his notebook. The expression of dislike on his face made it clear that he didn't like Bryan's cocky attitude.

'We will need to take a formal statement from you back at the station. And I will probably need to talk to you again. Can you meet me there at ten o'clock in the morning?'

'Sure,' Bryan said nonchalantly, giving a half shrug of his shoulders as he got up to leave.

Outside the interview room, there was a lot of whispering going on between Mrs Jones and the cleaning lady, Sharon, who was from the rougher part of Ludlow.

'What do ya fink 'appened to 'er then?' she asked.

'How the hell should I know?' Ann snapped, shuffling some papers around on her desk.

Sharon was standing over her chewing some gum. Her hard face looked as though it could be the result of a rough upbringing.

'I just fawt you might 'ave 'eard sumink, that's all. Keep your 'air on.'

'Look, Sharon, the best thing we can do is carry on as normal.'

Reluctantly, Sharon left Ann's office and went about her duties. The house was out of bounds for the time being, due to the police still treating it as a crime scene. Sharon was an expert at looking busy and carried a plastic cleaning container with her everywhere. It was packed with cleaning sprays and various cloths and dusters. It looked impressive, but got very little use.

Mr Boden had made a brief appearance earlier that morning, calling all the staff together. Everybody waited around sullenly and there was an awkward atmosphere.

'I'm sure you've all heard by now that my wife, Marsha, is missing.' He cleared his throat and wiped his brow with a red and white spotted handkerchief before stuffing it back into his trouser pocket. 'I'm sure that there is a perfectly logical explanation as to where she is, but for now, I think it best that we all try and pull together. As a team. And I just wanted to say that it's business as usual.' His voice faltered and he cleared his throat again. 'She's probably gone away for a few days. She'll turn up, I'm sure.' He stopped, his voice breaking. Taking the handkerchief from his pocket, he blew his nose very loudly. 'I'm sorry. I will let you know if there's any news and of course. It goes without saying. If any of you hear anything. I mean anything, that might help the police with their inquiries, please come and tell me or go directly to the police. Thank you.'

Ann ushered everybody back to work.

'Don't worry, Mr Boden,' she said, knowing that the others could hear her, 'We'll keep things moving along. Won't we Bryan?' who happened to be standing nearby and was deep in thought.

'Er, yeah, sure.' Bryan felt bad because now was not the right time to tell Mr Boden that he was going to be leaving. Billie's job offer couldn't have come at a better time.

CHAPTER 19

LUCY

Lucy was upset when Bryan didn't respond to her WhatsApp of a selfie outside Ashcroft Estate Agents captioned, 'Got an interview here tomorrow!'

As luck would have it, business was booming following the unprecedented rise in house prices following the Covid-19 pandemic. It seemed that city dwellers were flocking to the seaside or migrating to the countryside. Shropshire and the surrounding areas had some stunning properties for sale, including a gorgeous one-bed flat in Castle Square in the heart of Ludlow. Lucy had spotted it in the window before she went in for her interview. She was excited when she saw the price and would tell Bryan all about it later. She had a good feeling about it, but they would have to act fast. It would make a perfect holiday let and was sure to be snapped up.

Dropping her off outside The Swan in Little Twichen, Lucy's Mum told her, 'Just text me when you want me to pick you up.'

'Thanks, Mum!' she shouted, clambering out of the car and waving enthusiastically as her Mum drove off, excited at the prospect of a romantic date with Bryan. She couldn't wait to tell him about the flat.

'Would you like to order some drinks?' the waiter asked the young couple seated at a corner table in the dining area. Both were studying the menu.

'What are you going for?' Bryan asked, still trying to decide.

'I'm going for the Herefordshire beefburger, so I'll go with red wine, please.' She looked across at Bryan who was still deep in thought, browsing the delicious array of dishes, all made with locally sourced produce.

'I fancy a steak, so I'll go with red too, please.'

'Is that a bottle, sir?' the waiter asked.

'Sure.Why not? Thanks.'

Lucy smiled across at Bryan and thought he looked gorgeous. Even though she had taken an age to get ready, he hadn't commented on how she looked. Then she remembered something her Mum had said in the car on the way down. This was the village where a lady had gone missing.

'God, wasn't it awful about that woman going missing? Did you know her? She was the Funeral Director's wife. That's where you work, isn't it?' The realisation dawned on her.

'Yeah. She's the boss's wife. Nice lady.'

'So. Have you heard anything? You know. About what happened to her?'

'No. We were all questioned by the police yesterday. Mr Boden looked pretty cut up.'

Lucy appeared shocked. 'Does that mean you're a suspect?'

He looked uncomfortable. 'I guess so. From what I can make out, I was one of the last people to see her.' Then the realisation dawned on him too.

'Oh, my God.' Lucy studied him with a worried look on her face.

'I only had coffee with her,' he said defensively. 'I'd cycled over to collect my car. That's all.'

The waiter appeared with their wine and they stopped talking.

'Anyway. Here's to us!' Bryan said, raising his glass in the air.

'Cheers,' Lucy chimed, clinking his glass with hers, her eyes sparkling.

'So,' Lucy continued, looking directly at him. 'You do remember us talking about looking for somewhere to live so that we could move in together, don't you?' Lucy had mentioned it previously, just prior to a particularly rampant sex session at The Feathers Hotel in Ludlow. They had both chipped in for the room because they were desperate to do it anywhere other than in the back seat of Bryan's car. He would have said yes to anything at that point in time.

Bryan shrugged. 'I don't remember,' he responded, sipping his wine. His eyes were drawn to a very attractive woman seated at the next table. She was wearing a see-through blouse and no bra.

The atmosphere suddenly turned icy between them as Bryan continued to stare lasciviously at the young woman.

'But we talked about it. Buying somewhere together,' Lucy explained, soldiering on. She sighed. 'Honestly, Bryan! And will you stop looking at that woman,' she hissed.

'I never agreed to anything, Luce,' he said, dragging his eyes away from the woman. 'You must have dreamt it.'

Irritated, Lucy pushed back her chair and flounced off to the Ladies. When she came back a few minutes later, Bryan and the woman in the see-through blouse were actually flirting with each other.

Lucy had had enough and left the restaurant. She waited outside for a few minutes, expecting Bryan to follow, but he didn't. 'Mum. Can you come and get me?' she asked stonily. 'I've just finished with Bryan.'

CHAPTER 20

MISS MOORCRAFT

Helena Moorcroft had never been interviewed by the police before and was surprised at how quickly they came knocking on her door.

'Oh, I'm so glad you came, officer. I was trying to telephone the local police station but they don't seem to have one in Ludlow anymore.'

'No, everything is centralised now. It's called streamlining.'

'Oh dear. It's a damned nuisance. That's what I would call it, because I couldn't speak to anybody. I almost gave up in the end. Please, take a seat.'

The plain clothes policeman obediently perched himself on the edge of the two-seater settee, which was covered in cat's hair. Miss Moorcroft sat with her hands folded neatly in her lap on the threadbare armchair opposite, next to the open fireplace.

'So, Miss Moorcroft,' the officer began, flipping open his notebook. 'How well do you know Mrs Boden?'

The spinster looked like she was being questioned on Mastermind. 'Well, actually officer, we know each other quite well. I mean, I often stop for a chat when she is out walking her dog. She's a very kind person and is always happy to help out, if she can. I last saw her a few days ago. In fact, I've been quite worried about her.'

'Go on,' the officer urged.

'Well, she's always out with her dog. Rain or shine. I think I saw her dog on Saturday. Around lunchtime.'

'Go on,' the officer prompted, fixing his gaze on the elderly woman sitting opposite him.

Miss Moorcroft was in her element and became quite animated. 'Well. I was out in the kitchen making a cup of tea.' She shifted in her chair because that was a lie. She had been topping up her sherry glass but didn't want the young police officer to think that she was an alcoholic. 'I saw Mrs Boden's dog up at Dovecote Manor. If you come through to the kitchen, I can show you.' She sprang up in a sprightly fashion and led the way through the dark narrow passageway to the outdated kitchen at the back of the cottage. She was standing at the stainless-steel sink in front of the window. The sill was cluttered with plants and knick-knacks that were covered in a thick layer of greasy grime. The officer stared at the mess and judging by the look on his face, he was not impressed with Miss Moorcroft's housekeeping. He wrinkled his nose at the smell which was a cross between boiled cabbage and damp, and was most unpleasant.

'You see, over there?' Miss Moorcroft volunteered, pointing a bony finger towards the hillside where the officer could see a grand house. He nodded.

'But how could you be so sure it was Mrs Boden's dog?'

'I would recognise that Golden Retriever anywhere; it's a beautiful sandy gold colour. And if the dog was there, Mrs Boden wasn't far behind. They went everywhere together.'

The officer kept looking out of the window and then turned and looked at the spinster dubiously.

Miss Moorcroft was pleased, wringing her small, bony hands together, as though she had provided a piece of key evidence in the puzzle to solve Marsha Boden's disappearance. She had a glint in her eye as she beetled off back to the sitting room, leaving the officer to find his own way back. But not before he had had a good look around.

'Have you interviewed Mr Boden,' she quizzed.

'I'm afraid I can't divulge any details about the investigation, which is still ongoing. Now if there's nothing else?' The young officer turned to make his way out through the old, creaky front door, which opened directly onto the street.

'Thank you for your help,' he said curtly, before making his way outside, taking in great lungfuls of fresh, clean air.

'Not at all,' Miss Moorcroft said politely, her hands clasped tightly together in front of her as she watched him leave. Shaken up by the fact that her friend was missing, the shabby old spinster decided that she had earned herself a treat, by-passing the schooner in the glass display cabinet, in favour of a small tumbler.

CHAPTER 21

LLOYD PETERSON

Lloyd Peterson sat at the small table in the Interview Room, opposite DI Clive Daniels. He had called his solicitor, Andrew Bistle, who was sitting next to him.

'Sir, can you just take me through the events of Saturday, 28th May once again. The day we believe Marsha Boden disappeared.'

Lloyd shifted in his chair. He spoke slowly and calmly in a clear, crisp manner. 'I received an e-mail from Marsha early in the morning, about 7:30 I think. She told me that she had told her husband that she was leaving him. The night before. Anyway, by all accounts, he threatened to strangle her and...'

'Sorry to interrupt, Mr Peterson, but are those the words that she actually used?'

Lloyd thought for a moment and then got out his phone. He started scrolling through his e-mails. 'She said, 'He grabbed me by the throat.'

DI Daniels nodded. 'Yes, we have located that e-mail on Mrs Boden's laptop.'

'Please. Go on,' the DI urged.

Lloyd's forehead was creased as he tried to recall the events of that terrible day. Clearly, he was having difficulty processing some parts of the information. 'I'm sorry, officer. I can't believe Marsha would have reneged on our agreement.'

The DI looked at him quizzically.'And what agreement was that?'

'The day before, we talked about her coming to move in with me. At Dovecote Manor. She said she was going to tell her husband she was leaving him.'He stopped briefly and looked down.'We were so in love with each other. I just can't believe that she wasn't genuine in her intentions. When our affair started...'

'When was that?'

Lloyd had to think for a moment.'About a year ago. She told me that her marriage was over. She said it had been dead for a long time. We were genuinely in love. I wanted nothing more than for her to move in with me. She was a wonderful woman.'

'Was?' the DI questioned.

Lloyd sat up straight in his chair. 'Is...is a wonderful woman. I keep waiting for her to come back. To say it's all been a terrible mistake.'

'What's been a terrible mistake, Mr Peterson?

'I don't know. Whatever it is that has kept her from starting a new life with me.'

DI Daniels studied the man sitting opposite him.

Lloyd turned and whispered something to his solicitor. 'Look. I love Marsha. I would never harm a hair on her head. Her husband threatened to strangle her. Don't you think it's him you should be questioning?'

'We're questioning everybody who was close to Mrs Boden or who saw her on that Saturday. Please carry on, Mr Peterson.'

Lloyd was deep in thought as he recollected what happened. 'In her e-mail, she told me that her husband had confiscated her phone. She was packing a few things together and would come to Dovecote Manor later that day. She also said something about her husband having disabled the phones. I e-mailed her back saying I would come and collect her but she told me not to. She said she didn't want any trouble. In case her husband came back unexpectedly. Thinking about it now, I should have jumped in my car and gone to get her. She sounded frightened of her husband. She said she had never seen him so angry.'

'Why do you think she didn't try and get the phones working? I mean, it was probably just a cable out of a telephone socket in the wall.'

Lloyds eyes looked tormented as he replied. Then he shook his head slowly from side to side. 'I don't know, officer. She was probably preoccupied. I mean, she was clearly afraid of her husband. She probably wanted to throw a few things into a suitcase and get the hell out of there. That's why I was so surprised when she hadn't turned up by early afternoon.' He had a wretched look etched on his face and looked strained around the eyes. 'And that's when I drove over to see if I could find her.'

'And what time was that?' DI Daniels snapped.

Lloyd thought carefully. 'I think it was about two-fifteen. I had been into Ludlow to buy something nice for a special supper.'

'So, let me just recap,' DI Daniels reiterated. 'The woman you adore goes missing, and you go shopping. Is that correct?'

Lloyd's head snapped up. 'I had to do something with my time. I couldn't just sit around waiting,' he said animatedly.'Besides, it was supposed to be a celebratory meal.' Lloyd's face clouded over. He had a faraway look in his eyes and there was an air of sadness about him.

Andrew Bistle leaned in and whispered something to his client.

'Am I going to be detained, officer?' he asked, his voice full of concern.

'No. Not at this stage. But, just to clarify, Mr Peterson,' the DI asked, looking Lloyd directly in the face. 'When was the last time you saw Marsha Boden alive?'

The question seemed to shock Lloyd.'Do you think she's dead?' he asked, panic shooting through him like an electric shock.

'I don't know. I'm just trying to ascertain what happened to her. I will re-phrase my question. When was the last time you saw Marsha Boden?'

Lloyd looked at the Detective Inspector. His side-kick, a young male officer, seated next to him, hadn't said a word throughout the entire interview. Now he had two pairs of eyes boring into him.

'Friday afternoon. The day before. Marsha said that she was going to tell her husband that evening.'

'And she was going to move in with you the next day? Just like that?'

Lloyd was clearly irritated at the tone of the DI's question. He pursed his lips together, as if biting his words back. 'No,' he said in a clipped voice. 'We hadn't got that far. But clearly, the chain of events that followed, when Marsha broke the news to her husband that she was leaving him, pre-empted that. She was clearly frightened and wanted to be with me. I'm just angry with myself that I didn't go to her. I should have gone to get her.' The regret was clear in Lloyd's voice, and his shoulders visibly drooped when he stopped talking.

'And, when you did go to try and find her, what happened then?'

Lloyd's head snapped up again. 'Nothing happened,' he said defensively. 'I drove across to Boden's. Marsha's car was outside.' He spoke slowly as if recounting the events in his head. 'There was nobody about. I tried the back door. It was open. I went inside and called out but there was no one around.' He stopped as if recalling the event was very painful.

'Take your time, Mr Peterson,' DI Daniels said, a warmth returning to his voice.

'I went upstairs, calling Marsha, but it was all...very ordinary. I checked all the rooms and when it was obvious that Marsha wasn't there, I left.'

'And did you see a suitcase anywhere? Half packed?'

Lloyd thought for a moment. 'No. I didn't.' He had a quizzical look on his face. 'Perhaps Marsha had lied to me. Perhaps she had changed her mind.' The realisation hit him like a train.

'I think my client has been more than helpful,' Lloyd's solicitor announced authoritatively.

'You have been very helpful, Mr Peterson. No further questions. But please. Don't leave the country.'

Lloyd looked completely baffled. He couldn't understand why the officer thought he would want to go anywhere. Other than home. Or to try and find Marsha.

CHAPTER 22

KATE AND ZELDA

It had been over a week since Kate Bursford had buried her husband. Although she was grateful to her parents for insisting that she and her boys stay with them, she was beginning to feel claustrophobic. She had cabin fever. Still reeling from the shock of Nigel's suicide, it was difficult not having her new partner on hand to support her. Zelda's lack of contact had got Kate wondering whether she really was in this relationship for the long haul. She had tried to call her several times, but her phone had gone straight to voicemail.

'Mum, I think it's time I thought about taking the boys back home,' she announced, sitting at the big wooden breakfast table. She looked worn out and had lost a few pounds in weight.

Mrs Bevan was busy at the Aga flipping pancakes for the children, who were upstairs playing. The vast rooms, filled with nooks and crannies, were perfect for a game of hide-and-seek.

When Kate's mobile rang, she answered the call and whispered, 'Sorry, Mum, I've got to take this. Hello. Yes. Hi, Mr Griffiths.' Her stomach was in her mouth. Her Deputy at the school sounded cold and distant.

'The Governors had a meeting last night, Kate. I'm afraid the decision to keep you on wasn't unanimous.' There was a deadly hush before he went on. 'However. Taking into consideration your past conduct and many years of service at the school, I managed to persuade them to keep you on as Headteacher.' Kate couldn't believe what she was hearing.

'Thank you, Michael. Thank you so much!'

As formal as ever, Michael Griffiths told Kate that he would expect her back behind her desk as soon as she felt up to the job. Kate assured him that she was more than ready to return to her post. A huge ripple of relief washed over her.

'Well, that's wonderful news, dear,' her mother enthused, tucking a plate of golden pancakes into the oven to keep warm. 'Now, come on, you must eat something. You're wasting away.'

Kate helped herself to some granola and poured oat milk over the top, scattered some blueberries into the bowl, and tucked in.

'Tea or coffee today, love?'

'Coffee. Thanks, Mum.' Kate was grateful for everything her parents had done for her, especially her Mum. She had been an angel. They smiled at each other and Mrs Bevan's eyes began to fill up. She turned away quickly. 'Boys! Pancakes are ready,' she called out into the hallway. It had the desired effect. Her grandsons came bounding in and clambered around the table, eager for their favourite breakfast of warm pancakes topped with Nutella.

Kate finished her breakfast and headed upstairs to start gathering their things together, taking her mug of coffee with her. It was time to try and get back on with her life.

When she went upstairs, she tried calling her friend Marsha again. She had left several voicemails but hadn't heard back from her. It wasn't like her not to respond. She made a mental note to pop into Boden's on her way to school in the morning. She had a horrible feeling in the pit of her stomach.

***

Robbie and Chase joined their pals out in the school playground at first break, while Kate watched on nervously from the staffroom window. She waved and smiled encouragingly. She was relieved when the other kids paid no particular attention to them, but kept playing the games that made so much sense to them, but none whatsoever to her. There were two girls with a long skipping rope in one corner of the playground. Various other groups were all darting around haphazardly, making a lot of noise. To her delight, Robbie and Chase were absorbed into a small group of boys that she especially liked, who were playing marbles near the bike rack. Robbie, in particular, had been affected by his father's death. He had become very quiet and withdrawn and sauntered behind his younger brother, carrying his school bag like it was a lead weight.

After the school bell rang out, signalling the end of her first day back, Kate herded the boys along Snickets Lane, past the converted Wesleyan Chapel, onto High Street, and back to The Granary, where Zelda was waiting for them. There was orange squash for the boys and a welcoming cup of tea for Kate. The smell of home baking hit them as soon as they got inside. A plate of Nutella sandwiches and a tray of treacle flapjacks, still warm from the oven, sat on the kitchen worktop.

Setting her bag down on one of the barstools, Kate hugged Zelda, as if she were nothing more than a friend. They had agreed that they would be discreet for the time being. They each had their own bedroom across the landing from each other. Kate had told the boys that Mummy's friend was staying to help them out. They seemed fine with that. She was mindful of the delicate situation and didn't want to rush things. The boys had been through enough already.

Later, when Robbie and Chase were tucked up in bed, the two women were alone at long last.

'Sorry I haven't been here for you, Kate,' Zelda said, a serious look on her face. 'It's been crazy busy at work. I'm working on a paper my professor is encouraging me to finish. I know I should have been here for you. And the boys.'

'Oh, don't worry about it,' Kate said dismissively. She knew that Zelda's post as a Clinical Psychologist was full on. 'This pasta is amazing,' she said, scooping a forkful into her mouth and savouring the rich, creamy sauce. She drained her wine glass, realising that the bottle they had opened earlier, was empty. 'I'll get another one,' she volunteered, starting to get up from her seat.

'No. You stay there. I'll get it. You've had a long day. She smiled across at her. 'How was your first day back at school anyway?'

'Better than I thought,' Kate said, helping herself to another portion of the delicious Carbonara from the bowl on the table. 'Everybody's been so kind.' She smiled at Zelda and was so glad to be able to talk freely with her. Running her hand through her highlighted hair, tucking a few stray strands behind her ear, she felt herself relaxing for the first time in a while. 'It's so good to be together again. Properly,' she said, smiling.

Zelda topped up Kate's glass before sitting down opposite her. 'Did you find out anything about your friend? The one who went missing?'

'Kate put her fork down and stopped eating. 'No. I called round to her house this morning. On my way to school. I spoke to her husband. There's no news.'

Zelda shook her head. 'He must be in pieces. You said she has children?'

'Yes. Two sons. They moved away years ago. I think they live in Bristol. One's a high-flying tekkie. Works for Google. Earning a fortune, apparently, Marsha told me. She was so proud of him. She was proud of both of them.'

'If there's anything I can do,' Zelda volunteered. She remembered meeting Marsha at one of the quiz nights in The Sun. She liked her.

'Just being here is more than enough,' Kate said, sipping her wine.

'I've been thinking,' Zelda ventured, topping up her glass, 'Why don't we look for somewhere to live? I mean somewhere together. I'm happy to sell my place in Ludlow. You should get a pretty penny for this place. We can buy a place of our own. It'll be our home. Besides, once the development gets going, we're not going to want to watch houses spring up all around us.'

Kate knew that Zelda had a point, but she was also smart enough to realise that nobody would want to buy a property with a housing development in its back garden. If they did, they would expect a hefty reduction in the asking price.

'Can we talk about this another time? It's a bit soon yet.'

Zelda sipped her wine. 'Sure. I'm sorry. Do you want to talk about...what happened?'

'What do you mean?' Kate asked, bemused.

'Well, we've never really talked about what happened. I mean, do you think Nigel killed himself because of me? I can't stop thinking about it.'

Kate set her glass down on the table and had a pensive look on her face. Then she looked directly at the woman opposite her.

'No. You mustn't think that.'

'So why did he kill himself?' Zelda asked defensively.

Kate shrugged her shoulders. 'I don't know. He suffered from terrible mood swings which were related to his heavy drinking. There was something else going on though.'

'Oh? What do you mean?' Zelda's interest was piqued.

Kate thought carefully before saying anything. 'I don't know, but he and Billie Tidmarsh were pretty tight. If Billie Tidmarsh is involved, you can bet your bottom dollar it's something dodgy.'

Zelda was all ears. 'Go on.'

'I've known Billie since we were kids. We went out together for a while after we left school.' She sipped her wine before continuing. 'I thought he was the one but it turned out that a younger, prettier girl caught his eye and I was history.'

'Was he your first love?' Zelda asked perceptively.

Kate nodded. 'Yup,' she said sardonically. 'He broke my heart. But then, a year or so later, I met Nigel and we got married quite quickly. He was by far the better choice. So, when I found his body with the empty pill container by his side and the half-empty vodka bottle, I assumed he had committed suicide. But I've got a gut feeling Billie was involved somehow.'

'You have told the police all this?'

'Not yet. But I will,' she added quickly, seeing the look of horror etched on Zelda's face. 'My head's been all over the place. They did question me. Immediately afterwards. But I think I was still in shock, to be honest.' Kate's face clouded over, and for the first time since she had found Nigel's body, it dawned on her that she was now mother and father to her two boys.

Zelda's expression and body language said it all. She was not at all happy about the situation and the warm atmosphere between the two women plummeted, cooling drastically.

CHAPTER 23

GUY BODEN

G uy Boden hugged his sons, David and Simon, when they rendezvoused at David's smart house in Clifton. They had wanted to go home and talk there, but Guy wanted to get away. Clear his head.

'What the hell's going on, Dad?' Simon asked. He and his brother were dazed and confused at the news of their mother's disappearance.

'I don't know', Guy said, shaking his head. His eyes were welling up. 'It doesn't make any sense. I know she can be pretty feisty but it isn't like her to just go off like that. I'm really worried about her.'

'You said the police are doing everything they can. Have you rung around all her friends? Family? That kind of thing?'

Guy looked at him blankly. 'Yes, of course, I have. I've done everything I can think of,' he said, shifting in his seat.

'Had you and Mum had a row?' David asked, nursing his mug of coffee.

Guy looked sheepish. 'Things weren't great between us. Your Mum was acting a bit strange if I'm honest. She was getting busier with her bookkeeping and I think she was getting a bit too busy at one stage. She seemed a bit stressy whenever she came back from her trips into Ludlow. She was concerned about one of Billie Tidmarsh's businesses, but she wouldn't elaborate.'

Guy's sons looked at each other knowingly at the mention of Billie Tidmarsh's name.

'She was dead against the new housing development. He was behind that too. I think she thought something was going on but she didn't know what. Other than that, she had been distant towards me for some time, but I was busy with the business and we just got on with things.' He took out a navy and white spotted handkerchief and dabbed his eyes before blowing his nose very loudly.

'Did you tell the police all of this?' David asked, his bearded face full of concern.

'Yes. Yes, I told the police everything,' he replied, stuffing the handkerchief back into his trouser pocket.

'And have they been helpful? I mean, they are still looking for her?'

'I bloody well hope so,' Simon interjected, before Guy had a chance to answer.

'Yes, they've been doing all they can. Making door-to-door enquiries around the village questioning everybody who might have known her or had any connections to her. I heard that they even questioned all the ladies in the stitch-and-bitch group.' He smiled a lopsided smile and had a faraway look in his eyes. 'Marsha would go along to the sewing group in the Community Centre every now and again, but it wasn't really her thing. It was she who coined the phrase. She said the genteel 'In Stitches' sewing group was far from funny, and they gossiped more than they stitched. Have the police questioned you both?' Guy asked, focusing his attention back on the room.

'Yes, we told them everything we could, which wasn't much really. Mum was such an independent soul. We think she's just gone away for a while. You know. To think things through.'

Guy thought they might be right and a deathly hush descended as none of them knew what to say, each deep in thought wondering what had happened to such a beautiful, carefree, and spirited soul.

Suzie, David's wife, brought a tray of biscuits in and another cafetiere of coffee, breaking the awkward silence. She sat down next to Guy, a concerned look on her face. 'I'm sure she'll turn up,' she said compassionately, laying her hand over his and squeezing it gently.

CHAPTER 24

ANN JONES

B ack at Boden's, the tittle-tattle buzzing around was escalating daily as more and more theories were thrown into the proverbial ring for dissection and discussion. Sharon, the cleaning lady, who always turned up late and was extremely unreliable, suddenly started arriving on time, and loitering around when it was time for her to leave.

Mrs Jones had always thought that Sharon had a cushy number. When she saw her taking yet another ciggie break while gossiping with one of the other staff members, the red mist descended. 'What do you think you're doing?' she bellowed, marching across to the gazebo.

Sharon gave her one of her supercilious smirks. 'It's got nuffin' to do wiv you.'

'It's got everything to do with me!' Ann's Welsh accent came out stronger when she was angry. 'Mr Boden has left me in charge. If the business goes down the toilet because we're all sitting around shirking, then nobody is going to get paid, are they? Ever thought about that, you stupid fucking woman?' Ann blushed as soon as she had blurted the words out, embarrassed in case anybody else had overheard the outburst.

'How dare you talk to me like that!' Sharon screeched, stubbing out her half-smoked cigarette. She leapt up and stomped across the courtyard to her car, a Dacia Duster. 'Who do ya fink you are, anyway? Lady fucking muck? And guess what? You can feed the fucking dog and take it for a walk. You lazy bitch.'

Ann was mortified and in two minds as to whether to slap her across her silly, sanctimonious face. 'Oh no you don't! You told Mr Boden you would look after his dog while he was away. So you can bloody well look after it.' The two women stood glaring at each other in a stand-off. 'Go on! Go and get it. I'm not bloody looking after it.' Ann's face was like thunder and she stomped off back into the office and slammed the door so loudly, it was a wonder it didn't come off its hinges.

Sharon stood there, glaring in Ann's direction, then chucked her bag onto the passenger seat of her car, and then headed off to get Jasper. Clearly, she decided it would be easier to take him home with her and bring him back in the morning.

'Now,' Ann thought philosophically, tucking some wisps of hair that had worked loose from her bun after the fracas, 'Perhaps I can get on with my work now.' When her mobile buzzed - Boden's had a strict rule that all mobiles were to be kept on silent during working hours - she smiled before leaning in and whispering seductively into the phone, 'I'm so glad you called. How are you?'

'I'll be back tomorrow,' Guy informed Ann matter-of-factly, which put her completely off her stride, but she was still fizzing with excitement at the thought of seeing him.

Everything had gone like clockwork and she was proud of how well she had kept things going during his absence. He would be so pleased with her, she thought smugly, and couldn't wait for things to die down so that they could get back to how things were before Marsha went missing.

The following afternoon when Guy appeared, his first thoughts were for Jasper. Ann was spitting feathers because Sharon had looked after the dog well. She couldn't bear the thought of another woman wheedling their way into his affections.

'How are you? How did it all go?' she whispered furtively, fussing around when Guy came into the office, closing the door behind him.

He looked at her, his brow furrowed. 'I can't really say,' he said, settling into one of the chairs near her desk. He had a far-away look in his eyes and was deep in thought. He was shaking his head. 'I don't know what to do, I honestly don't. The boys are beside themselves with worry and it's like a bomb has gone off, blowing our lives to smithereens. We're living in a vacuum. That's the only way I can describe it. We're all in complete limbo. We can't go forward and we can't go back.'

Ann listened intently, wording her response very carefully. 'Yes, it must be so difficult. It would be good to have closure, whatever the outcome.' Then she handed him the monthly accounts that she had worked diligently preparing, in time for his return. She knew the distraction would do him good.

Guy studied them intently. He had noticed that there had been a marked downturn in orders following the disappearance of his wife. Village tittle-tattle had dented his profits substantially, but thankfully, the graph had bottomed out. Ann had experienced a downturn in business once before at Boden's. It was back in the early days when she had just joined the business. She remembered Mr Boden calling in some members of staff and telling them that he would have to let them go. It was awful. The business had almost folded, but she recalled how Mr Boden had soldiered on, determined to keep things going. And to his credit, he had. She had even offered to take a pay cut, but thankfully that hadn't been necessary.

Orders had started trickling in, but that was probably due to her quick thinking in getting Golden Leaves, a pre-paid funeral plan, up and running. People would pay into the plan on a monthly basis. Ann tried to persuade people to sign up for the Platinum Plan, which was £7,000. Most people opted for the mid-range package, or the Gold Plan, at £5,000. Some people actually paid the money upfront in one go, but most people opted for the monthly payment scheme.

'That was a close call, wasn't it?' Ann commented, studying the concerned look on Guy's face. 'All we need to do now is find out what happened to Marsha.'

'Yes. Let's hope the police can find out what happened to her so that we can all get on with our lives. I keep waiting for her to walk through the door, or for the police to turn up and tell me something awful has happened. I wish I knew, one way or the other.' He ran his hand through his hair and momentarily closed his eyes as if trying to block out the inevitable.

'Oh, Guy,' Ann cooed sympathetically. 'I'm so sorry. If there's anything I can do to help. You must be exhausted. Why don't I come round and cook for you this evening? Bring some wine. Tom's away again.'

Guy glared at her. 'My wife is missing. I don't think it would be a good idea for you to come skulking around when everybody knows that I am on my own.'

Ann balked at Guy's response. She was convinced that he would jump straight into her open arms.

'I'm so, s, sorry, Guy,' she managed, 'I just thought...'

'What? You thought what? That the minute my wife was no longer around we could carry on where we left off and live happily ever after?'

Ann's blood ran cold and the colour drained from her face. Shifting uncomfortably in her chair, she looked horrified. Then she blushed, feeling the warmth in her cheeks. How could she have been so stupid? she thought, her heart sinking, the weight of Guy's rebuttal weighing heavily upon her.

CHAPTER 25

BILLIE AND BRYAN

Billie Tidmarsh was the only child of Mr and Mrs Tidmarsh, the owners of the village shop, and everybody knew that he was a rum 'un. He had broken his mother's heart when he got in with a rough crowd from the wrong side of town as a teenager. He was expelled from school and then he was involved in a car accident in which two local lads were killed, but he survived with minor injuries. He only ever parachuted in and out of his parents' lives when he wanted something. He could be very persuasive and was trying to convince his father that the new housing development was a boost to the community, and much needed in Little Twichen.

'All I'm doing is building houses for people to live in. I don't know why everybody is so against it.'

'You don't live here,' Roy Tidmarsh told his son tersely. 'Because if you did, you would get a sense of the outrage of the locals. It will spoil the equilibrium of the village. All those outsiders adding to our numbers. It's alright for you, living in a swanky apartment in Birmingham, over an hour's drive away. When was the last time you came to visit me and your mother? You know how much she misses you.'

There was a short silence. 'You know how busy I am, Dad. Running my businesses. I send her flowers. I'll try and call round when I get a chance,' he retorted, the irritation in his voice clear.

'And when will that be?'

'I don't know. I told you. I'm busy,' he snapped.

'You've broken your mother's heart so many times. I know that she would prefer five minutes with you than have a dozen bouquets.' Roy cut the call and hovered his finger over 'block this caller,' before moving it away. It was nearly the end of the road as far as he was concerned with his wayward son. But Millie still adored him. He was her blue-eyed boy, even after everything he had done.

Despite his rougher side, Billie had always been the popular kid at school. Everybody wanted to be his friend, including Bryan Jamison. Kids followed him around like the Pied Piper. The bigger kids watched out for the younger ones and although Billie left school, and Little Twichen, as soon as he could, Bryan had stayed behind but had not done very well. He still lived with his Mum just outside the village. He had applied for the job at Boden's because his Mum had seen the job advertised in the Shropshire Star and nagged him to apply for it. She said it was better than stacking shelves in Tesco's. He wasn't lazy but he wasn't proactive either and hadn't done terribly well at school. When Mr. Boden told him that as long as he had a driving licence and was prepared to work hard, he would give him all the training he needed to be an undertaker. It hadn't been at the top of Bryan's wish list of careers, and when he had told Billie, he had nearly pissed himself laughing.

'I can think of worse jobs,' he had quipped.

'Such as?' Bryan had asked.

'Working in a slaughterhouse. It stinks. Or, a pathologist. At least all you have to do is put the dead body in a box. You don't have to cut it open or analyse stomach contents or weigh the organs.'

Bryan grimaced at the thought but was chuffed that he had Billie's seal of approval. And that was all he ever wanted.

CHAPTER 26

THE INVESTIGATION

The second briefing in the case of the disappearance of Marsha Boden was held at West Mercia Police Headquarters. Sergeant Damien Henshaw kicked off the proceedings after the introduction by his superior officer, Detective Inspector Clive Daniels.

'I spoke with Mrs Boden's GP. I wanted to find out whether she was taking any antidepressants or had any mental health issues. It turns out that Marsha Boden was in rude health. The GP's words, not mine.'

DI Daniels smiled. 'Thanks, Damien.' He liked the young officer. Then he turned serious again. 'Now, what did we find out?' He sat on the edge of the desk and looked around his team expectantly.

'Sir,' Sgt. Henshaw began tentatively, 'I spoke to Miss Moorcroft. I think she's a bit of a busybody but other than that, I think she's harmless enough. She was quite friendly with Marsha Boden, by all accounts. She reckons she saw her dog up at Dovecote Farm on the Saturday which is the day we believe Marsha Boden went missing. She seemed to think that if the dog was there, so was Marsha.'

'Carry on,' DI Daniels said, encouragingly.

'Well, she seems pretty sharp. And she seemed eager to help and was genuinely concerned for Marsha's well-being. But honestly, I think she just saw the dog and assumed that Marsha was there too.'

'Okay. Thanks.' Hitching up his trousers and perching on the edge of a desk, DI Daniels continued, 'What do we know about the family? Della, how did you get on?'

'Not much to report, sir. Both sons were baffled and concerned about their mother's whereabouts. Both of them mentioned that they thought their parents were going through a rough patch in their marriage.'

'Okay. Right,' he announced, standing up and walking around the room, 'We haven't got very much to go on, other than we think that Marsha Boden was in the process of leaving her husband for another man. Therefore, our number one suspect is the husband. We're arranging a search of the stretch of river where Guy Boden went fishing and the surrounding area. We searched the woodland area where we know Mrs Boden used to walk her dog, but found nothing. We have a couple of other leads. Bryan Jamison is an employee at Boden's and we think he was one of the last people to see Marsha. Do a bit more digging around and see what you can find out about him. Also, have we been able to find out any more about Mrs Boden's suspicions about the various income streams that Billie Tidmarsh had? She mentioned this to her husband and Mr Peterson.'

Some shaking of heads and murmuring indicated that nobody had followed this up.

'Well, what are we waiting for then?' he barked.

CHAPTER 27

KATE

'Sir, there's a lady here who wants to talk to you. Says it might have something to do with that missing lady, Marsha Boden.'

DI Daniels went straight through to the front desk. 'Mrs Bursford. How are you? Come on through.'

'I'm okay, thanks.'

DI Daniels showed her into one of the interview rooms, offered her a seat, and sat down opposite her. 'What's this all about?'

Kate had a confused look on her face. 'Well, I'm worried about my friend Marsha. It's not like her to go off the radar. Is there any news?'

'No. I'm afraid not. We're following up on all the leads that we get, but so far we haven't been able to ascertain her whereabouts. But rest assured, we're doing all that we can. Now, you didn't come here to ask me that, did you?'

Kate shifted uncomfortably in her chair. 'No. I didn't.' She bit on her bottom lip. 'I think Billie Tidmarsh might have had something to do with my husband's death.'

The DI looked at her, then nodded encouragingly. 'Go on.'

'Well, I know Billie of old and he's got a reputation for being...' she stopped and chose her words carefully, 'Not always being on the right side of the law. He's the village boy who left for the bright city lights and did good. He's supposed to have made his money from property developing, but I think he and my husband were involved in something.'

'Like what?'

'I'm not sure. I think Nigel might have been obtaining prescription drugs for him.'

'To sell, or deal? That doesn't seem very likely to me.'

'No. I don't think huge amounts were involved. Just the occasional package here and there.'

'And what evidence do you have to support this claim?'

'I overheard them talking. They didn't realise that I had returned to the house. I'd forgotten my phone. Anyway, I was surprised to hear Billie's voice. He and I hadn't been in touch for years, so I was shocked when I heard him in conversation with my husband. I heard them talking about Rohypnol. Nigel was telling Billie that it's difficult to detect, so would probably go unnoticed in food and drink.'

'Yes. It was popular for spiking drinks in nightclubs, back in the day,' DI Daniels said calmly.

Kate turned pale.

'You don't think he was using it on women, do you?' DI Daniels asked, his voice very serious. 'I mean, you do know it's called the date rape drug?'

'Yes. I mean no! God, no. Billie had no need to drug his women. They were already putty in his hands. I don't know what he did with it.'

'And did you confront your husband?'

'Yes. Of course, I did. But he denied everything. He said I must have misheard.'

'And you didn't think to go to the authorities about it?'

Kate slouched down in her chair. 'I didn't know what to do. I had the boys to think about. I mean, if Nigel had lost his job...'

'And how long do you think your husband was supplying these drugs to Billie for?'

Kate thought, pursing her lips trying to recollect the timeframe. 'I think about a year.'

'There's something else.'

'Go on.'

'Well,' she began tentatively. 'Nigel parked his car in the garage the night he died. He never used the garage. Yesterday, I went in there for the first time since...' She stared ahead of her into space then came back into the room mentally. She looked straight at DI Daniels. 'I noticed the front of his car was badly damaged and was covered in what looks like blood.'

CHAPTER 28

LUCY

Lucy was still waiting for a phone call about the job at Ashcroft's and was beginning to think she hadn't got it. It had been nearly a week since her interview, which she thought had gone well. She was pleased with what Alex, the Property Team Leader, had told her. He had said that most of the young girls he employed moved on quickly, realising that it wasn't for them. He also told her that she seemed different and liked her enthusiasm. As she was leaving, he mentioned that he knew her father, and asked her to pass on his regards.

While she was in the queue at Greggs, her mobile rang. It was Alex. 'Hi, is that Lucy?'

'Yes,' she replied tentatively.

'It's Alex here, from Ashcroft's. We would like to offer you the job!'

It was all Lucy could do to stop herself from squealing out loud. 'Oh, that's amazing. Thank you so much!' she enthused, stepping out of the queue and heading out onto King Street.

'I'll get a formal letter out to you today and we can get you started as soon as possible. You said you only had to give a week's notice with your current employer. Is that right?'

'Yes, a week.'

'Okay, well, we'll be in touch with a contract but, this is a bit of a longshot. I'm about to meet the guy behind the new development in Little

Twichen. I thought it might be a good idea if I introduced you to him. It's just that I think you would be perfect to man the show home. You wouldn't be available later, around five? I'm meeting him for a drink at The Church Inn.'

Lucy knew the pub well. 'Sure. Yes, that's fine,' she blurted out, desperately trying to think whether she had any plans for later.

'Great. See you then,' Alex said smoothly, ending the call.

She was over the moon. She had always wanted to work in property and now she had got the job at Ashcroft's, she felt like there would be no stopping her. She was a little disappointed that she didn't have someone special to share her good news with. She and Bryan had split up after the flirting fiasco at The Swan when she realised that he hadn't been serious about their relationship at all. Even more disappointingly, he hadn't contacted her but had completely ghosted her.

Quickly tapping out a message, she sent a group WhatsApp to her friends inviting them out for a drink later to celebrate. She could meet up with them after meeting Alex and the mystery man at The Church Inn.

The rest of the afternoon passed in a blur. She rang her parents to tell them the good news. Then she decided to treat herself to a shopping spree. She would need some smart new clothes and was keen to make a good impression.

When she got to The Church Inn, she quickly spotted Alex at the bar with another man.

'Ah, Lucy,' he said, turning to introduce his young, soon-to-be Sales Negotiator. 'This is, Billie Tidmarsh, the owner of Green Circle Housing Group.'

Lucy stretched out her hand to shake Billie's and felt as though an electric shock had passed through her entire body.

'Hey, nice to meet you,' she managed to say.

'Likewise,' he said, his eyes meeting hers. 'Can I get you a drink?'

'No, this one's on me,' Alex said, turning to the barman at The Church Inn to order a round.

Billie's eyes swung back to Lucy and he clearly liked what he saw.

Lucy felt herself blush and tried to compose herself, 'So, how do you guys know each other?' she asked, feeling very self-conscious.

'Oh, we go way back,' Billie said dismissively. 'Alex tells me that you've just landed a job at Ashcroft's. I think he's got high hopes for you,' he schmoozed, studying her intently as he spoke, his voice smooth and silky.

'Yes, he wanted me to meet you. Something to do with a new housing development in Little Twichen?'

'Yes, that's right. We've got sixty-five houses going up there. Building has already started.'

Alex handed Lucy a gin and tonic and they decided to head out into the beer garden, where they found a free table and sat in the shadow of St. Laurence's Church. Lucy couldn't stop sneaking surreptitious glances at Billie, admiring his toned physique and swarthy features. He was smoking hot.

'So, I'm thinking of putting Lucy in charge of the show home at the new development' Alex told Billie.

Billie looked at Lucy studiously.

'What experience in marketing do you have?' he asked

Lucy blushed and felt as if she was being put on the spot. 'I'm good at sales,' she managed to say. 'And I have always wanted to work in property. I'm fascinated by the property market and what drives it. I'm good at marketing and since my interview, I have been researching property trends in the area and have already drawn up a list of potential purchasers to target.'

Billie took a sip of his beer and then smiled at her, his eyes sparkling as he did so. 'That's very impressive.'

'She's enthusiastic. And full of ideas. I think she'll be great,' Alex chimed in.

Billie looked Alex in the eye and said calmly, 'I trust you, Alex. You've never let me down,' and he proposed a toast. 'Here's to Meadowbank,' he said raising his glass and clinking it with the others. And to you. Lucy.'

Strongly drawn to Billie, Lucy was reluctant to leave to go and meet her friends. It was as if he had a magnetic field around him that was pulling her in. She was keen to get his number but didn't want to come across as being too forward. She would ask Alex for it when she started work. But that was over a week away, which seemed like a lifetime.

Billie drained his glass. 'What's everybody having? It's my round.' He caught the eye of a pretty young waitress clearing glasses from a nearby table and whispered something in her ear, which made her giggle. Within a few minutes, she was back with their drinks.

'I'm sorry, guys, but I'm going to have to love and leave you. I'm meeting up with some friends to celebrate.' She looked coyly at Billie and flashed one of her cutest smiles at him. 'That's a shame,' he responded. 'We'll have to keep in touch.'

Lucy's heart skipped a beat. Then Billie said, 'I'll need regular updates on the new development. What's your number?'

She told him and he tapped it into his phone and called her. 'There. You've got my number now,' he said matter-of-factly, tucking his phone into his inside jacket pocket.

'Job done!' she thought triumphantly, even though Billie had made it clear that it was purely from a professional perspective.

'Oh, Lucy, don't mention anything in the office next week,' Alex said conspiratorially as she got up to leave. 'I don't think the others will take kindly to me putting the new girl in charge of the show home.'

'No. Of course not.' She smiled knowingly, pleased that Alex had introduced her to Billie. It was a nice touch. 'Nice to have met you, Billie,' she said, feeling herself blush again.

'Likewise, Lucy. Likewise.' She could feel his eyes following her every step of the way as she headed down Harp Lane. She was as high as a kite with excitement, even though Billie was probably way out of her league. But at least now she had his number.

***

'Ooh, Luce, what's going on? You look like the cat who just got the cream.' Her girlfriends huddled around her when she met up with them at The Rose and Crown.

'I don't know what you're talking about,' she said coyly.

'Come on. You can tell us. Who is he?'

Lucy blushed furiously.'Nobody. There isn't anybody. I've only just finished with Bryan. Remember? Leave me alone,' she said petulantly

'Ooh, spikey,' Alicia cooed. 'What's he like?'

'Enough!' Lucy shouted. 'Now, whose round is it? We've got some celebrating to do.'

Her pals all glanced at each other knowingly and when Lucy felt her phone vibrate in her bag, she was desperate to check who it was. But, of course, she didn't dare.

CHAPTER 29

MR TIDMARSH

Roy Tidmarsh was replenishing the fresh milk in the cold counter at the shop, and couldn't stop thinking about Marsha. He often stopped for a tête-à-tête while taking a short break during the day or out walking in the evening. She was generally upbeat and always happy to stop and chat. It seemed so out of character for her to go off without saying anything. He wondered whether the last conversation he had had with her was connected to her disappearance. He hoped to God that wasn't the case.

Marsha had been crossing the bridge on her way back into the village and was heading down to the river. Jasper had bounded on ahead, keen for a dip in the cool, running water. Marsha was following on jauntily behind.

Roy caught up with her and they had talked about the weather and then the conversation had turned to the new housing development. The topic of conversation was on everybody's lips and the villagers were in solidarity about not wanting it. As with most things of that nature, the developers steamrollered their way through all the red tape, and because of a national housing shortage, the Government had eased their path significantly. The locals had had little say in the outcome. Marsha clearly had concerns about the development. She was also very much against the person behind it. She had been tactful when she broached the subject. Roy recalled how strongly she had felt about Billie making money off the back of bringing misery to the village. Decimating the habitat of flora and fauna in the process. Without a second thought.

Thinking back to that evening, his disgust at the way his son had turned out was clear. It saddened him deeply. Their chat had been cut short when Jasper had decided that it was time to go. He bounded off up the pathway which led out onto the green. Marsha had skipped after him leaving Roy with a heavy heart. That was the last time he ever saw her.

'Roy! Do you want a cup of tea or not?' Millie was asking, hands on hips with a quizzical look on her beaky little face. 'You were miles away. What's the matter?' she asked, taking advantage of a lull in the shop to seek out her husband, having been busy stock-taking out the back.

'Nothing, dear. I can't stop thinking about Marsha, that's all.'

'Mm, it's all very odd, isn't it? Do you think she had some kind of a breakdown? She might have jumped in the river or...'

'Who knows?' Roy interrupted, not wanting to think about such terrible things. 'But it was odd the way she just upped and left without telling a soul. Apparently, her husband is beside himself with worry.'

'Yes,' she said, absent-mindedly.

Looking around him to make sure the shop was clear of customers, Roy asked, 'What's the matter?' as he slid the cold counter door closed.

Millie avoided her husband's gaze. 'I heard that Billie fired her. You know that I recommended her to him? To help with the bookkeeping. Well, Kate told me that Marsha had told her that she thought something odd was going on. With Billie's business. The one in town.'

Roy picked up a cardboard box and stared at his wife.

'Well, let's keep this between ourselves. We both know that Billie likes to skirt around the law. Make things work to his advantage whenever he can. If the villagers knew how much he'd got from the Government to build those 'ouses, they'd be up in arms.'

When they saw Bert Humble walk in they both clammed up, glancing at each other conspiratorially.

Chapter 30

Guy Boden

Guy Boden settled down to another evening at home alone. He poured himself a large Scotch and settled into his favourite leather wing-backed chair. Marsha's Skechers were just visible under the matching chair opposite. Jasper, who was lying at his feet, had taken to carrying one of her slippers with him everywhere he went. His big brown eyes were swimming with sadness, and he looked up dolefully every time a door opened.

Guy's mind was working overtime. He kept wondering whether a mobile phone would still be traceable if submerged in water for any length of time. He felt wretched and wished he hadn't been so hot-headed. He also regretted taking it out on Ann earlier. He would give her a call later and try to make amends. He was pretty sure that she would acquiesce to his charm.

Then his thoughts turned dark again and he jerked himself back into the room. He downed his glass in one, wincing before getting up to pour himself another. He was just settling back down into his chair again when the telephone rang.

'Boden's Funeral Directors,' he said, answering it very formally.

'Mr Boden?'

'Yes. Who is this?'

'It's Helena. Miss Moorcroft.'

'Oh, hello Miss Moorcroft. Is everything alright?' he asked, his voice softening.

'Yes, I'm sorry to bother you, but I forgot to give a donation at Dr Bursford's funeral. I wondered if you knew which charity he wanted donations to go to.'

'Oh, right. Okay. Well, if you want to drop an envelope in and leave it with me or Ann, we'll make sure it gets to the correct charity.' He knew that Helena Moorcroft would never entertain making an online payment. She had probably never heard of JustGiving.

'Oh, that's very kind of you, Mr Boden. I appreciate that very much. I'll drop something into the office.' She hesitated. 'I don't suppose there's any news about Marsha, is there? I'm getting more and more worried about her.'

Guy clenched his jaw and his demeanor changed instantly. 'No, Miss Moorcroft, there isn't.' He slammed the phone down. 'Bloody woman,' he muttered.

When his front doorbell rang, he wondered what was going on. He half expected to find Ann standing there, so was surprised to see that it was Detective Inspector Clive Daniels.

'Guy Boden', he said sternly, holding up his warrant card, 'I'm arresting you on suspicion of murdering your wife, Marsha May Boden. You do not have to say anything but it may harm your defence if you do not mention when questioned something which you later rely on in court. Anything you do say may be given in evidence.'

Guy was flabbergasted. 'I don't know what on earth...'

'Mr Boden. If you could accompany us to the station, please?'

'What about my dog? I can't leave him! How long is this going to take?'

'Don't worry,' DI Daniels assured him, noticing a strong smell of alcohol. 'We'll get somebody to look after your pet for you. I'll ask one of my officers to stay here.'

Guy seemed appeased. Poor Jasper had been through enough already. It was clear that Marsha's disappearance had affected him deeply.

***

In the interview room at West Mercia Police Station, DI Daniels began his cross-examination of Guy Boden.

'Mr Boden. You said that your marriage was going through a rough patch. You knew that your wife was having an affair, didn't you?'

A nerve in Guy Boden's cheek twitched and his face clouded over. 'No comment.'

'You knew, but you didn't know who it was.' DI Daniels goaded.

Guy remained tight-lipped, refusing to answer the question. 'No comment.'

'It has also come to our attention that you are having an affair with Ann Jones, your Office Manager.'

Guy sighed and resigned himself to the fact that it was doing him no good by not answering the questions. 'Things hadn't been great between my wife and I. That's hardly a reason to kill her,' he said wearily. 'We hadn't been intimate for a couple of years.'

'Did your wife have any life insurance?'

'No. Not that I'm aware of.'

'Well, we will need to confirm that one way or the other. We will also need full access to the records in your office again. We are going to exhume some bodies from the time your wife went missing.'

Guy was horrified. 'You can't do that! What on earth are those poor families going to think?'

'We are also arranging for DNA samples to be taken from any remains we find at the local crematoria.'

'You can't get DNA from ashes,' Guy said matter-of-factly.

'No, you can't. You're quite right. But you can sometimes get DNA from teeth and bones that have not been destroyed,' DI Daniels retorted, making a mental note of Guy's reply. 'It's highly unlikely that we will find anything of significance, but we will try. Now. Tell me exactly what your wife told you about the antiques business or anything else to do with Billie Tidmarsh.'

Guy crossed his arms over his chest and leant back in the hard, plastic chair. He dredged his memory, trying to remember what Marsha had told him. 'She always seemed on edge when she came back from her bookkeeping sessions in Ludlow. It was Mrs Tidmarsh who got her the job. She was fine with everything at first, but as time went on, she seemed more and more disgruntled. She was very stressed out when she got back. As if something was really bothering her.' He scratched his jaw. 'Then suddenly, Billie told her he didn't need her anymore. As if he wanted her out of the picture. She told me she was suspicious about his incomes streams but said she would have to be certain before she could go to the authorities.'

'Do you think she intended to go to the police?'

Guy shrugged his shoulders. 'I don't know. She wouldn't talk about it. She clammed up every time I tried to bring it up.'

'Well, we have your wife's laptop, so we will see what we can find out. Now, this friend of yours who vouched for you on your fishing trip. We have spoken to him and he corroborated your statement. However, that doesn't mean to say that you didn't drive back earlier, kill your wife, then dispose of her body. Then return at the time you told us that you got back home.'

Guy's head snapped up. 'I told you. I wouldn't...didn't...kill my wife. I wanted us to make a fresh start. To try and rekindle our marriage. I left her a note on the kitchen table the morning I left. On the Saturday.'

'You didn't mention that you tried to strangle your wife, though did you, Mr Boden?'

Guy's mouth dropped open.

'Your wife sent an e-mail to Mr Peterson telling him this. Apparently, the phones weren't working. Did you disable them?'

'No. No, I didn't,' he replied indignantly. 'Why would I do that?'

'Well, according to that e-mail, your wife also told Mr Peterson that you had taken her mobile phone.'

'That's nonsense. I did no such thing.'

DI Daniels slid a sheet of paper across the desk. 'Would you mind reading that e-mail, please?'

Guy reluctantly picked up the sheet of A4 paper and read what Marsha had written to her lover. His face looked taut and anger burned in his eyes. He slapped the paper down on the desk and looked at DI Daniels with disdain.

'It seems your wife was frightened of you, Mr Boden. After you tried to strangle her.'

'I did not try to strangle her. An argument got out of hand and I lunged at her. That's all.'

'What have you done with your wife's body?'

Guy lowered his head into his hands, rubbing his face before he looked up again.

'I have not done anything with Marsha's body. As far as I know, she is alive and well.'

'I'm keeping you in custody for forty-eight hours and then we're going to charge you. We're just tying up a few loose ends.'

'Jeezus Christ! I didn't kill my wife! You can't do this. What evidence do you have? You haven't got anything to prove that I killed her.' He turned and whispered something to his solicitor.

CHAPTER 31

ASHCROFT'S

Alex was a big noise in the locality and full of himself. He had started out with a small estate agency business and had built up quite an empire. Lucy enjoyed working with him and he had asked to meet her at an old warehouse in town.

'Hi, Alex' she called out breezily, jumping out of a black Audi A3 with Ashcroft's logo plastered all over it.

'Hey Lucy. Did you bring the keys?'

She smiled knowingly and shook a bunch of keys in the air as she made her way to the door of the unit on Station Road. Once inside, she let Alex go ahead.

'It's deceptive, isn't it?' she said, taking in the vast space that was full of old bric-a-brac.

There was a wall of boxes stacked up at one end and some old chairs, sofas, dining tables, and other oddments of furniture. Alex referred to them as antiques but she thought it looked like a load of old tat.

After a few minutes of browsing around, Alex turned to Lucy.

'Make sure you only give the keys to Billie. No-one else, is that clear?'

Lucy nodded. She felt proud to be associated with such an astute and handsome businessman, although she was desperate for their relationship to turn into something more.

'Come on, let's get back to the office,' he instructed.

Alex kept to his word and offered Lucy the position of Head Sales Negotiator based in the Marketing Suite at Meadowbank. It would be a while before the show home was ready, but at least she could start planning her marketing strategy. He assigned Jed from the office to work alongside her. He didn't want her working alone on the site.

'Bitch.' Lucy overheard one of her colleagues say when she returned to the office with Alex.

'Excuse me?' she said to the office in general, which consisted of half a dozen females and one male sales negotiator.

'You heard,' one of them said. 'You didn't take long to climb up the ladder, did you? We all know how you got the job in the first place though.'

Lucy's hackles were well and truly up. 'And just how did I get the job?' she spat at the spiteful girl who had started the flare-up.

'Don't you know?' The young woman sneered. 'It was Daddy who got you the job, deary, not your hidden talents or should I say talons?'

'How dare you!' Lucy shouted back. 'I got this job fair and square.'

'Yeah, right,' the other girl said, chewing gum. 'If that's what you want to believe, that's up to you, but we all know it was because Daddy pulled some strings to get you in.' The girl looked at her sanctimoniously.

Lucy was furious. The girl had hit a raw nerve. Instead of fighting back, she turned on her heel and went back to her desk. Burying herself in her work, she diligently started working through a list of tasks that Alex had given her to do, all the while wondering why he had delegated the jobs to her. Suddenly, she didn't feel quite so happy about getting the job based at Meadowbank, and rather than a promotion, it felt like she was being side-lined.

She started creating e-mail lists and mailshots to drum up interest in the new site. She knew that there was hardly any wriggle room on the prices, so she would have to make it sound as though each and every purchaser had bagged a bargain, despite them paying over the odds. That was the skill of a good salesperson; making the buyer think they had a bargain. It was all a game that Lucy was pretty good at. Perhaps she had inherited that side of things from her father, who had retired as a Land Agent. The other girl's words were still ringing in her ears, '...Daddy got you the job...' and her ego had been well and truly bruised.

CHAPTER 32

MARSHA'S DISAPPEARANCE

M arsha Boden's disappearance made headline news in the local newspaper, The Shropshire Star. Mr. Tidmarsh had had to order in extra copies because they were flying off the shelf. Little Twichen had been shaken to the core by the sudden and mysterious disappearance of one of their residents.

Miss Moorcroft had done a good job of letting people know that her friend was missing. She was clearly concerned and told people to be vigilant. She even got a local printer to make up some flyers which she had started to display on telegraph poles and lamp posts around the village. She had contacted the nice young man at West Mercia Police Headquarters. She wanted to know which number she should use for people to contact if they had any information which led to the discovery of Marsha Boden. She even suggested putting up some of her own money for a reward, but Sergeant Henshaw had advised against it.

Villagers were edgy and felt uncomfortable with the thought of a possible perpetrator in their midst. Some had taken to locking their doors again, especially at night. Mothers of teenaged girls insisted they could not go out alone, and were to be accompanied at all times. People looked over their shoulders a lot more than they ever used to. There was an air of mistrust around the village.

Ann Jones was distraught when she heard the news of Guy's arrest. Instinctively, she knew what she had to do. Stand firm at the helm of the Boden ship during her boss's absence, even though she was finding it difficult to concentrate. Fielding phone calls and side-stepping customers' awkward questions, she did her best, but she only had one pair of hands. Sometimes, she wished she had more help in the office. Over the years, Guy had placed more and more trust in her. Initially, she had been flattered, but now that he was no longer here to keep a watchful eye on the other side of the business, nobody seemed to know who was in charge. As far as she could tell, most of the other staff members were wandering around doing their own thing. There was no direction from anybody. Although she was confident in the office, she didn't feel that it was her place to oversee the staff in the other buildings. That was Guy's domain.

'What a turn-up for the books! Who would have thought it?' Sharon announced, flouncing into the office with a puppy in tow.

'What the hell?' Ann barked, seething at how brazen the woman was. She despised her.

'My daughter has started breeding dogs and she's asked me to try and sell the last one. Would you like him? He's a bargain. Only eighteen hundred quid. He's so cute, isn't he?' She was snuggling up to the Cavalier King Charles Spaniel puppy, who was madly licking her face with its pink, floppy tongue.

Ann could not believe her ears or her eyes. The minute the boss was away, Sharon took advantage and kicked right back. 'You're paid to clean, not to sell dogs, so why don't you go and put the dog in the car and start work, like everybody else around here?'

Sharon jumped up as if she had been stung by a wasp. 'Ooh, touched a raw nerve, did I?' she said and then realised she may have gone a step too far when she saw the look on Ann's face.

'I'm warning you, Sharon,' Ann growled.

'What?' she taunted with a supercilious grin planted on her hardened face. 'You'll do what? Loverboy ain't 'ere to watch your back anymore, is he?'

'That's it. Get out! Take your bloody dog with you and piss off. Don't bother coming back either.'

Sharon was completely non-plussed by Ann's outburst. She scooped up the puppy and teetered outside with it, purposely allowing the door to slam loudly behind her.

Ann ran after her, seething with anger. 'And don't bother coming back!' she repeated. 'You're a waste of bloody space. Do you hear me?' She was bellowing at the cleaner who was busy putting the dog into the back of her car. 'Keep your 'air on,' she said, her supercilious smirk turning into a full-blown grin. 'We'll see what old man Boden's got to say about you firing me when he gets back, shall we? I don't suppose he'll be too pleased, do you? After all, you're not going to get off your arse and look after his dog, are you?'

Ann's face was like thunder and it was all she could do to stop herself from slapping the woman across the face, although she knew that that was exactly what Sharon was goading her into doing. She had to keep the moral high ground. As the two women stood a few feet apart glaring at each other in a showdown waiting for the other to back down, a black Audi scrunched to a halt on the pea gravel drive right next to them. In the back seat, with a face as thunderous as a mid-west tornado sky, was Guy Boden. The vehicle was an unmarked police car.

'Both of you. In my office. Now,' he said getting out of the car. His voice was so low it was barely audible.

'What the hell's going on?' he demanded. The two women stood in front of his desk like two naughty schoolgirls.

Ann explained that everybody had been doing their best to keep things on track. When she had seen Sharon blatantly skiving again, she saw red.

'Honestly, we've been so busy. The phones haven't stopped ringing and we had two funerals to arrange. Then an old lady from Worcester died and we were contacted by the care home to ask if we could arrange her funeral. She had no family, and you know how complicated it gets with all the paperwork we have to deal with.' Ann didn't draw breath and was keen to tell her side of the story. 'So when I saw that Sharon had no intention of doing any work today, because you weren't around to keep an eye on her, I told her to leave.'

Sharon piped up to give her side of the story. 'I've been working 'ere longer than you and Mr Boden's always been happy with me, so it's none of your bloody business.' She glared at Ann.

'Well that's where you're wrong,' she said through gritted teeth. 'You see, it is my business because Mr Boden left me in charge and if we don't keep things going while he's away, we will all be out of a job. Including you,' Ann said pointedly.

Sharon chose to ignore Ann's comment. 'I've got work to do,' she said and flounced off with the importance of somebody who was about to greet royalty.

Guy was speechless. He let the cleaning woman leave. He had far more pressing things on his mind.

'Sorry. She just winds me up. She never does any work and when she does, it's always half-hearted. She doesn't deserve the wage you pay her. She's a complete waste of space.'

Guy heaved a huge sigh. 'Marsha asked me to take her on. Somebody approached her in Ludlow and I said I would give her a job. I'll deal with it. But not today.' He took off his glasses and rubbed his eyes with his thumb and forefinger.

'How are you anyway?' Ann asked, turning her focus onto him. 'What did the police say?'

Guy sighed again and rubbed his hand over his face. 'They didn't have enough evidence to charge me.' He looked exhausted. 'But I'm still a suspect. They could re-arrest me.'

'Oh, that's awful,' Ann said, clearly worried that her beloved Guy could be taken away from her. 'What do you mean? Still a suspect?'

'They are exhuming some bodies and doing some DNA testing on ashes from the local crematoria. They think I might have put Marsha's body in a coffin with another body.'

Ann's eyes nearly popped out of her head. 'Oh my goodness!'

Suddenly, there was a commotion outside and they went out to see what was going on. Jasper had head-butted the King Charles Spaniel puppy. Sharon was screaming at the top of her voice. 'Get off! Get away!' Thankfully, the minute Jasper spotted Guy, he lost interest in the puppy and bounded over to greet his master. Then, before Ann could register what was happening, the dog turned to her, growling loudly and baring his teeth. The whites of his eyes were showing. In a split second, he snapped and sank his teeth into her forearm, instantly drawing blood.

Ann let out a blood-curdling scream.

CHAPTER 33

MEADOWBANK AND LUCY

E arthmoving works began in earnest carving out the plots for the new houses. Residents still voiced their objections about the development, berating the fact that Little Twichen would never be the same again. But with the acute shortage of houses and an avalanche of people needing somewhere to live, expanding the village was inevitable, and something they would have to accept. It was a case of moving with the times. It was strange without Marsha. She had been the loudest voice against it. She would have hated the carbuncle on the beautiful meadow, which had now been decimated.

The social housing aspect worried some snootier members of the community. They questioned why people who can afford to pay upwards of £400,000 for a house, would choose to live next door to a house worth a fraction of that. But, of course, they had no say in the matter. Whether these diverse sectors of the social strata could live harmoniously side by side, was yet to be seen.

As with the previous smaller developments, additional patients had been absorbed at Coppice Lane Surgery, children were added to classes at Little Twichen Primary School, and families were integrated into the wider community. It was called progress and the villagers had had no option but to go with the flow. Feelings ran high because of the person behind this particular development. The bad boy of the village who was steamrollering his way through their lives in the name of profit.

Lucy couldn't see what all the fuss was about and, to her mind, Billie was a hero, providing much needed housing for a cross-section of the community. She felt a huge loyalty towards him and was very protective of his name.

Alex had hinted at a handsome bonus if she sold twenty of the houses off-plan. She had seven earmarked already, all of which were in the process of being legally signed off to their new owners. She would use her bonus to buy an apartment in Castle Square, different from the one that she thought she and Bryan were going to buy. This one was a top-floor penthouse, no less. Rather a grand description for a two-bedroom light, bright and airy flat at the top of a former drapers in a beautiful Edwardian building. She had fallen in love with it and was looking into getting a mortgage to buy it. Her life had taken on a whole new meaning since she had started working at Ashcroft's. She was upset when she and Brian had finished, but had eventually moved on. Her life had moved in the direction she had planned, although she wished her father hadn't intervened, if that was true. It could just be bitchy office gossip though, she reflected.

When she saw Billie's number come up on her mobile, her heart skipped a beat and she tried to keep calm and played it cool.

'Hey, Billie. What can I do for you?'

'I need an update on the development and was wondering if we could meet up later?'

'OK. What were you thinking?'

'How about The Riverside? We can sit out on the balcony, say seven-thirty?'

'OK. Great.'

'Cool. I'll book us a table.'

'See you then,' she purred. Her life was just getting better and better.

***

Lucy arrived at The Riverside Bar and Restaurant a few minutes late, having had trouble finding a parking space in the popular eatery. When the sun comes out, everybody flocks to the upmarket pub on the river, which has a reputation for its delicious cuisine. Billie had chosen well and had even secured a table on the glass balustraded deck with views straight across the River Dunne. She was most impressed.

'What can I get you to drink,' he asked, brushing her cheek with his. She caught a waft of his delicious aftershave.

'A lime and soda would be great, thanks. I'm driving.'

Billie disappeared, leaving Lucy to settle into her seat and admire the view. As she sat back, basking in the warmth of the evening sun, a Kingfisher darted out from the riverbank. It settled on a rock in the middle of the slow-flowing river, did a three-hundred-and-sixty-degree turn, as if parading its exquisite plumage, and then flew back into the undergrowth, disappearing as quickly as it had appeared.

Billie returned bearing drinks and menus. He was very easygoing and had a laid-back air about him that Lucy liked.

'I hear the steaks here are fantastic,' he said, browsing the menu.

Lucy tended towards being a vegetarian but hadn't committed one hundred percent.

'I think I'll go for the monkfish with a mango salsa,' she announced, deep in thought studying all the delicious options. She looked up and smiled at the gorgeous man sitting opposite her.

'Ooh, good choice. I think I'll join you. A perfect meal for such a beautiful summer's evening. Cheers.' Billie had the most amazing smile which made his chocolate brown eyes crinkle around the edges.

'Cheers!' They chinked glasses, Billie opting for a pint of lager.

'So, how was your day?'

'Oh, very busy. There's been a lot of interest in the development in Little Twichen.'

'Yes, Alex was telling me. That's great news. I've invested heavily so I'm pleased to hear that. Is everything going okay up there?'

'Yes, everything's going really well. No problems at all.'

Billie smiled at her. 'Yes, Alex was right about you. I'll arrange for that bonus he mentioned to be made available.'

Lucy blushed and dismissed his comment. 'Where are you based?' she asked, taking a sip of her drink and tucking a stray wisp of blonde hair behind her ear.

'Birmingham. I've been staying here at The Riverside for a few days while I sort out some business leads in the area.'

Lucy got the impression that Billie was a bit of a wide boy, but she thought he was amazing all the same.

'You're from Little Twichen, aren't you? Your parents run the village shop there.'

'Yeah. I left as soon as I could. Way too parochial for me. I prefer the city life. Bright lights and all that.'

'Did you know the lady who went missing, Marsha Boden?' Lucy took another sip of her drink.

A mouth-watering waft of fried onions floated out onto the balcony where they were sitting.

'Yeah. She's married to the Funeral Director. My Mum recommended her to me and she did the odd bookkeeping job for one of my businesses.

Here in town. Anyhow, I didn't come here to talk about that.' He looked at her seductively. 'I've got a beautiful room with views over the river...'

Lucy blushed.

'And, I'm leaving in the morning...' He left the sentence hanging. A waitress arrived to ask if they wanted wine with their meal before Lucy had a chance to respond.

'I think we'll have a bottle of Chablis, thanks,' Billie said, handing back the wine list to the waitress. He gave Lucy another smoldering glance and she felt her insides turn to jelly. She knew the inference that he was making. She was beside herself with excitement. And anticipation.

After her hurried couplings with Bryan, Billie's lovemaking was on a whole new level. He was very experienced and Lucy fell completely under his spell. By the time the sun rose over the Shropshire hills the following morning, she was well and truly smitten.

'I'd best get a move on,' she said dreamily, lying naked under the white sheets, not wanting to break the spell.

'I'll call you,' Billie said, collecting up his things. 'And if you give me your bank details, I'll ping the deposit over for that flat you're after.'

'No way, Billie! I can't possibly take it,' she protested, sitting up and holding the sheet up to cover her modesty.

'Hey, we talked about this last night. It's your bonus. You've earned it.'

'That's very generous. Thank you.' She fluttered her eyelashes at him.

'It's not a problem. Honestly.' That smile again. 'I've got some calls to make. Meet me in the dining room when you're ready.'

After breakfasting together, Billie checked out and paid the bill while Lucy hung back in the smart reception area. She blushed when the young waitress, who was back on duty behind the desk, looked at her and then at Billie. She was very proud to be with this gorgeous man and knew the young woman was envious.

They walked hand-in-hand to her car and Billie hugged her, kissing her tenderly one last time. He slid into his black Porsche and glided slowly out of the car park before roaring off, leaving Lucy in complete and utter awe.

CHAPTER 34

GUY BODEN

The tinny, cheap-sounding theme tune from the 1980's advert, 'Just One Cornetto!' chimed out from an ice-cream van that trundled around Little Twichen every Sunday, around lunchtime.

Guy and his two sons were sitting around the dining table. They were trying to enjoy a roast chicken dinner that they had all helped to prepare, in an attempt to try and get some normality back into their lives. Normally ones to wolf their food down, today all three of them sat pushing pieces of meat and vegetables around their plates.

'Do you think we should assume the worst by now?' David asked, resting the knife and fork on the edge of his plate. 'I mean, she could have made contact with any of us by now.'

The silence was oppressive and Guy wished that he could be eliminated as a suspect. The worry was taking its toll. 'Let's keep positive. We have to. For your Mum's sake.' He smiled, trying to be strong for his boys. 'Come on, we might as well clear this lot away,' he said wearily.

The three men busied themselves with sorting out the leftovers; depositing cling-filmed dishes in the fridge, stacking greasy tins and gravy-stained plates into the dishwasher, and tidying up the kitchen. They had done this so many times before, but Marsha had always been at the helm of the family home, preparing them delicious meals and making them feel loved. Today, it just wasn't the same. The soul of the modern, timber-framed house was missing and no longer had a heartbeat. It felt empty and hollow without her.

Guy turned to his two sons, folding a National Trust tea towel covered in game birds, one that Marsha particularly liked. 'I might have to lay off some staff. Business has dropped off the edge of a cliff since the police arrested me. Things are not looking good,' he said solemnly.

The boys had never taken an interest in the funeral business, preferring instead to make careers in technology and finance. Although they were a close family, once they had left home, they only visited for birthdays, Christmas, and on special occasions. Guy got the distinct impression that now that their mother was no longer around, he would see less and less of them. They had their own families to think about now. Kids grow up, get married, and have children of their own, and so the cycle of life continues. Although he and Marsha hadn't been made grandparents yet, he got the impression from the boys that they wouldn't be long before they started producing their own offspring. He knew that Marsha would have loved to have been a grandmother. She often talked about it when the boys weren't there.

'Sorry to hear that, Dad. You will be alright though? I mean financially...' Simon asked, a concerned look on his face.

'Yes, I've weathered storms in the past, son. I'm sure everything will be fine.' He said, raising his eyebrows. He put on a brave face but inside, he was in turmoil.

'Well, if you ever need any help, I've got some friends who might be able to offer some financial advice. You know, if things get bad.'

'Oh, good heavens no! I'm sure everything will be fine,' he lied, 'But I'll bear that in mind. Thanks. Now, how about we take Jasper out for a nice long walk?' He desperately needed to get out of the house for some fresh air.

'Excellent idea,' Simon and David reiterated. The three of them set off down the High Street with Jasper straining on his leash. When they reached the butcher's shop, Jasper started to behave very oddly. He stopped dead and started barking.

'Come on, boy,' Guy said, trying to coax him to move but Jasper was having none of it. He sat rooted to the spot.

'What's all the fuss about?' Ann asked, emerging from a side door. Jasper growled when he saw her, but she held out her hand with a juicy steak on it which the dog sniffed and took reluctantly. As soon as he started eating it, he golloped the tasty treat down quickly, licking his lips afterward and turning away.

'Thanks, Ann,' Guy said. 'How's your arm?'

'Oh, it's fine,' she said dismissively, waving her bandaged arm in the air. 'If it wasn't for that stupid woman and her silly dog....'

'Yes. It's so unlike Jasper to do something like that. He's usually such a sweet-tempered dog. I think he's missing Marsha.'

Jasper started to strain at his leash when he spotted David and Simon, who had gone on ahead and were going into The Swan.

'Enjoy the rest of your weekend,' Guy called out, as Jasper tugged him away.

'You too,' Ann replied, smiling sweetly. She watched until they were completely out of sight.

CHAPTER 35

LITTLE TWICHEN

T he unusually hot weather had created bedlam in the small village. Camper vans, cyclists, and families disgorging from four-wheel drive vehicles, laden with picnic hampers, camping chairs, and inflatable dinghies, created a bottleneck at the green just off the High Street. A journalist had published an article in The Sunday Times about wild swimming in the area. Ever since then, the village had become a mecca for people wanting to sample the wonders of dunking themselves into a freezing cold river in the middle of a meadow. The shingle area near the old arched bridge, which the locals called 'the beach,' was the most popular spot. Visitors had been known to arrive as early as eight o'clock in the morning to bagsy their coveted spot.

Throughout the day dogs could be heard yapping, kids screeched as they plunged into the cold water, and boomboxes blared out across the tranquil countryside. It was a Sunday and people were becoming more and more fractious due to the intense heat, which was fierce, even for July.

The riverside garden of The Swan was crammed with people lunching out and drinking Pimms and ice-cold lager while watching the antics of the visitors playing on the river. A local man paddled a coracle sedately past the pandemonium of the pleasure seekers, oblivious to the dozens of pairs of eyes trained on him, as he slowly and skillfully propelled the small bowl-shaped boat forward, by moving a single oar in a figure of eight motion in front of him.

The scene was joyful for the revellers but not so for the villagers, some of whom resented the influx of day trippers, spoiling their quiet and idyllic lives in the countryside. Just as they were opposed to the new housing development for the very same reason. One villager had taken to posting their distaste on FaceBook, only to be caught up in a backlash of venom and spiteful comments.

'Get a life! These people have probably never enjoyed wild swimming before.'

'Share and share alike you boring person.'

'Count yourself lucky to live in such a beautiful place. Those visiting probably live in a concrete jungle. Give them a break.'

Tidder's benefited from the influx of visitors and ice-cream sales soared and party packs of beer flew off the shelves, making it almost impossible to keep up with demand.

All the fun and frivolity were in stark contrast to the underlying mood in Little Twichen. One of their residents was missing, but the visitors either didn't know or if they did, they didn't seem to care.

CHAPTER 36

BRYAN

Bryan had never really been interested in making his job at Boden's long-term; he had only applied for it because his Mum had badgered him into it. When Billie rang him up one day out of the blue and offered him a job as a delivery driver, he had jumped at it.

'The police have been digging around a lot at Boden's,' Bryan reported to Billie.

'I expect they'll come snooping around me now. Throw them off the scent if you can. Just keep them away from me. I wish I'd never given that bloody woman a job now. I knew she was trouble.'

Bryan winced at the edge in Billie's voice. 'Leave it to me.' He pocketed the burner phone that Billie had instructed him to buy. He taught him never to trust anybody and to always cover your tracks.

Bryan could tell that Billie had been preoccupied when they spoke. He suspected he was schmoozing another unsuspecting muse. He was such a womaniser.

He had heard that Lucy was dating him now. He hoped she wouldn't get hurt because she deserved better. The more he thought about it, the more he realised that his feelings for Lucy were stronger than he cared to admit. In retrospect, perhaps he should have fought for her rather than letting her slip away. Right into Billie's arms.

***

'I've come to talk to somebody about Marsha Boden.'

'Wait here,' a police constable told the young man who had presented at the front desk.

'DI Daniels. I'm heading up the investigation into Marsha Boden's disappearance. Come on through.'

Bryan followed the man through the police station where he was taken into an interview room.

'What's this all about?' DI Daniels asked.

'Well, I've remembered something. On the day that Mrs B disappeared, she asked me if I had seen her dog. I hadn't. It probably doesn't mean anything but I thought it might be important.'

'Right. Anything else?'

'Yes. I saw a van parked in the layby just down the road when I left.'

'Did you get a registration number?'

'No. I didn't think anything of it at the time but since...you know.'

'What colour was this van?'

'White, I think.'

'Any signage or anything distinctive about it?'

'No. Not really. I can't remember.'

'Right. So, it could have been a delivery guy checking on his next drop-off? Or some random person checking their satnav or using their phone?'

Bryan shrugged. 'Yeah, I guess so. But I thought I'd mention it.'

DI Daniels made a note of what Bryan had told him and looked at the cocky young man with a look of disdain on his face.

'Well, thanks for dropping by,' he said in a clipped voice, pushing the swing door open and letting Bryan back through to the front desk. 'You've been most helpful,' he lied, and watched as the young lad rode off on his bike at top speed.

As soon as he was out of sight, Bryan dismounted from his bike, pushed it through an alleyway, and fed it into the back of a van that Billie had given him the use of for his new job. He headed back to the yard as he was working out his last few days of notice at Boden's.

He was just changing out of his jeans and hoodie into his formal wear when he heard Mr Boden's voice.

'Bryan! Have you finished prepping that car yet?'

'Yes, Mr Boden. We're all ready for the off at eleven-thirty,' he shouted, zipping up his flies and checking his appearance in the mirror before making his way to Mr Boden's office.

'Good lad. Good lad. You can drive today. Remember, keep her slow and steady.'

Bryan looked very serious. 'Thanks,' he said, taking the keys from him. He assumed one of the other staff members would be accompanying him and became a little edgy.

'I've got this, Mr Boden. You must have other things on your mind. Leave this to me.' They walked out to the courtyard and stood next to the gleaming hearse.

'No, this will be a quick in and out. Come on. You know my rules, though. No radio. Respect for the dead and all that,' he said, climbing into the passenger's seat of the hearse.

Bryan shuffled from one foot to the other. 'Got it' he replied, climbing in and nudging the hearse gently out onto the main road. He kept his eyes straight ahead and periodically checked his rear-view mirror. There were no cars following on today. It happened like that occasionally, if the family couldn't afford to hire extra cars or sometimes, like today, the old lady on board was so old that she had outlived most of her family and friends. Hardly any mourners would attend her funeral. The pungent scent from a beautiful bouquet of pink tiger lilies on the coffin was quite overpowering. He wondered who had arranged for them to be put there.

When they pulled up outside the Wyre Forest crematorium, Mr Boden said, 'As soon as we've taken the coffin inside, Bryan, I would like you to go straight back to the yard and wait for me there. We've got a very big funeral this afternoon at three o'clock. I'll get a lift back with Mr Peabody. You get on and make sure all the cars are gleaming and ready to go.'

'Okay,' Bryan said and wondered why Mr Boden needed to wait around. Secretly, though, he was pleased to be able to drive back alone. As soon as he pulled the hearse out of the crematorium onto the main road, he tuned into Radio 1 and turned the volume up full blast.

CHAPTER 37

KATE AND ZELDA

K ate had thought about what Zelda had said about buying a property together. It made perfect sense, so she had picked up a glossy brochure for the new development, Meadowbank. She had had a lovely chat with the sales assistant, Lucy, while she was there. She was most helpful.

'Are you serious?' Zelda asked excitedly when Kate handed it to her.

'Well, I wasn't thinking of leaving the village because of my job and the boys' school. What do you think?'

'It's fine by me. But I'm not happy after our conversation about Billie Tidmarsh. Have you been to the police yet?

'Yes. I told them everything. Don't worry, Zelda. Everything's going to be fine. We have each other now and I want to take things to the next level.' She smiled across at her and knowing the boys were outside playing, leant in and kissed her tenderly on the lips. Smiling mischievously, Kate spread the brochure open on the granite worktop at the colourful page containing the plan of all sixty-five houses. 'So, which one shall we call ours?'

After a short discussion, they both agreed that a corner plot would be perfect.

'Okay. Leave it with me. I'll go and speak to my new friend in the Marketing Suite. Now, the boys have a surprise for you. It's outside.'

The boys were out in the garden playing with their new inflatable water slide, which Kate had splashed out on and thought they deserved. As luck would have it, a hot spell coincided with the long, school summer holidays.

'Happy birthday, darling,' Kate said, pouring her a glass of champagne.

'But my birthday's not until tomorrow,' she said, closing her eyes. She looked as though she was savouring the cool bubbles as they slid down easily.

'I know, but I thought we would make the most of this lovely weather, while it lasts.'

The boys came scampering into the kitchen and Robbie took Zelda's free hand while Chase led the way out into the garden.

'Come on, Auntie Zeld', he chirped, his blue eyes sparkling mischievously. 'Come and see your surprise!'

'Ooh, I love surprises,' she said, smiling at Kate as she allowed herself to be led out into the garden.

'Close your eyes!' the boys shouted.

'But I won't be able to see where I'm going?'

Kate took Zelda's champagne flute and she obediently closed her eyes as Robbie took her hand in his, making their way gingerly across the lawn, having kicked off her shoes on the terrace beforehand, as instructed.

'Okay. Open your eyes now!' the boys shouted in unison.

'Oh, my God! A hot tub. I love it! I've always wanted one.'

Kate appeared by her side and handed back her glass and whispered throatily in her ear, 'How about we get in naked later? I've arranged for Mum and Dad to have the boys tonight.'

Zelda smiled. 'Can't wait,' she whispered.

'Okay, guys. Who's hungry? Shall we light the barbecue?'

'Yeah! Burgers and sausages. Yippee!' The boys stopped momentarily, then carried on with their horseplay.

Kate and Zelda quickly changed into their costumes and submerged themselves in the hot tub, sipping on their champagne, and enjoying the warm summer evening. A fat pigeon cooed on the fence nearby, and a pair of Cabbage White butterflies flitted magically above them in formation. They watched the beautiful display in awe before they fluttered away as quickly as they had appeared.

'Life doesn't get much better than this,' Zelda said dreamily.

'I'd better get this food cooked before I get too tiddly,' Kate said, guessing the barbecue was probably just at the right temperature after lighting it earlier.

'Boys! Guess what? Nanny and grandad are coming to pick you up to have a sleepover,' she announced, clambering out of the hot tub and reaching for a bright beach towel. 'What do you think?'

'But what about the burgers and sausages?' Chase asked with a worried look on his face, clearly concerned that he was going to be deprived of his favourite food.

'We're still having the barbecue. We can eat first and then nanny and grandad will pick you up later.'

'Hooray!' they both shouted. They continued their boisterous game of running, chasing, and shoving each other down the water slide, their skinny, white legs slipping and sliding all over the place, like newly born foals, as they tried to clamber back up the wet slide.

'I'll go and pack a few things for the boys,' Zelda whispered to Kate.

'That would be great, thanks.'

'Christ, I can't wait to get my hands on you later,' Zelda whispered, her eyes sparkling.

Kate smiled coyly and they reluctantly peeled themselves away from each other to get on with the tasks in hand, eager to get the boys fed and ready for collection.

As soon as they had finished waving them off, the two women topped up their champagne flutes and made their way back out into the garden, which was strewn with discarded water pistols, towels, and other paraphernalia that the boys had left lying around.

Climbing naked into the tub, they kissed passionately. Zelda took one of Kate's pert, rosebud nipples into her mouth and flicked her tongue over it back and forth, causing her to groan in ecstasy. Then she held it in her mouth and grazed it, very gently, with her teeth.

'God, you have a gorgeous body,' she whispered throatily, her eyes burning with desire. She admired her partner's sensational curves, slowly taking in every inch of her smooth, creamy-white skin, before moving her gaze down to the delicious triangle of dark hair submerged in the water. 'Let's carry on inside.'

Lying in bed naked, after enjoying each other's bodies for several hours, the two women finally laid back panting. 'God, I needed that,' Kate exclaimed.

'Me too,' Zelda said dreamily.

CHAPTER 38

LUCY

Tucked away in the pretty hamlet of Little Twichen giving a sales spiel to people who, in all probability, had already made up their minds to buy a house there, was Lucy's idea of a dream job. She had had one customer today already. Kate Bursford, the Headteacher of the village school, had shown an interest in one of the corner plots. After a little encouragement from Lucy, she had paid a deposit there and then to secure it. Selling the new houses was so much easier than she had first envisaged. On her way back to the office, she swung by Boden's. There was a lady who worked there who had shown an interest in one of the other corner plots, and she was keen to reel her in too.

'Hi, Mrs Jones. I thought I would drop in a brochure for you.'

Ann Jones had a puzzled look on her face and was clearly not expecting a visit from the young saleswoman. 'Oh, there was no need, lovey, I could have popped in to collect one.' She all but snatched the brochure from Lucy and slid it into her desk drawer.

'You used to go out with Bryan, didn't you? Mrs Jones said.

Lucy was taken aback by Mrs Jones' directness. 'Yes, how do you know?'

'Oh, Bryan told me when you broke up. He was pretty cut up about it. Nice lad. I think you made a bad choice though.'

Lucy looked surprised. She had only stopped by to drop something off and now she was being given the Spanish Inquisition.

'Billie Tidmarsh. Bad news, he is. I wouldn't touch him with a barge pole. You be careful with that one.'

Lucy felt herself getting flustered. 'I thought you and your husband...'

'Oh, it's nothing serious. We're only thinking about it. You know, for when he retires.' She looked around her conspiratorially. 'No need to mention this to anybody else, lovey, he doesn't know about it.' She smiled warmly at the young girl in front of her. 'I haven't spoken to him about it yet, so...Mum's the word!'

'Right, okay,' Lucy replied, backing away. 'I'd best be off. I've put one of my business cards in the brochure, so if you need anything, just give me a call.'

'Right. Will do. Thanks, lovey.'

After catching up with various other matters she was dealing with in the office, Lucy headed out at lunchtime into the sunshine, feeling lighter the moment she stepped over the threshold of the office out onto the busy street. She loved the small town, not only because of its beautiful black and white timbered buildings, ancient castle, and historic church, but because it had a lovely vibe.

An open-air market filled Castle Square every Tuesday and Thursday where you could buy anything, from artisan cheeses to homemade fudge, all locally produced. As she was heading to the vegan burger stall, her mobile phone rang.

'Hi, is that Lucy Holden?'

'Yes, it is. Who's this?'

'It's Maggie from Barnett Walters Solicitors,' the very young-sounding voice informed her, 'I was just ringing to say that we have completed on your flat and you can collect the keys from Ashcroft's.'

Lucy smiled. The young girl had no idea that she worked at the agents involved in the sale.

'That's great news! Thank you.'

'You're welcome,' the girl said in a monotone voice, ending the call.

Sitting on a wooden bench in the square by the castle, which was as pretty as a picture, with several cascading flower displays making it feel like summer had properly arrived, she decided to skip the veggie burger and give Billie a call instead to tell him the good news.

There was no reply, so she left him a voicemail. Picking up a wedge of cheese-and-onion quiche and a Pastel de nata from the Harp Lane Deli, she thought she deserved a treat. She was, after all, celebrating her very first foray into the world of property ownership. She headed back to the office where she bumped into Alex, who was just leaving.

'Hey! I wondered where you were,' he said.

'I'm on my lunch break,' she responded defensively.

'Have you got a minute?'

'Oh, okay,' she said cheerily, tucking the goodies she had bought into her bag to eat later.

Instinctively, they both headed down the street and turned left under the old clock tower, where a local artist had set up a stall displaying watercolours of local landscapes. They carried on along the cobbled alleyway and into The Church Inn.

Alex ordered a pint and Lucy asked for a coffee. She didn't want to go back to the office smelling of alcohol and give the old crones more ammunition against her.

'Are you sure?' Alex asked, bemused.

'Yes, absolutely. A coffee would be great, thanks.'

'You go and find a table outside and I'll bring the drinks through.'

As luck would have it, a couple got up to leave just as Lucy entered the beer garden, and she dived into one of the empty seats to secure the table.

Alex came through shortly after and settled into the seat opposite. 'Congratulations!' he said, beaming at her and raising his glass.

'Thanks.' Lucy bumped his glass lightly with her coffee cup and Alex held out his hand with a set of keys on it.

'I believe these are yours, Miss Holden,' he said in an overly formal voice, which made Lucy giggle.

'Thank you kindly, sir,' she mocked, taking the keys. 'I'm so excited!'

'You deserve it, Lucy. You've worked hard these past few weeks and that's why you got the job at the Meadowbank show home. I knew you would be an asset to the company.'

Lucy smiled, embarrassed, and sipped her coffee. 'Thanks.'

'I know the other ladies in the office are not happy about it, but they'll just have to live with it. Besides, you've earned it.'

Lucy didn't know what to say and blushed. She was grateful to Alex for giving her a chance.

The atmosphere suddenly turned serious. 'That warehouse we went to the other day. I don't want you to talk to anybody about it. Only Billie. Is that clear?'

'Sure. I'm not one to gossip.'

'Good. That's what I thought. The less people know, the better. Besides, it's nobody else's business except Billie's. He's putting a lot of faith in you.'

Once again, Lucy was flattered that Billie trusted her. She really had hit the jackpot when Alex had introduced them.

When they finished their drinks, they headed back to the office and Alex held the door open for her. She felt buoyed up by his protectiveness and hoped that it wasn't going to fuel the fire of animosity against her any further.

CHAPTER 39

THE INVESTIGATION

'Settle down, please. Right. What do we have so far on the missing person, Marsha Boden?' Detective Inspector Clive Daniels walked purposefully among his team like an invigilator patrolling a sixth-form exam.

Della Carlton was first to speak. 'The sighting that Miss Moorcroft reported of Mrs Boden's dog at Dovecote Manor on Saturday has been substantiated. Lloyd Peterson said he found the dog asleep on his porch sometime late on Saturday afternoon.'

'Right. So that all ties in, except that nobody actually saw Mrs Boden with her dog. And just because Miss Moorcroft spotted the dog, she perhaps mistakenly assumed that Marsha was also around. She could already have been missing by then.' His voice tailed off as if he was piecing things together in his mind as he spoke. 'Does anybody have any more information on the mobile phone?'

'Yes, sir,' PC Leila Bridlington responded timidly, blushing as she spoke.

Seeing how nervous his colleague was at addressing a room full of people, despite the fact that she should be used to it by now, Detective Inspector Daniels encouraged her to continue. 'Go on.'

'Well, as we know, Guy Boden hasn't been completely honest with us. He didn't tell us that he had tried to strangle his wife.' The young policewoman said the words with irony. 'Nor did he tell us that he had confiscated her mobile phone. And tampered with the landlines to prevent his wife from raising the alarm. I think he must have panicked when she went missing and either destroyed it or discarded it somewhere.' Leila hesitated momentarily, looking all around as if waiting for a response from somebody. 'So, the phone records show that Lloyd Peterson called her several times throughout the day, six times, in fact. Kate Bursford also called, and Miss Moorcroft.' The young PC was reading from a list. 'And Simon Boden, one of her sons. There is one number that we are still trying to identify. After that, there is no more information, indicating that the phone was destroyed or catastrophically damaged.' She flicked through a few pages and then said, 'The last position tracked on the phone was somewhere in Little Twichen. The tech guys could only give us a rough estimate. It wasn't anywhere near the Bodens' residence, sir.'

DI Clive Daniels nodded at her and smiled. 'Good work. Carry on.'

'Well, it was only due to Marsha's quick thinking to send an e-mail from her laptop that she was able to get a message to Lloyd Peterson.'

'So, why didn't she just jump in her car and drive over to Dovecote Manor as soon as her husband left?' DI Daniels asked, a pensive look on his face as he stroked his chin between his thumb and forefinger.

Leila answered quickly, without hesitation. 'She was obviously frightened. Perhaps she thought he would be waiting for her and might follow her, and who knows what she thought he might be capable of. Maybe she was protecting Lloyd Peterson. The man she loved.'

There seemed to be a general consensus of agreement amongst her colleagues.

'Good point, Leilia. Let's conduct a search to try and find the phone. Also, contact all mobile phone shops in the area, including as far afield as Leominster and Hereford, to see if we can ascertain whether Marsha might have bought another phone. It could be that she dropped it while out walking the dog. Let's see what else we can find out.'

'Yes, sir,' Leila responded, pleased with her performance.

'And what if she did go to Dovecote Manor as she and Mr Peterson planned?' DI Daniels floated. 'And why isn't she there now? Did something happen to her beforehand? Henshaw. You took Lloyd Peterson's statement. What did he say?'

The officer checked his notes and then said, 'He said she told him in the e-mail about her husband's violent reaction to her telling him their marriage was over. Mr Peterson said that he wanted to jump in his car and go and collect her immediately, but she insisted on packing some things together first. She told him that she would be over as soon as she had finished. She asked him not to come over in case her husband came back. She didn't want any trouble.'

'Right. So, we have a possible scenario here of Guy Boden driving back from West Wales and killing his wife. We know that he went fishing that day because his alibi checked out. But we all know that loyal friends can sometimes be persuaded to lie or deceive. Anybody got anything else to go on?'

There was a collective shaking of heads.

'Henshaw. Did you find out whether Mrs Boden had any life insurance?'

'I did, sir and she didn't have any.'

Detective Inspector Daniels perched on the edge of a desk and addressed his team in a serious tone. 'It could well be that Marsha Boden was finding everything a bit too much and just wanted out. Although we are following up every avenue we can, we must bear in mind that she might have wanted to 'disappear' of her own accord. When somebody goes missing, it doesn't always mean the inevitable has happened to them; it could be that they just don't want to be found. It's something to bear in mind.'

There was a collective nodding of heads and a flurry of activity as the team set to work to continue the investigation into Marsha Boden's disappearance.

CHAPTER 40

BERT HUMBLE AND MISS MOORCRAFT

While Miss Moorcroft was rooting around in the chilled cabinet at Tidder's for some clotted cream to go with the scones that she had baked for Bert, she heard two young women in the queue for the till regurgitating the news of Mr Boden's arrest.

'It's terrible, isn't it!' one of them exclaimed, cradling a jar of coffee in her hands.

'Murder!' the other responded, an armful of crisps and snacks at the ready. 'Who would have thought it? Here. In Little Twichen.'

If Miss Moorcroft hadn't been so preoccupied with getting everything just right for Bert's visit later, she would have said something. Instead, she kept quiet; she had never liked Mr Boden. She thought him distant and cold. A Funeral Director was to her mind a most peculiar career, even though her former job as a Tax Inspector wasn't perhaps the most popular career choice either. She reasoned that Guy Boden was good at his job because he was able to detach himself. And for that very reason, she also thought that he could have murdered his wife without any remorse. She hoped that she was wrong. But what other explanation could there be as the days ticked by and still there was no news of Marsha? As she was paying, she noticed Bert Humble across the street, deep in conversation with Kate Bursford.

Having just collected his paper from Tidder's, Bert had bumped into Kate and was mulling over what she had just told him. Deep in thought, he ambled across the road, forgetting to do what his mother had drilled into him as a boy. 'Always use a pedestrian crossing to cross the road.' There were none in the village. She also told him, 'If you cross near a bend, get as much visibility either way as you can.' But Bert was deep in thought. He lost Dorothy two years ago to cancer. He had never really thought about the possibility of having another relationship. Not at his time of life. But the other evening, after the meeting at the village hall, Helena Moorcroft had been so kind to him. He liked it when she had linked her arm through his. And now, after what Kate had just told him...

Customers enjoying a quiet drink or meal in The Swan, heard the squealing and hissing of brakes as the lorry skidded and screeched to a halt. There was a terrible thud. And then silence. A car travelling in the opposite direction had swerved and mounted the kerb, ending up embedded in the wall of Little Twichen Manor. There was twisted metal, lots of broken glass and debris everywhere. The driver of the car was bleeding profusely but managed to stumble out of his vehicle before collapsing onto the road.

A quick-thinking patron, who happened to be a doctor enjoying a rare, quiet lunch with his wife, grabbed the A-board, advertising the lunchtime menu, from outside The Swan, and plonked it in the middle of the road to alert oncoming traffic of the collision around the corner.

'Somebody call 999!' he shouted, going into triage mode. A crowd trickled slowly out of the hotel and gathered around to see what was going on.

'Sit on the wall over there and don't move,' the young doctor instructed the lorry driver, who was clambering out of the lorry cab and was about to check on the old man that he had hit. He looked as though he was going to vomit. 'Somebody stay with him!' he shouted, pointing at the lorry driver. His next priority was the injured driver of the car, who he helped to stand

and sat with him on the kerb. A young woman materialised at his side and told him that she was an off-duty nurse.

'Do what you can to stem the bleeding. And stay with him,' he instructed. Then he called out to some bystanders, gesturing authoritatively, his sleeves rolled up and ready for action. 'I need four or five people to stop the traffic and tell people to stay in their vehicles. Hurry!' There was already a stream of cars with drivers' heads poking out of open windows, rubbernecking to see what was going on. There was a danger of cars slamming billiard-ball style into the back of each other. A queue had already formed near the bridge.

Next, he knelt alongside the belly of the HGV and saw a man's mangled body near the back axle, covered in blood. The lorry had clearly run right over him. He hurried around to the back of the stationery vehicle and knelt alongside the body. He felt for a pulse but there was nothing. He checked his watch, making a mental note of the time.

The young fire crew, stationed on Laburnum Lane, were quickly at the scene. One of them placed his jacket over the top half of what was left of Bert's torso. Some of them sat in shock on the old seat under the old oak tree on the green, one of Bert's favourite places to sit and have a natter to whoever would listen. Others stood nearby watching over their friend's body. Several sheets of newspaper were fluttering around in the breeze, blowing along High Street. They were splattered with blood.

***

Miss Moorcroft heard the commotion just as she was leaving Tidder's.

'Helena!' Kate called out from across the street, quickly back-tracking when she heard the squealing and hissing of the lorry's brakes, and noticing Miss Moorcroft heading down to the scene.

Helena Moorcroft looked across at Kate Bursford with a confused look on her face. She waited while Kate gingerly made her way across the road to speak to her.

'What's going on?' she snapped, as forthright as ever.

'I don't know, but it didn't sound good. I think somebody's been run over.'

The two women hurried down the road to the corner where quite a crowd had gathered. Kate stopped in her tracks when she overheard somebody say that a man had been killed. Hit by a lorry.

'Oh, God,' Miss Moorcroft said, the realisation hitting her as she took in the scene before her. She had also heard the shocked ripple of whispers from the onlookers. 'I must have been in the shop when it happened. Is it Bert? Bert Humble,' she clarified. People in the crowd were shaking their heads. Nobody seemed to know what was going on, but they were all jostling for poll position to see if they could get closer to the grisly scene before them.

'Come on, Helena. Let's get you home,' Kate instructed, steering Miss Moorcroft away, preventing her from getting too close.

Miss Moorcroft uncharacteristically burst into tears. 'Is it Bert? Somebody. Please. Tell me!'

Kate tried to calm the old spinster down, but Miss Moorcroft was having none of it.

'You can't go down there,' Kate called out as Miss Moorcroft slipped free and beetled off through the crowd making light work of it.

The young doctor who had taken control of the situation, spotted the old lady approaching and guessed from the expression on her face that she knew the victim. 'I'm afraid you can't come any closer. You must go back over the road. Now.'

Kate appeared and guided Helena reluctantly away from the traumatic scene, which had now become one massive sightseeing area, with people converging from all directions.

Kate took Miss Moorcroft into The Swan and sat down with her on one of the squishy leather sofas in the reception area. Neither of them spoke as they both tried to process the awful news.

'When I saw Bert earlier,' Kate began tentatively, 'He was telling me all about how he was going to call round and fix your mower. He told me he was looking forward to seeing you.'

'And what did you tell him about me?'

The guilty look on Kate's face said it all.

'I told you that I had feelings for Bert Humble in confidence,' Miss Moorcroft admonished. 'I told you not to say anything!'

Kate put her head in her hands. She obviously felt wretched about what had just happened.

CHAPTER 41

ANOTHER FUNERAL

B oden's Funeral Directors were called upon to give Bert Humble a good send-off and Guy was grateful for the business.

'It's so sad. I can't believe that old Bert's gone,' Ann said, tidying away some brochures that she had open on her desk. She had started wearing her hair down in the office.

'Death doesn't get any easier to accept, particularly when it's in such tragic circumstances,' Guy responded with a faraway look in his eyes. 'Poor old Bert. I wonder what was weighing on his mind so heavily that he didn't see the lorry.'

'I think his hearing was deteriorating. Everybody knows you have to keep your wits about you on that nasty bend if you cross over by the bridge. Some locals are up in arms at the developers because they reckon that if the lorry wasn't in such a hurry to get to the site, old Bert would still be with us.'

'I think that's stretching it a bit, Ann, don't you? I mean the lorry could have been passing through but it just so happened to be heading for the Meadowbank site.'

'Yes, I know. But because of the fierce opposition to the new houses, you know what people are like. They want to lay the blame at the feet of the developers and in particular, Billie Tidmarsh. Everybody knows he owns the company behind it. He's not a popular character around here. Never has been.'

Guy noticed Bryan Jamison outside washing the cars in readiness for Bert's funeral.

'Have you noticed Bryan's been very quiet lately?' he asked.

Ann was busy filling in some online forms. She stopped what she was doing and took off her glasses. 'He's always been a quiet lad. He was big pals with my youngest, Dylan, and as a teenager, he was always the quietest one in the group. Nice lad, though.'

Guy watched the young lad as he buffed off some residue of car polish with chamois leather and recalled how Marsha used to invite him into the house for coffee sometimes.

'Anyway, he's moving on. He came in this morning to tell me he's leaving. Got another job in Ludlow. Some delivery driving job. He was a bit vague. Said the funeral business wasn't for him after all.'

Guy looked surprised. 'Oh, that's a shame. I had high hopes for him. I wonder why he didn't come and speak to me first?'

'Oh, I told him not to bother you. What with everything that's going on.'

'I wonder whether he's jumping ship before the ship sinks,' Guy reflected gloomily.

Ann gave him a lopsided smile. 'Who knows? He seemed pleased to be going. Said he would be earning a lot more too.'

'Well, in that case, I can't say that I blame him,' Guy said philosophically. 'I'd better get going. Lay old Bert to rest.'

As the pallbearers lowered Bert's coffin into the ground, a light drizzle fell steadily over the churchyard in Little Twichen. A bedraggled robin perched on a nearby tombstone, as if to oversee the safe resting place of a new soul. The closer members of Bert's family stepped forward to toss a handful of soil onto the coffin while taking a few moments of silent reflection. The cold, wet, and dismal day only added to the air of gloom.

A crowd of mourners had come from far and wide and passed their condolences to Bert's family, who were all still in shock at losing him so suddenly, and in such tragic circumstances. Although the mood was sombre, Bert's family were uplifted to see so many people gathered to pay their respects.

CHAPTER 42

MOURNING BERT

Miss Moorcroft was wearing an ancient black two-piece suit teamed with a cream blouse and had even found a hat at the back of her wardrobe. It was all crushed and dented, but nothing that a good shake and brushing couldn't fix. She stared down at the coffin and stopped for a few moments, reminiscing that she and Bert were supposed to enjoy an afternoon tea together on the day that he died. She had hoped that it may have led to something more. Now, she would never know. 'God bless you, Bert,' she whispered, fighting back the tears.

'Helena, how are you doing?' Kate asked softly. She linked her arm through Miss Moorcroft's and gently led her away from the graveside. The two women shared an unspoken bond because they had both been at the scene when Bert met his untimely death.

Miss Moorcroft's movements were slow and mechanical, her eyes full of sadness. She didn't need to answer Kate's question. Her face said it all.

'Have you met my partner?' Kate asked as a beautiful young woman materialised by her side.

Miss Moorcroft dabbed her eyes with a white, cotton lace-edged handkerchief and looked Zelda up and down. Before she had a chance to say anything, Kate steered her towards the cinder path leading out of the church.

'I'll walk with you down to The Sun,' she said, averting any confrontation, clearly sensing Miss Moorcroft's disapproval.

'That's very kind of you Kate. I might have a sandwich and a quick sherry to say my farewell to Bert.' Her voice was shaky and she blew her nose as they walked slowly along the winding path, down some steps, and under the metal archway leading onto Mill Street. Suddenly she turned to Kate and announced sharply, 'Don't ignore your friend on account of me.'

Kate smiled. When they reached the pub a short walk away, the three of them found some empty seats around one of the big, wooden tables in the spit-and-sawdust bar, settling in alongside some fellow mourners, who were deep in conversation. They were regaling stories of when Bert was a lad and how he had loved to help out on local farms after school and during the school holidays. He had had a reputation for being the best vegetable grower in the area. There were lots of smiles and nods of agreement and a warm, nostalgic feeling in the air. Bert Humble was very well thought of, highly regarded, and would be sorely missed. Not least by Miss Moorcroft.

When Kate's mobile phone vibrated, she stepped outside to take the call.

'Mum. Is everything okay?'

'No, love. I'm worried about Robbie. He's shut himself in his room and won't come out.'

Chapter 43

Billie and Bryan

Bryan watched as Ann Jones spotted his mate's flashy new Porsche pull up outside. She knew it could only be one person. 'You've got a nerve showing your face around here,' she shouted, stomping outside before Billie was even out of the car.

'Well, if it isn't Mrs Jones,' he said, feigning a Welsh accent as he unfolded himself from the car, sliding off his Aviator sunglasses.

Ann's face went puce with anger. 'You're not welcome around here. You're bad news,' she spat vehemently. 'Don't you let Mr Boden see you here. What have you done to his wife?'

Billie leaned nonchalantly against his car, crossing his feet at the ankles. 'What the hell are you talking about?' He was clearly unperturbed by her outburst.

'You haven't been welcomed in this village ever since that terrible accident. My boy still hasn't got over losing his best friend. He didn't pass his test until he was twenty-six. Too frightened, he was. And the families of those poor lads. They never got over it.'

'I was exonerated of any wrongdoing, remember? Why does everybody still blame me for what happened? It was an accident. Why can't people just accept that?'

Billie was barely listening, busy looking all around him. 'I didn't come here for a telling off,' he said casually. 'I've come to collect Bryan. It's his last day and I bet he can't wait to leave this place.'

'How dare you!' she spat, the hatred in her voice plain. 'And what do you think you're doing dumping all those houses on us? All in the name of making more money for Mister Big Shot Tidmarsh. One day, you'll get your comeuppance. Mark my words!' She was on a roll now and was waving her glasses around, as if trying to shoo him away.

Just as Billie was about to walk into Ann's trap of a slanging match, Bryan mooched up to the car wearing his uniform of jeans and a hoodie, carrying a rucksack, 'Nice wheels, mate.'

'Yeah, get in Bry.' He slid his Aviators back on and calmly addressed Ann. 'You know what? You're one of the reasons I couldn't wait to get away from this place.' His parting shot was to spray her with a shower of pea gravel as he roared off, leaving her standing in the courtyard, screeching and flailing around as if she were trying to fend off a wild animal.

Bryan thought it was hilarious. He wasn't sorry to be leaving Boden's, although Ann Jones had always been as nice as pie to him, but only because he was mates with Dylan. He missed seeing Mrs B about the place. She was very easy on the eye.

'We're just gonna pick Lucy up then it's into town for a few beers and a celebration. You joining the crew. Welcome aboard, Bry!'

Bryan's smile almost split his face in half, it was so wide. 'Cheers, bro. Feels good. Bit awkward with Lucy though...'

Billie looked across at him. 'It's all cool. She'll be fine. Besides, I'm taking her away tomorrow. It'll do her good to have a change of scenery. Shake off this dump. Spread her wings a bit. Can't understand why anybody would want to live here.' He pulled the Porsche Panamera into one of the Meadowbank show home parking spaces and leapt out. 'Won't be a minute, Bry.'

A minute or so later, he was back with Lucy in tow and opened the back door for her. She clambered in and buckled up. 'Hi,' she said to Bryan awkwardly.

He turned round from the passenger's seat and gave her an equally awkward half smile. 'Alright, Luce.'

Billie pulled stealthily out of the site, driving slowly along Laburnum Lane and then opening her up as he turned right onto High Street, despite it being a thirty-mile-an-hour speed limit. The deep, throaty burbling of the car's four-litre V8 engine could be heard reverberating around the entire village as it roared off and away, heading into town.

CHAPTER 44

LUCY AND BILLIE

Billie dropped Lucy outside her new flat, parking his car up for the night outside. 'Back later, babe,' he announced. 'Slight change of plan. I'm taking Bryan out for a few beers. Celebrating him joining the crew. I'll be back later to crash at yours.' He skimmed her cheek with a perfunctory kiss and was gone, he and Bryan swaggering off into the bowels of Ludlow for a boys' night out.

Lucy's heart sank. She thought she would be invited. Then again, it would have been pretty awkward. She resigned herself to an evening on her own and let herself into her new apartment. She had lovingly dotted a few pieces of second-hand furniture around the top floor flat, which she had teamed up with an eye-catching rug that she had bought from a stall on the market. A few modern prints on the walls, and some well-positioned houseplants and it already felt like home.

If she craned her neck out of the bedroom window, she could see the castle walls and loved the location, right in the heart of Ludlow. It was handy for all the wonderful eateries and bars for when she met up with friends, which she reflected, she hadn't done since she had been dating Billie. She thought about him every single waking moment.

It was late by the time Billie got back. She had waited up for him but finally caved into tiredness. Slightly irritated, she got up to let him in.

'Remind me to give you a key in the morning,' she said, her voice thick from sleep.

'Hey, babe. What's up?' Billie quipped, clearly having sensed her irritation.

'It's late. I thought we were going to spend the evening together. You didn't say anything about going out with Bryan.' She padded barefoot back to the bedroom and he followed her.

'Hey. I missed you,' he whispered, planting delicate kisses all the way up the nape of her neck. She nuzzled against him and closed her eyes enjoying the wonderful sensation. He peeled her skimpy nightdress off slowly and began planting tiny butterfly kisses all over her body, starting at her feet and working all the way up to her breasts, skyrocketing her into a dizzying orbit of ecstasy.

The following morning before she was barely awake, Billie said, 'How do you fancy a few days away in Dubai?'

'What? she asked, confused, still in a post-coital haze.

'It's a surprise. I got a good deal. I've booked you a ticket but if you don't want to come...' That smile again. The one that made her go weak at the knees.

'Billie! What about work?' Her stomach lurched at the thought of what the witches in the office would say if she took off for a few days without warning.

'We'll only be away for a couple of days. Well, three. Besides, aren't you working up at Meadowbank this week? Just tell Alex you'll be working remotely.'

'I'll need to call him to run it past him first.'

'Sure, but I've already spoken to him. Now, are you coming to Dubai or not? The flight leaves tonight.'

'Bloody hell,' Lucy thought. She decided to ring Alex anyway to get his approval. If he said no, she wouldn't go. But Dubai! And three whole days with Billie all to herself. It was too tempting.

'It's your call, Lucy. If you think you can handle it, go ahead,' Alex told her curtly. 'Personally, I think it's bad timing. But, like I said, it's your call.'

Lucy decided she would go anyway. She would take her laptop with her so at least she could check her e-mails. She knew the spiteful bitches in the office wouldn't check them.

She wondered why Billie hadn't mentioned Dubai before. Then again, she reflected, he'd been out all evening with Bryan and then they had been busy for most of the night.

'Here. I've been meaning to give you this,' he said, handing her a Platinum Amex card. 'Treat yourself to something nice when we get there. And I mean anything, babe.' He smiled and then he leant down kissing her, a long, lingering kiss. Despite the intense night of passion they had just enjoyed, Lucy felt herself getting aroused again.

'Billie. You spoil me,' she cooed, taking the card and examining it.

'Here's the PIN. It's in my name, but, use it like it's your own.'

Lucy laid the card carefully on the bedside table.

'Oh. And can you just sign this document? It's just a record of the bonus I paid you, that's all. My accountant needs it.' Billie stood over her holding out a document while handing her a pen. Scanning the execution page briefly, she signed on the dotted line where Billie was pointing, but he whipped it away before she had a chance to read anymore.

'Right. Get those bags packed. Dubai, here we come! I've got to nip out. Things to do. I'll pick you up at two.' He picked up his car keys from the chest of drawers and was gone, leaving Lucy in a blind panic about what to pack for her trip.

She showered and washed her hair, looked out her dolly trolley and as she was pondering over where to start with her packing, the door buzzed.

'Shit', she thought, 'I forgot to give Billie a key.'

When she answered the telephone entry system, it wasn't Billie's voice that she heard.

'Come on up,' she said.

'Hey Bryan,' she said awkwardly, wrapping her short dressing gown tightly together, wishing she didn't have wet hair.

'Hey, Luce. Can I come in?'

'Sure, but you've just missed Billie.'

'I know. I saw him leave.'

'Can I get you a coffee? You look like you need one.'

'Yeah, thanks. We had a bit of a heavy night. Billie left early though.' Bryan watched Lucy as she busied herself in the kitchen. She didn't use a cafetière like Mrs B but used instant instead. It was much quicker, he reflected.

They sat at the small circular table Lucy had managed to squeeze in behind the settee just off the kitchen. 'So, what do you want?'

Bryan looked at her as if studying every contour of her face. 'I came to apologise. I'm sorry for the way we broke up. I was way out of order. I miss you, Luce.'

Lucy's face clouded over. 'It's a bit late for that, isn't it? I mean, I'm with Billie now. Does he know you're here?'

Bryan blanched at her words. 'Yes and no. He's asked me to drive you both to the airport later so that I can look after his car. He doesn't want to leave it at the airport. I knew you'd be alone. I wanted to talk to you, that's all. I mean,' he looked coy. 'We were good together, Luce, weren't we?'

Lucy looked surprised. 'Why didn't you call me? You've had plenty of time,' she said sarcastically. 'Anyway, like I said, I'm with Billie now. Do you know how much you upset me?'

'I'm sorry. I really am.' He looked at her knowingly. 'We were really good together. I miss you, Luce.'

'Well, it's too late now. Yes, we were good together. Very good. But I've moved on and you should too.' She reached across the table and touched his hand. 'If you had called me or got in touch sooner, I might have thought about us getting back together. But not now. I'm sorry.'

Bryan got up to leave. 'Well, if you ever change your mind, you've got my number.' His shoulders sagged as he walked away. 'Anyway,' he said, turning to face her when he reached the front door, 'I'll see you later.' He smiled and left.

Lucy felt confused.

CHAPTER 45

THE INVESTIGATION

There was an air of despondency at the West Mercia Police Headquarters at the Team Meeting to discuss the findings into the disappearance of Marsha Boden.

Detective Inspector Daniels looked exhausted; he was heading up two 'sudden death' investigations, one being the young lad in Upper Markle, who was the victim of a hit-and-run. The other was the sudden death of Bert Humble in Little Twichen. An anonymous caller had contacted the incident room. They thought that Bert might have been killed because of his vehement opposition to the new housing development, which in turn, they said, could have been connected to Marsha Boden's disappearance. DI Daniels was not so sure but would have to investigate the claim anyway. He rubbed his hand over his face in an attempt to focus his attention and was conscious of the fact that he hadn't shaved, due to pulling an all-nighter.

'Right, what have we got so far? The timeline of the day Marsha disappeared is looking grey in some areas, so either someone is lying, or perhaps the residents of Little Twichen have closed ranks. It's quite possible and it's our job to find out. We have had Billie Tidmarsh under covert surveillance and have evidence to suggest that the antique business is involved in something other than dealing antiques... Our surveillance team has logged activity in the dead of night on several occasions. I'm keeping the team low-key for now, until we can gather enough evidence to carry out a raid.'

There was a general nodding of heads but the team knew that it wasn't easy to obtain evidence that would be admissible in court.

DI Daniels also knew that if money laundering was involved, which was a possibility, then the source of the money being laundered would have to be established, in which case, he would have another case to try and unravel. Manpower was down, resources were even tighter and he sometimes wondered how his department managed to function at all.

'We have some new evidence. Bryan Jamison, the young lad who works at Boden's and was one of the last people to see Marsha Boden on the Saturday she went missing, said he saw an unmarked white van parked up in a layby on the day Mrs. Boden disappeared. Unfortunately, he didn't get a registration number, so not very helpful. So far, we haven't been able to find out anything more about the van or the driver. He also mentioned something about Mrs Boden's dog, the Golden Retriever. She thought the dog was outside but he hadn't seen it. I've got a feeling that dog might be key to this investigation.'

'If only dogs could talk, a Guv?' Henshaw quipped.

'Yes, that would be very useful at this point. Thanks for that,' DI Daniels said sarcastically.

'Did we get the results back on that dog biscuit that was found at the scene?'

'Yes. It was nothing, sir. Just an ordinary dog biscuit,' Henshaw responded.

'OK. Let's look at some of the possibilities: One. Things just got too much for Mrs Boden so she took off to start a new life somewhere on her own. Possible but not probable in my opinion. Two. Her husband killed her, perhaps in a fit of rage because she was leaving him for another man. Three, Bryan Jamison murdered her because as far as we can tell, he was the last person to see her alive. Four, the man Marsha Boden was having an affair with, Lloyd Peterson, had something to do with her disappearance. Or five, and this is a long shot but it is a possibility. She slipped and fell while out walking her dog. We know that she didn't have her mobile phone with her on the day she disappeared. We also know that there are several old lime kilns in the area. It is possible that she slipped and fell, but the dog would have raised the alarm and somebody would have seen or heard something.'

'My money's on the husband,' PC Leila Bridlington said.

'I wonder if those sudden deaths are connected?' Damien Henshaw volunteered.

'Go on,' DI Daniels urged.

'Well, it's only a small place and it seems odd that three people died suddenly, both around the time Marsha Boden disappeared. Two just before, Dr Bursford and Jamie Lyle, the lad killed in the hit and run incident, and one just after, Bert Humble.'

'Have you found any connection?' the DI asked, rubbing his chin, mystified. 'One was a suicide and the other two were RTA's.'

'Not yet, Guv, but I'm looking into it. I mean, we know that Mrs Boden was friendly with Bert Humble and was helping him out with various ways of trying to stop the new housing development. So what if she had confided in him about something? Or perhaps he'd been poking his nose into the planning application process and made some enemies along the way?'

'It's possible, I suppose. I mean, the anonymous caller seems to think there might be a connection. See what you can find out,' DI Daniels instructed.

'By the way, I've looked through all the statements taken from the staff at Boden's but I couldn't seem to find one for Ann Jones. I spoke to her briefly but we will need a formal statement. Did anybody take one?'

There was an embarrassed ruffle of paper and lots of side glances.

'Right. Somebody get on to it. Straight away! I'm going to organise another search of the woodlands and surrounding area, although I don't hold out much hope. Local farmers and land owners would have reported it, if they had seen or heard Mrs Boden. Or found her mobile. And her dog was at home. In my experience, a dog would stay with its owner, especially if they were hurt or injured.'

DI Daniels scooped up some papers and turned to his team. 'One last thing. Kate Bursford told us she had discovered her husband's car in the garage with some damage to the front bumper. It was covered in what looked like blood. We examined the car and it turns out that the blood was from an animal, so he probably hit a deer, judging by damage to the vehicle At least that rules him out from the hit-and-run. Mrs Bursford was relieved when I told her.' He stood up. 'Right, if there's nothing else, let's get back to it, keep asking questions. Keep digging. Let's find out what happened to Marsha Boden.'

He wrapped up the session keen to head off home to get his head down for a couple of hours.

CHAPTER 46

ANN JONES

'PC Damien Henshaw' the young police officer announced in the Interview Room of West Mercia Police Station. 'Please state your full name and occupation for the tape.' PC Leila Bridlington was sitting next to him, opposite the person being interviewed.

'Ann Elizabeth Jones. Office Manager.' Ann's Welsh accent seemed stronger than ever. Her signature red glasses were halfway down her nose and she peered over the top of them expectantly. The scent of cheap perfume permeated the air. She was wearing her hair up today, in a Chignon.

'Can you tell us where you were on Saturday the 28th of May.'

'Yes. I was working in my husband's butcher's shop. He was away. His mother's not too good. They think it's Alzheimer's. His father's poorly too. They're getting on, you know. In age.'

'Yes. Thanks for that,' PC Henshaw interrupted.

'So. What time were you there? And, are there any witnesses?'

Mrs Jones sat back in the hard plastic chair. 'Let me think. Right. Craig was helping out that day. Been with us for years, he has. I was there all morning. Till around one. Then we closed. Only open half days on Saturdays.'

'And you were there the whole time?'

'Yes. Might have nipped out for a coffee. Or a loo break.'

'And how well do you know Marsha Boden?'

Ann pushed out her bottom lip. 'Known her for years. Her boys went to school with our two. And I see her sometimes when she pops in the office to speak to Guy. But that's not very often.'

'So, you're not close then?'

'Well, not really. I say hello to her when we bump into each other. I sometimes pop round for a coffee if things are quiet in the office. But not very often. We're very different.'

'What do you mean by that?'

'Well, I mean, some people you just get on with like a house on fire and others you can take 'em or leave 'em.' She was leaning forward, her forearms on the desk. 'I wouldn't call her a friend, but I didn't dislike her. If that's what you're getting at.'

'And after you finished work. In your husband's shop. What did you do then?'

Ann sat back again. 'I went into Ludlow.' She looked into space, thinking. ' I remember now,' she said perking up. 'I needed to get a birthday present for my niece.'

'And where did you go?'

'Gosh! I don't know! Well, I wandered around for a bit. Then I bought something in The Silver Pear.'

'Would you have a bank statement or receipt to prove that?'

Ann looked affronted. 'Somewhere, yes. I suppose I must have.'

'I must ask you to produce that. When you can please.'

'Right. Okay.'

'Is there anything else you want to add to your statement, Mrs Jones?'

'No. Not really. Only that I hope Marsha comes back soon. Guy's been like a bear with a sore head since she went missing. Understandably,' she added, as if it was an afterthought.

CHAPTER 47

LUCY AND BILLIE

'Mister Tidmarsh. I have a reservation for eight o'clock.' The maître d'hôtel at the Eau Zone restaurant nodded, checked his reservation list, and then said, 'If you would like to follow me, sir. Ma'am.' He ushered the handsome young couple through a set of huge plate glass doors, opened by a bell boy in a striking red, gold, and black uniform, who smiled and nodded as they passed. They were greeted by a glass structure suspended over a small lagoon of the most exquisite shade of blue that Lucy had ever seen. Under-lighting accentuated the beautiful setting. She couldn't take her eyes off the gigantic flower arrangements of virginal white gladioli in two-foot-tall vases, strategically placed in eye-catching formations to enhance the opulent setting. She had never been anywhere so luxurious.

They were seated at a small circular table set for two people. It had a dazzling white linen tablecloth and an exquisite table decoration, matching the décor of the fine establishment. Minimalist with a slight clinical feel, which worked perfectly.

'Can I get you a drink, sir, madam?' the waiter asked, a white linen cloth draped over his forearm.

'Do you have a wine list?' Billie asked.

'Certainly, sir.'

A few seconds later, a wine waiter arrived with a wine list and said he would return to take the order in a few moments.

It was a warm, sultry evening and Lucy had never been to such a swanky restaurant. She loved the decadence of the setting but was shocked when she saw the price of the dishes. The bill would probably come to more than what she earned in a month, but that wasn't her problem. Billie was picking up the tab and didn't seem in the least bit fazed by the off-the-scale prices.

'Here's to us,' Billie toasted after the wine waiter had poured it for them, letting him taste it first.

'Cheers!' Lucy said, feeling light-headed. She had never been so happy. Billie certainly knew how to treat a woman she thought smugly, as she sipped the delicious wine in the opulent setting, feeling as though she had finally found her calling. She could definitely get used to this lifestyle.

Billie smiled at her. 'I've got a meeting tomorrow, out at the Dubai Creek Golf and Yacht Club. You don't mind, do you?'

Lucy's heart sank. She had been hoping to spend every waking moment of every single day with this gorgeous man. But she was having such a good time, she nodded with a half-smile that didn't quite reach her eyes. Besides, she had the Platinum Amex credit card burning a hole in her pocket. What better place to do some serious shopping than Dubai, she reflected, sipping the delicious wine.

'Has anyone ever told you how beautiful you are?'

Lucy blushed as she took another sip of her wine, which was way over and above the usual cheap plonk that she usually drank. Emboldened by the alcohol, she accepted Billie's compliment, basking in the adulation.

After their incredible dining experience, they headed back to the Address Hotel in a limousine and couldn't keep their hands off each other. Lucy didn't want the evening to end and they enjoyed a nightcap at the Azul Bar and Lounge, before heading back to their serviced apartment on the forty-third floor.

The following morning, on Billie's instructions, they were up at the crack of dawn and heading out to the Dubai Creek Golf and Yacht Club in a private limo, ready for his tee-time at seven-thirty. Lucy was made to wait in the clubhouse while he played his round of golf.

'Billie! Don't keep doing this!' Lucy cried when he told her his plans

'Hey, babe. Come on. Didn't we have a great time last night?' He cupped her face in his hand and pressed his head against hers.

'Yes, but why can't I go shopping while you're playing golf?' she asked petulantly, pulling away from him.

'Because I like it when you're with me. Order a coffee, enjoy that beautiful view and before you know it, I'll be back.' He swaggered off leaving her smarting.

'Is anybody sitting here?' a very elegantly dressed young woman asked in an Australian accent.

'No. Go for it,' Lucy replied distractedly, feeling incredibly pissed off.

The young woman sat down. 'On your own?'

'No. My boyfriend is playing golf.'

'On holiday then?'

'Yes. Just for a few days. Do you live here?' Lucy enquired, knowing that Dubai was a popular place for expats.

'No. I work in London but I come here for a break quite often. It's a brilliant place. Guaranteed wall-to-wall sunshine,' she said smiling. 'I'm thinking of making the leap to move here permanently.'

'Really?'

'Yeah. I was in a relationship back home in Oz and my boyfriend wanted to work in London, so I followed him. It turned out that he preferred the company of an English woman and he left me.' She put her hands in the air, making a 'c'est la vie' gesture.

There was something about the tone of the woman's voice that resonated with Lucy. Bryan hadn't fought for her at all, instead letting her slip away like a minnow in a stream, allowing her to float away in the slipstream of life. As she thought about Bryan, she remembered their conversation the day before and realised that he hadn't been a bad catch after all.

'I'm Sapphire, by the way,' the tall, willowy woman offered, stretching out her hand.

'Nice to meet you. I'm Lucy.'

The two women chatted for a while, striking up an instant rapport. Eventually, it was time for Sapphire to leave. She had only been checking the place out for a possible corporate event. 'Here's my business card. I'm in property.'

'Me too!' Lucy enthused, taking the fancy business card. High-end property sales, she deduced looking at the company name and the Kensington location.

'If you're in London, give me a call. Or if I can help in any way, just let me know.'

'Thanks. I will.' Lucy took the card and tucked it safely into her handbag, reflecting on how much she had enjoyed the young woman's company. She doubted that their paths would ever cross again, but very much hoped that they would. There was something about Sapphire. She was sassy and gutsy. Qualities that she admired.

By one o'clock, Billie still hadn't returned and Lucy was beginning to feel as though he was really taking the piss. She ordered lunch of a Lakeside yellowfin tuna salad nicoise, accompanied by a large glass of wine. Honestly, she thought to herself. Coming all this way to Dubai to sit on my own in a restaurant. She decided that if he wasn't back by the time she had finished, she would leave.

Just in the nick of time, Billie swaggered in. 'Babe. I'm sorry. I got chatting with this guy and...oh, you've had lunch. I thought you'd wait for me.'

Completely out of character, buoyed up by the wine, Lucy said, 'I couldn't wait any longer. In fact, I was about to order a taxi to take me back to the hotel. At least I could have enjoyed sitting by the pool.'

Billie's face clouded over. 'No need to get stroppy. I've been in a meeting. It's not all pleasure you know. This trip.'

'That's not what you sold it to me as,' she replied petulantly. 'I was bored. I wanted to go shopping but you wouldn't let me.'

'I thought we could go together, that's why. Besides,' he said, smiling and rubbing his hands together. 'I've just done the deal of the century so how about I get you another glass of wine and order myself a bite to eat? Waiter!' He turned around and snapped his fingers in the air.

Before Lucy had a chance to reply, Billie had ordered himself a Lakeside club sandwich and two glasses of wine.

Succumbing to his charms once more, Lucy got stuck into her second glass of wine, her anger dissipating with every sip.

'What's this deal of the century then?' she asked.

'Oh, no need to worry that pretty little head of yours with things that don't concern you, babe. You just sit back and enjoy the ride.' He smirked at his own joke and instantly regretted it.

Seeing the look on Lucy's face, he realised that it was the wrong thing to say, and gave Lucy one of his sexiest smiles.

'Hey, come on babe. Why the long face? From now on, I'm all yours. How do you fancy a trip down to the marina tonight? I know a great restaurant there.' He tucked into his sandwich and ordered another glass of wine for them both.

Lucy was about to protest but then thought, sod it. She had earned it, waiting around like a spare prick at a party. She would make sure they stopped off at one of the fancy shopping malls on the way back to the hotel. She was determined not to let Billie off the hook with that one.

The waiter brought her a beautiful fresh orchid when Billie paid the bill. 'Enjoy your stay in Dubai ma'am' the young Goan said, smiling warmly at her as he set the exquisite flower gently down onto the table next to her.

'Thanks, I will.'

CHAPTER 48

KATE AND ZELDA

Zelda was pouring some coffee when Kate sauntered into the kitchen wearing her short-sleeved nightie and Ugg slippers, her blonde hair all ruffled from sleep.

'Mm, that smells good.'

Zelda took another mug out of the cupboard and poured her one. 'Here you go. Are you okay? You look a bit pre-occupied.'

'Yeah, I'm okay, thanks,' she lied. 'Just worried about Robbie. I think he's taken losing his Dad harder than I realised.'

'How's Chase doing?' Zelda asked, cupping her mug in both hands.

'He seems okay but you can never tell. I'll keep an eye on him.'

'If anybody knows kids inside out, it's you,' Zelda told her warmly.

Kate smiled. 'Yeah, but all the training in the world doesn't prepare you for dealing with your own children.' She hitched herself up onto one of the bar stools.

'Have you heard anything more about your friend, Marsha Boden?' Zelda asked, perching on the stool opposite.

'No.' Kate's face clouded over. 'It's all very odd. She told me she'd been doing some work for Billie Tidmarsh...'

'What? Do you think he's involved, somehow?' Zelda interrupted, suddenly on full alert.

'I don't know.' Kate stared down into her coffee cup. 'You haven't seen anyone hanging around, have you?'

Zelda looked concerned. 'What do you mean? Hanging around here?'

She nodded. 'Yes. I've got a horrible feeling that Billie Tidmarsh might have something to do with Marsha's disappearance.'

Zelda quizzed Kate. 'Why do you say that?'

'I don't know. I think Marsha might have discovered something. She was doing some work for him in Ludlow. Something to do with one of his businesses there. She told me once that something was going on but she wouldn't elaborate. You can never be too careful where Billie Tidmarsh is concerned. I wouldn't put anything past him.'

'Christ, Kate,' Zelda exclaimed. 'You don't think we're in danger, do you? I mean, you've said it yourself many times, Billie can be a nasty piece of work. I don't know the guy, only from what you've told me. I had no idea...' she trailed off, deep in thought.

'I told Marsha to go to the police but I don't know if she did or not.'

Chase came bounding into the room wearing his Spider-Man pyjamas, wielding a Transformer pretending to shoot Zelda.

'Chase! Please, calm down,' Kate admonished. 'I can't hear myself think. Where's your brother?'

Chase shrugged. 'In his room,' he said despondently looking down at his feet and forgetting all about shooting anybody.

Zelda looked across at Kate. 'Do you want me to go and have a word with him?'

'Would you? Thanks.'

'How about a Thai takeaway tonight? I could pick one up at The Purple Elephant later if you like. We could have a quiet night in?'

Zelda smiled. 'Sure.'

'Shall we all go into town later then? Try and get Robbie out of his shell a bit. Or perhaps we can take them to that trampoline place in Hereford.' Kate put her mug into the dishwasher and then went over to Zelda. 'Why don't you ask Robbie what he wants to do?' she said, hugging her from behind.

'That's a good idea,' Zelda responded, feeling all warm and fuzzy. 'I'll see if I can persuade him.'

CHAPTER 49

LLOYD PETERSON

L loyd Peterson was beside himself with worry. The woman he loved had gone missing and within the space of a few short weeks, his friend, Bert Humble, had gone too. He couldn't stop thinking about the terrible way that Bert had died, but at least he knew that he was never coming back. With Marsha, every time his phone rang, he thought it might be her; every time a car pulled up outside, he ran to the window hoping to see her.

He looked out across the fields to the valley beyond. Autumn had burnished the trees with a golden bronze hue. He noticed the sheep huddled together under the old oak tree in the middle of the top field. He was losing interest in the estate. In fact, he was losing interest in everything.

When he heard a Gregory Porter song playing softly in the background, his thoughts instantly turned to Marsha. He suddenly felt overwhelmed with grief. She had lit up his life in a way he had never thought possible. He was looking forward to being with her so much, living together as man and wife. Now he was on his own again and was beginning to wonder what life was all about. Or even whether his life had any purpose now at all.

As he cleared his breakfast things away, he heard a vehicle pull up outside and ran to the window to see who it was, then disappointingly saw the red Royal Mail van. He went out to greet the postie in the hope of having a chat.

'Loov-lee die,' the butch young woman said in her thick black country accent. She was wearing a red tee shirt and grey shorts and seemed in a hurry.

'Yes, it's a lovely day,' Lloyd responded flatly. The young woman thrust a bundle of colourful flyers at Lloyd and turned on her heel, sifting through other pieces of mail as she went.

'Thanks for that,' he said sarcastically, taking the bunch of brochures and pamphlets, knowing that he would sling them straight into the recycling bin. The postwoman was obviously in a hurry and dived straight back into her van, spinning the wheels in her haste to get away, hardly taking time to close the door as she went.

Lloyd stood in the courtyard holding the sheaf of papers and watched the van drive away until it was out of sight, breathing in the autumnal air, drawing in a deep lung full. He listened to the bleating of sheep from the surrounding fields; the soundtrack of his life. His shoulders drooped as he turned and went back inside to start sifting through the mail. There was a bill from Severn Trent Water, which made his eyes water, and a bank statement that he didn't bother to open. He knew he had plenty in there and besides, he used the First Direct Banking app, so the statement was way out of date. He opted for paper statements because he had to keep meticulous records for the Estate; it saved him printing them out. The printer ink was expensive. He would file the statement when he was in an 'admin mood,' as Marsha used to say. He almost missed the small white envelope tucked between a pizza parlour flyer and a glossy brochure advertising the new Meadowbank development. It was handwritten and had a stamp on it. Curious, he slit it open with a letter-opening knife and pulled out a single sheet of paper. As he started to read the letter, his hands began to shake and he couldn't believe his eyes.

CHAPTER 50

MISS MOORCRAFT

Miss Moorcroft hadn't been going out much at all lately. Still reeling from the shock of Bert's death and the mysterious disappearance of Marsha, she was finding it all a bit too much. After the way Guy Boden had treated her the other evening, slamming the phone down on her, she wouldn't be in the least bit surprised if he had something to do with her friend's disappearance. He seemed like a nasty little man and Miss Moorcroft wondered to what extent her friend had suffered at his hands. A shiver ran through her bony body. It didn't bear thinking about.

Taking five twenty pound notes from a stash of cash that she kept in an old desk, she placed the money in an envelope and scribbled, 'In memory of Bert Humble' across it. Underneath, she wrote, 'In loving memory, from Helena Moorcroft.'

Striding purposefully down Snickets Lane towards High Street, she was glad to find Ann Jones alone in the office.

'Hello. I've brought a donation in memory of Bert Humble.' She thrust the envelope unceremoniously at Ann, who was peering at Miss Moorcroft over the top of her glasses, which were halfway down her nose.

'Oh, that's very good of you. Thank you. I'll make sure it gets to the family.' She tucked it into the top drawer of her desk. There was an awkward silence.

Miss Moorcroft looked around the smart office. 'Do you mind if I sit down?' she asked, not waiting for an answer. Slowly lowering herself purposefully into one of the leather armchairs, clutching onto her handbag as if it was a lifeline, she scrutinised the hefty woman before her. She had probably been quite a looker in her day, she surmised, but was clearly reaching her sell-by date. Her long mousey brown hair, flecked with grey, was tucked up away from her face and she had an air of being a cut above everybody else. Her silly red glasses were perched halfway down her nose and looked as if they were going to fall off at any minute.

'I'm really rather busy, Miss Moorcroft,' Ann said testily, shifting in her seat and shuffling some papers around on her desk.

'Oh, this won't take long, dear,' Miss Moorcroft said matter-of-factly, peering at her studiously over the top of her gold-rimmed glasses. 'Now, what do you know about Marsha's disappearance?'

The question clearly caught Ann off guard. Her face clouded over and she removed her glasses. 'What do you mean? What do I know about Marsha's disappearance?' she repeated slowly. 'I know the same as everybody else. She was here one minute and the next...she was gone.'

Miss Moorcroft studied Ann through narrowed eyes and watched her eyes, which were darting around all over the place.

'Now, if you don't mind. I'm terribly busy and Mr Boden will be back any minute. He won't take kindly to me chit-chatting with you.'

'Oh. But we're not chit-chatting, my dear. I'm merely asking you some questions. You see, Marsha was a friend of mine. A dear friend, in fact,' Miss Moorcroft knew she was pushing it a bit with that last statement, but she said it anyway. 'And, what with you working here, at Boden's, I thought you might have seen or heard something. It's all rather odd, don't you think? The way she just disappeared like that? And what did you think of Mr Boden being arrested? Do you think he killed her?'

Ann Jones had had enough. 'I've told you that I know as much as you do. And that is just what I've heard around the village. Mr Boden went fishing one Saturday and when he got home, she was gone. That's it.'

'Ah. You see, I heard that he didn't report her missing until the Monday. Two days later. Rather odd, don't you think? Why do you think that was? Do you think he was busy disposing of her body?'

Ann Jones stood up and Miss Moorcroft thought she was going to blow a gasket. Her face was thunderous as she stood behind the desk, her Amazonian frame towering over Miss Moorcroft. 'How dare you! Mr Boden could never have done something like that.'

'And how would you know?' Miss Moorcroft asked, very slowly. She got up to leave. Ann Jones was clearly protecting her boss and for a split second, she thought she was going to frog-march her out of the office.

'Well, I'd best be off. Oh, and don't forget to pass on my donation, will you?'

If looks could kill, Miss Moorcroft would have been dead on the spot.

CHAPTER 51

LLOYD PETERSON

Lloyd recognised the handwriting on the sheet of pretty stationery paper, which had a border in the William Morris lemons design. It was Marsha's. His heart sang. She was still alive! He never thought that he would see her again. According to the note he was holding in his quivering hands, she was still alive: 'My dearest Lloyd. I am going to stay with my husband. Please forgive me. Marsha. xx'

He was confused. What the hell was going on? He sat down, not able to process what he had just read. It didn't feel right. It was too terse. Not Marsha's style. Had she been forced to write it, he wondered. Or gone into hiding because she feared his reaction? Why the time lapse between him receiving the letter and her disappearance? Nothing made any sense. He kept re-reading the letter, hoping for something to jump out at him, to give him a clue as to her whereabouts, but the more he read it, the more confused he felt. He checked the envelope but it gave no clue as to where it was posted. He pondered over when, way back, if you posted a letter in a certain place, it would be post-marked with the name of that town. He figured that the Royal Mail had moved with the times in protecting the privacy of its customers with the advent of the Data Protection Act.

His mind was wandering all over the place and touching the paper made him feel close to Marsha. He couldn't explain it, but he felt her presence through her words. He looked again at the handwriting; it looked like hers.

Had her husband threatened her? Worse still, had her husband harmed her in any way? He decided there and then to take some action. He had waited far too long as it was.

Jumping into his Range Rover, he sped through the village and headed to Boden's Funeral Directors. Pulling up hurriedly on the courtyard, he leapt out. There was nobody about. He headed to the office and knocked on the door. A woman with a Welsh accent called out, 'Come in!'

'Is Mr Boden here?' Lloyd demanded. He had his hands on his hips, his arms akimbo.

'No, he's at a funeral. Won't be back until after three, at the earliest. Can I help at all?'

'No. I'll catch him later.'

'Can I give him a message?'

Lloyd turned on his heel. 'No. Thanks.'

Ann got up from her desk and started to follow the man she recognised as the Estate Manager from up at the manor, but before she could catch him up, he had jumped into his vehicle and was pulling off the drive. She wondered what he had wanted with Guy, but he clearly wasn't in the mood to chat.

From Boden's, Lloyd drove straight into Ludlow. Not knowing Marsha's whereabouts was killing him.

Parking up in a cul-de-sac near West Mercia Police Station, he made his way to the door and pressed a buzzer. Eventually, somebody answered.

'Yes. I'm here to hand something in. It's relating to the disappearance of Marsha Boden.'

He heard a buzzing sound and the door clicked. He pushed it open and was met by a very young-looking police constable.

'Is DI Daniels around, please?' Lloyd asked.

'No, sorry. You just missed him.'

Lloyd let out a sigh of frustration. 'Damn. Listen, I've just received a letter from the woman who's missing from Little Twichen, Marsha Boden. I think it's important. It could mean that she's still alive. I must speak to him.'

The young PC looked nonchalant. 'I can give it to him when I see him next.'

'And when will that be?' Lloyd asked, sensing that the young man was attaching no sense of urgency to the matter whatsoever. He seemed completely devoid of any interest in it at all.

'Dunno.'

'Do you have his mobile number?'

'Wait here.'

After what seemed like an eternity, as Lloyd waited impatiently in the slightly run-down foyer of the former police station, now just a hub manned occasionally, the PC returned with a small card.

'Here you go,' he said, handing the business card across.

'Thanks.' Lloyd turned and left the building. punching the number in on his mobile as he walked back to his vehicle. He was seething with anger.

CHAPTER 52

THE INVESTIGATION

Detective Inspector Clive Daniels headed up the team briefing. 'The discovery of a letter purported to be written by Marsha Boden has surfaced. Lloyd Peterson received it in the post and dropped it straight into us. He seems to think it's kosher. Do we have anything?' He looked expectantly at his team gathered around him.

Della stepped up to the plate. 'We've got the DNA results back from the lab which matches that of Marsha Boden. The handwriting has been compared by an expert and it all points to it being the real deal.'

'Right. So where is she then?' DI Daniels asked sarcastically, his hands thrust into his trouser pockets. 'If she changed her mind about moving in with Peterson, Guy Boden must have been cock-a-hoop. Let's say he and Marsha had words and he threatened her that unless she ended her affair with Lloyd Peterson, things could get nasty and then they did.'

'But why did she write the note?' Della asked, confused.

Damien Henshaw piped up. 'What if he forced her to write it?'

'None of this makes sense. Why was the letter posted so long after Marsha disappeared? Why the delay?' We went through the place with a fine-tooth comb and found nothing. We even dredged through some remains of ashes that we were able to find at the local crematoria. And we exhumed two bodies from the local churchyard, but we found nothing. And we don't have anything substantial to go on, other than she didn't have her mobile phone with her the day she disappeared. And, Kate Bursford thinks Billie Tidmarsh might have something to do with her husband's death. Which, in turn, could be connected to Marsha's disappearance. Let's bring him in for questioning.'

The mood in the room at West Mercia Police Headquarters was upbeat. The more the team members learnt about Marsha Boden, Della in particular, the more they wanted to find out what had happened to her. They all thought that she sounded like a thoroughly decent person.

CHAPTER 53

LLOYD PETERSON

E ver since he received Marsha's letter, Lloyd Peterson desperately wanted to believe that she was still alive. He was baffled. Why would she suddenly want to end their relationship? He recalled how they had talked about her moving into Dovecote Manor with him. She was worried that it might have been awkward, but, as with most situations in Little Twichen, once the gossip died down and somebody else was in the lime-light, people would soon come to terms with them being a couple. He could not, for the life of him, work out what had happened to suddenly make her change her mind. He had his own suspicions about the note.

Deciding to check on Bert's house to keep himself busy, his heart felt like a lead weight in his chest. On the way, he passed the development that had caused so much consternation in the village. It was now well on its way to being an estate. Marsha would have hated it, he thought. She had often talked about the ecology of the site and how certain species of orchids were being endangered, not to mention all the other wildlife that had been displaced.

Passing the 'For Sale' sign that Ashcroft's had erected near the gate of Bert's former home, he inserted the key into the front door of his old friend's house. Stepping over a sea of scattered envelopes and flyers on the mat, he gathered them up and took them through to the small sitting room and placed them neatly on the sideboard. The curtains were drawn, making the place feel dark and even more depressing. Walking across the living room to the patio doors leading out onto the small back garden, he drew them back and was shocked at what he saw. Instead of the small lawn, usually the texture of a billiard table, today it was unkempt and overgrown. A massive heap of dark soil obscured any view that was once visible from the room. A sadness overwhelmed him. It was a good job Bert wasn't around to witness the decimation of the once beautiful meadow. It would have been enough to put him in his grave if he weren't there already. The cottage had a sad air about it, the emptiness feeling strange and unfamiliar. It already smelt musty. The kitchen had been tidied up. The refrigerator had been unplugged and the door left open. Bert had lived a simple life and it showed in his home. Basic, old-fashioned, dark furniture that was solid and dependable. A bit like Bert, Lloyd reflected. He checked the upstairs and everything was in order. He flicked on a light switch and was relieved to see that it was still working. He wondered how long it would be before the utility company cut the electricity off if the bill wasn't paid. He would mention it to the solicitor who was dealing with Bert's estate.

As he locked up, Lloyd felt even more depressed and wished he hadn't gone there. He couldn't face going home. Instead, he headed up to Boden's on the edge of the village. When he got there, the yard was empty and the office was all locked up. He had missed Guy Boden again and wondered whether he was deliberately avoiding him.

CHAPTER 54

ANN JONES

Ann Jones was sifting through a pile of unpaid invoices at her desk. She was familiar with the way things worked. If the deceased had sufficient funds in their bank account, the bank would sometimes settle Boden's invoice. If not, then it was down to the family to stump up the money. Not so easy if Probate was being applied for, which could take several months before it was granted, and, as she knew only too well, the death of a loved one brought out the worst in people. Why should one sibling pay over the other? Why not split the bill? If one sibling couldn't scrape the cash together another would sometimes pay their share with the promise of reimbursement once the estate was settled, but that wasn't always the case. Ann knew only too well that money could bring out the worst in people, and that was when the arguments started and rifts formed. She knew too that the funeral debt was just the beginning. After that, the wake had to be paid for, then the stone mason, and more often than not, the Local Authority stuck their hand out for a fee to secure a plot in the cemetery too. It all added up.

Dying could get very expensive and that was why she had advocated the alliance with Golden Leaves Funeral Plans. The idea was that mailshots of leaflets and glossy brochures were delivered in the area through a third party. When somebody signed up to the plan, Boden's were the nominated Funeral Directors. People paid into the plan and eventually, a tidy sum was accumulated which would be enough to pay their funeral costs. It was a win-win situation for all concerned, and Guy had praised Ann's forward thinking.

Ann knew that Marsha had never taken much of an interest in the business because Guy had confided in her on several occasions how it irritated him, even though she was a bookkeeper by trade, she refused to get involved. In the beginning, when Guy had first set up the business, Ann knew that he had found that a bitter pill to swallow as he struggled alone, but as time went on and the business flourished, he had employed her to lighten the load, which freed up some of his time to do the things that he enjoyed. He often talked about his love of fishing. How he loved sitting on the riverbank with a packed lunch, enjoying the quiet and solitude of the great outdoors on a riverbank. She could always tell when he had been away on a fishing trip because he returned happy and relaxed.

Ann recalled how Marsha had poked fun at him once when he returned home from one such trip without any fish.

'What's the point of sitting still for hours on end and then returning the fish to the river?' she had teased. Ann remembered how Guy had told her that he enjoyed the thrill of the chase. The point wasn't to catch the fish to eat it, but his enjoyment came from luring the fish to take the bait and then ensnaring it. That was the thrill.

'What should I do about Bert Humble's outstanding invoice?' Ann enquired when Guy appeared in her office with a cup of tea and a tray of chocolate digestives.

'Have we sent the first reminder yet?' he asked, settling into the leather chair next to her desk, one leg crossed over his other knee, holding a mug of tea.

'Yes. No response.'

'I thought I heard that that Estate Manager was a friend of his. It might be worth checking to see if he's an Executor. He's got plenty of money. He can bloody well settle my invoice.'

Ann peered over the top of her glasses at Guy, surprised by his outburst. 'I'll try,' she said. 'Otherwise, we'll have to wait until Probate is granted.'

Ann placed the invoice on a different pile and stopped what she was doing to enjoy the tea and Guy's company. 'How are you bearing up anyway?' she asked, munching on a biscuit.

'Well, at least Bert's family knows what happened to him. As sad as it was, they can draw a line and move on. I can't.' He looked strained and tired but Ann still thought him extremely attractive.

'It's the not knowing, that's the worst,' he went on. 'I keep thinking she's going to walk into the kitchen of an evening or come out of the bathroom when I'm getting ready for bed.' He was looking out of the window. Across to the house that he and Marsha had shared.

Ann flinched.

'Thanks for chasing up those invoices' he said, changing tack. 'What's the latest on the Golden Leaves plan? Any more takers?'

Accepting that Guy was uncomfortable talking about his wife's disappearance, Ann filled him in on the Golden Leaves plan, which was continuing to gather momentum. She told him that word-of-mouth recommendations were producing several new sign-ups a week. She knew that it was due to her quick thinking in getting Boden's on board with the franchise, that not only was the business surviving, but it was actually starting to prosper for the first time since Marsha disappeared.

Guy was relieved and pleased in equal measures and when he left Ann to get on with her work, she was deep in thought and seemed very preoccupied.

CHAPTER 55

LUCY AND BILLIE

The moment Lucy walked into the office at Ashcroft's, she knew she had been sent to Coventry. Nobody asked about her holiday in Dubai, even though she was sporting a nice tan. She put on a brave face and could almost hear the claws being sharpened behind her back.

'Lucy! Have you got a minute?'

It was Alex calling from his office.

'Hi Alex,' she said breezily, feeling slightly awkward. 'What's up?'

'I need you to help the others out for a while. We're behind with sales this month, despite having plenty in the pipeline. Get a list from one of the ladies and start calling round the solicitors to see where we are. We need to close more sales.'

'Okay. Will do,' she responded, hurt by the way he was talking to her. He was offhand and not his usual, friendly self. She backed out of his office, waiting for him to ask about her trip, but he was completely engrossed in his computer screen.

Just as she had predicted, nobody had checked her e-mails so it was a good job she had been on top of them. Nobody had checked her voicemails either, and there was a stack of messages waiting for her.

At lunchtime, she went out for some fresh air to escape from the horrible atmosphere. She called Billie on his mobile but there was no reply, so she left a voicemail.

***

'So, Mr Tidmarsh. 'Tell me what it is exactly that you do,' DI Daniels asked.

'I own several property development companies, one of which is the Green Circle Housing Group.'

'The Green Circle Housing Group, DI Daniels repeated. 'That's the one building the new development in Little Twichen, isn't it?'

'Yes.' Billie was not going to expand.

'And were you aware of the fierce opposition in the village?'

Billie sat back, rested his hands on his hips, and looked the Detective Inspector straight in the face. 'New houses being built anywhere get fierce opposition from the locals. It goes with the territory. I don't get involved with any of that. I have a planning team who sort everything out for me. I just stump up the cash.' He smiled and cocked one eye at the Officer. 'People think it's easy running your own business. Glamorous, even. It's neither. It's bloody hard work and I spend most of my time answering questions and sorting problems out. Even though I pay people to do that for me.'

'Tell me about the antiques business.'

Billie sat up straight. 'What do you want to know?'

'How does it work? Why the big warehouse?'

Billie thought before answering and then whispered something into his solicitor's ear. 'It's basically a storage area. When I get a call from a local estate agent, usually Ashcroft's, they put me in touch with a local clearance firm and I send a van round to collect all the stuff.'

'And where does this 'stuff' usually come from?' DI Daniels asked, clearly not buying Billie's story.

'House clearances of people who've died, mostly. There seems to be a bit of a revival of people wanting second-hand furniture. Some of it is much better quality than the new, modern stuff.'

DI Daniels could clearly see that Billie was a slippery character and was choosing his words very carefully.

'And how well did you know Marsha Boden?' The DI watched Billie's response very carefully.

'I knew her from the village. My mum recommended her to do some bookkeeping. Thought she was doing me a favour.' He looked at DI Daniels as if to say, 'Dear old Mum.' My team was in the process of employing a full-time bookkeeper, so I didn't need her anymore. We had to let her go.'

'I put it to you that Mrs Boden started asking questions about your income streams and you got rid of her.'

Billie looked bemused. 'I take it you mean fired her...? She was asking a lot of questions. Then I found out that she had been the main voice in the opposition to the development in Little Twichen, so yes, I got rid of her.' He had a steely look on his handsome face.

'And why did you feel that was necessary? Was it because she rumbled you? Worked out what you were really using the warehouse for?'

'I have no idea what you're talking about. I told her I wouldn't be needing her again because I didn't need the hassle. I surround myself with 'yes' people. Marsha Boden was definitely not one of those. She was getting involved in something that didn't concern her. I would never have taken her on, but like I said, my mum recommended her and my team appointed her.'

'What would you say if I told you that Mrs Boden thought you might be people trafficking?'

Billie didn't flinch. 'I would say that Mrs Boden didn't know what she was talking about, Officer.'

Much to DI Daniels' annoyance, since the surveillance unit had been in place, nothing out of the ordinary had been spotted. He needed to find people in the warehouse before he could arrest Billie. Reluctantly, he let him go.

CHAPTER 56

LLOYD PETERSON

Lloyd Peterson had been sitting in a layby in one of the white estate vans for the last hour, watching the comings and goings at Boden's, waiting for his chance. When he saw Mrs Jones' car pull out of the drive, which he had clocked on an earlier visit, he waited a few minutes and drove the short distance to the entrance, parking up next to a hearse. Taking a deep breath, he got out of the van and walked the short distance to the house, which he had visited on the day Marsha disappeared. This time he went to the front door and rang the bell. He waited. When Guy Boden opened the door, he wanted to grab him by the throat. It was clear from Guy's face that he knew who he was.

'What do you want?' he asked gruffly.

'Where's Marsha?'

Guy's hackles were up. 'Look, if you've come here to make trouble, you'd better forget it. If you've got any questions, I suggest you go to the police.' His jaw was pulsating and he drew himself up as if trying to make himself taller.

Lloyd was having none of it. As Guy started to close the door, he jammed his boot against the door frame.

'Did you make her write that letter?' he shouted, leaning against the door.

A struggle ensued and Lloyd, clearly much stronger than Guy, pushed his way in and the two men were now standing opposite each other in the hallway, glaring at each other. Lloyd had lost his hat in the struggle. It was lying on the floor between them.

'What letter?'

'You know bloody well what letter!' Lloyd spat out between clenched teeth. He had his fists balled ready.

'I don't know what you're talking about,' Guy lied, 'And if you don't leave right now, I'll call the police.'

Lloyd glared at him and knew that he was lying. 'I ought to punch your bloody lights out,' he said, the anger rising up inside him like a volcano about to erupt. 'What have you done with her?!' he shouted, stepping forward and raising his arm above his head, about to rain blows down on the man in front of him.

Guy cowered and stepped back, clearly afraid. 'I've told you, I don't know what you're talking about. Now get out. Now! Before I call the police! And if anybody should be punching lights out, it should be me punching yours out, matey.' He puffed himself up again as Lloyd towered over him.

'Go on then. Call them,' he said belligerently. Let's see what they've got to say about this. Marsha would never have written that note! You forced her to write it. You bastard!'

Guy held up his hands in front of him as if trying to stop traffic. 'Listen, you're the one who tried to steal her from me, matey!' He puffed his chest out, glaring at Lloyd, and clenched his fists, holding them up in front of him like a boxer.

Neither man spoke as each waited for the first punch to be launched. They glared at each other, the hatred oozing out of every pore in their bodies, the tension palpable.

Lloyd kept his eyes trained on Guy as he bent down and picked up his hat.

'You haven't heard the last of this,' he growled, moving so close to Guy's face that he could smell the fear. He turned and headed for the door. 'You better not have done anything to Marsha. Do you hear me? Because if you have, I will kill you.' He stormed off, leaving Guy trembling with a combination of fear and anger.

CHAPTER 57

TOM AND ANN JONES

Tom Jones had adapted to life in England, but, being a true Welshman, regularly had hiraeth, and every time he visited his homeland, felt the pull to return stronger than the time before. Now that his parents were failing in health, he was seriously considering relocating. Things between him and Ann hadn't been good for years but, like a lot of marriages, they tolerated it on the basis of 'better the devil you know.'

Ann could be so overbearing at times, sometimes bordering on bullying. It went against his grain. He was kind and thoughtful but Ann could be quite callous at times. Like when the dog breeding business had got out of hand. She kept assuring him that she had everything under control but greed had got the better of her. He had tried to step in. Sort things out. But she was having none of it. She was a force to be reckoned with and as he headed towards retirement, he could think of nothing worse than Ann bullying him the whole time.

He knew Ann was flawed. The animal cruelty business had been a bitter pill to swallow. She had assured him that she was a reformed character and that was the reason they had moved to Little Twichen. She had been supportive of him and his business in the beginning but had soon lost interest. Now that the children had flown the nest, and he and Ann weren't getting any younger, he thought more and more about moving back home. To Wales.

'We'd get a pretty penny for the business,' he had said to his wife, broaching the subject one evening, but it fell on deaf ears. The more he thought about it and the less interest his wife showed in moving, the more irritated he became. He signed up to Right Move and got daily updates on properties in Pembrokeshire that they could never have dreamt about buying when they had lived there. He would leave sales particulars lying around in the hope of persuading his wife to take an interest, but she was adamant that she wanted to stay in Little Twichen.

'I like it here,' she had told him petulantly, 'And the Golden Leaves initiative which I set up is snowballing.' What she hadn't told her husband was that she had devised a great little wheeze whereby she skimmed a small percentage off the top of every payment she received, calling it an 'admin fee.'

'What do you think about this place?' Tom had asked, showing his wife a beautiful house with spectacular views of the Preseli mountains. He had made sure that it was far enough away from where they had lived previously, but close enough to his parents' home, who were ailing fast.

'Mm. Looks lovely,' she had said noncommittally.

'Do you fancy going to see it?' He thought she was warming to the idea.

'Not really.'

That had been a few days ago.

He was already winding the business down and would be closing the shop soon. He would never give up on moving back home. Even if it meant that Ann didn't go with him.

'You're back late,' Tom observed as his wife tumbled in through the front door looking very flustered. She was carrying her laptop and a big, heavy file.

'Yes, I've been working late helping Guy out. Trying to keep him busy, you know. Distract him from all that's going on.'

'What's all that?' he asked, nodding towards the laptop and file that she had dumped on the table, scattering some paperwork that he was poring over.

'Mr Boden has asked me to see if I can pinpoint a discrepancy in the accounts. It seems as if some burial paperwork has been wrongly entered and the ledgers won't balance. I want to take a closer look at them here, without all the distractions at the office.' What she meant was that she couldn't concentrate fully with Guy around.

'Do you want a cup of tea? I was just about to make one.'

'Go on then,' she said, easing off her shoes and rubbing her feet.

'Busy day at the office?'

'Yes, you could say that,' she replied, still rubbing her feet. 'Miss Moorcroft came snooping around under the guise of dropping in a donation in memory of Bert. The atmosphere is very strange. It's as if everybody is looking over their shoulders the whole time. It's odd without Mrs Boden. Even though she didn't work there, she was always pottering around somewhere, or out with her dog.'

'Yes, she was a lovely lady. It must be difficult to carry on as if nothing's happened. I can't imagine what that must be like. What do you think happened to her?' Tom watched as his wife sipped her tea.

'Who knows? Why does anybody just disappear? It's those left behind that I feel sorry for.'

Tom's brow furrowed. 'I wonder if she fell while out walking her dog. There are quite a few old lime kilns in some of the woods around here. Do you think the police have thought of that?'

'I'm sure they have,' Ann replied with a certainty in her voice. 'I know they searched the surrounding areas because I was talking to one of the police officers that day they all arrived in vans. Don't you remember?'

Tom made a face that said, 'Not really,' and carried on with what he had been doing before his wife interrupted him.

Ann sipped her tea again, a faraway look in her eyes.

CHAPTER 58

LUCY AND BILLIE

'Hey babe. Fancy a weekend away?' Billie asked as he managed to catch Lucy on the phone as she was leaving the office on a Friday evening.

Honestly, she thought. He was like the bloody Scarlet Pimpernel. 'What?' she said, trying to keep the irritation out of her voice.

'You heard. Pack a bag and I'll pick you up in an hour.'

Lucy barely had time to throw some things into an overnight bag before Billie was letting himself into the flat with the key she had given him.

'Where are we going?'

'North Wales. It's beautiful at this time of the year.'

'No golf?' Lucy said, a serious look on her face.

'Nope. No golf, I promise. I do have some business to attend to but it won't take long.'

Lucy looked perplexed. Being with Billie was like being on a roller coaster. Sometimes she loved the ride and at others, she hated it. Like now. When all she wanted to do was put her feet up, order a pizza, and binge-watch Married at First Sight Australia with a glass of wine.

'Why can't you give me more time? Why is everything so last minute?' She was seriously thinking of not going but was very tempted and as usual, was being torn in two.

'Babe. Come on. You'll love it. I've booked us a great place to stay. It's right on the beach.'

Lucy caved in and packed her things and before she knew it, she and Billie were tearing along the A49 in his Porsche, heading north.

They arrived just in time to catch last orders for food at the bar of The Jolly Sailor, which was right on the beach. Thankfully, Lucy had worn a warm puffa jacket; the breeze on the beach was brisk.

'Do you mind if we eat inside?'

Billie smiled at her warmly. 'Sure. I just thought it would be nice to watch the sun going down.'

'Well, we can do that from inside. I'll try and grab us a seat by the window.'

After their meal, they walked hand in hand back to their cottage, a short walk along the beach. It was heavenly. Cosy and romantic. Billie poured some wine. When they eventually went up to the bedroom, they made love to the sound of the waves gently lapping against the shore.

***

The following morning when Lucy woke up, Billie was nowhere to be seen. She peered through the window which had a magnificent view of the rugged coastline. Seagulls squawked overhead, and it looked like it was going to be a glorious day. She showered and dressed and was about to put the kettle on when Billie came breezing through the door.

'Hey babe! I popped out to get some bacon. Fancy a full English?'

'Go on then.' Lucy was relieved. She thought he'd left her alone again.

'The forecast is great for today. I thought we could do a coastal walk,' Billie was saying as he rustled up breakfast.

'Yeah, sounds great. I bought my walking boots.' Lucy suddenly felt comfortable with Billie again, despite having reservations about his flighty lifestyle. When he was around, he was great company.

As soon as breakfast was over and cleared away, they set off along the beach, headed up onto the coastal path, and started their hike. It went for miles with spectacular views. When they had been walking for a while, Billie produced some binoculars from his jacket pocket and peered into the distance. Lucy took the opportunity to catch her breath. The views were stunning and the bird life was incredible. She had no idea what they were, but birds of all shapes and sizes circled and soared overhead, others settled on the cliff faces and behind her, on the windswept grasslands, smaller birds sang and hopped around on the hedgerows. She decided to sit down and drink in the view and despite the sea breeze, felt warm from walking.

Suddenly, Billie lowered his binoculars and got his phone out. He was talking quickly. Lucy couldn't make out what he was saying. Then he put his phone and the binoculars away and motioned for her to follow him. 'Come on! Let's head back. I think we've gone far enough.'

'Who were you talking to?' she asked, following along behind him on the narrow path. She didn't catch his reply because it got carried away on the wind. The fresh sea air smelled salty and Lucy was thoroughly enjoying herself. She would never have put Billie down as a walker.

The rest of the day passed in a blur as she and Billie had lunch at the pub on the beach, then headed back to their cottage for some afternoon delight, before walking hand in hand along the shoreline. Lucy had never been so happy and didn't want the weekend to end. All too soon it did though, and they were loading up the Porsche with their overnight bags and heading back home. Billie was staying the night before heading back to Birmingham, so it would be a week or so before she saw him again.

That was one thing Lucy hated about her relationship. The long distance between them.

CHAPTER 59

LLOYD PETERSON

As well as the gaping hole that Marsha had left in his life, Lloyd also missed her dog, Jasper. He had collected a four-year-old Golden Retriever from the Rescue Centre in Craven Arms and took her straight indoors to settle in by the warmth of the Aga. Her resemblance to Jasper was uncanny and he was glad of her company. They had become firm friends already. A companion is what he needed. As he held a chicken-flavored dog treat out on his hand, Bella looked up at him with her big, brown eyes and gratefully took the treat gently into her soft mouth. She closed her eyes as she scrunched on the biscuit as if savouring every last morsel, then quickly buffeted his hand for another, enjoying the affection that he showered on her.

He kept re-reading the note from Marsha. It didn't matter how many times he read it, he could not believe that she had written it. He had made a copy before handing it over to the police and held the single sheet of paper in his work-worn hands as though it were made of the most delicate porcelain. Whenever he held the note, he felt as though Marsha were there with him, in the same room. He swore he could even smell her delicately fragranced perfume, Cool Water, by Davidoff, which he had bought her on numerous occasions. His heart ached for the only woman that he had ever truly loved.

In the beginning, he had beaten himself up about sleeping with another man's wife. He had been trepidatious about taking their relationship to the next level, but Marsha had convinced him that her marriage to Guy was over. He had no reason not to believe her; she had been quite adamant. After his confrontation with Guy Boden, he felt no remorse whatsoever.

Cradling his mug of steaming tea, he looked out across the fields that made up part of the estate. He would have done absolutely anything to have Marsha with him now, sitting in the chair opposite, as she often used to do, drinking tea from a bone china cup with a saucer, as they chatted about this, that, and nothing in particular. She had opened his mind to music he would never normally have listened to and had shown him how to stream on Spotify, buying him a brilliant Bluetooth speaker. He thought of her every time he used it.

Marsha had also introduced him to the delights of exploring National Trust properties and their well-maintained gardens. He wasn't sure whether he would renew his membership or not when it ran out at the end of the month. There seemed little point in wandering around beautiful gardens on his own.

Checking his watch, he saw that the time was 10:30 am and he flicked on the television with the remote control. It was Monday, 19th September 2022 and he wanted to watch the funeral of HRH Queen Elizabeth II, having grown up with her at the helm of his country. He was touched when the coffin was lifted onto the shoulders of the Queen's Company, 1st Battalion Grenadier Guards, for her journey to Westminster Abbey, and then on to her final resting place alongside her beloved husband, Prince Philip, in the Memorial Chapel at Windsor Castle.

Watching the pomp and ceremony of the funeral, he marvelled at the scale, size, precision, and expertise of the people in charge of arranging the most important royal event in decades. Laying Queen Elizabeth II to rest after her seventy-year reign, which she had carried out with humility, compassion, and lots of laughter along the way. He felt extremely proud to be British.

If only Marsha was here with him, keeping him company, as he watched the procession making its way down the Mall as Royal Navy service personnel pulled the coffin along on a gun carriage. It was as touching and beautiful as it was sad and sombre. The end of an era.

His heart felt leaden with grief when he realised that he might never see Marsha again. What if she were dead? He had to believe that she was still alive. Keep that flame burning. Otherwise, he would sink into the depths of despair. More and more often, he thought how pointless his life was without her.

CHAPTER 60

GUY BODEN

As he settled down to another evening alone, his mobile rang. The caller display showed that it was DI Daniels. He braced himself.

'Mr Boden?'

'Yes.'

'DI Daniels. Can you come down to the Station, please? We have some more questions we would like to ask you.'

'Is somebody going to come and sit with my dog?'

***

Sitting in the interview room opposite DI Daniels, Guy was clearly irritated at being called in during the evening. It was seven-thirty.

'Why did you post the letter that you forced your wife to write to Mr Peterson?'

'I did not force my wife to do anything.'

'Well, we have reason to believe that you did. Bryan Jamison told us that when he called in for coffee with your wife on the day she went missing, the day you went on your fishing trip, he told us she looked distracted and she had been opening and closing drawers in the room off the kitchen. The bureau is near the door is it not, Mr Boden?'

Guy Boden had his arms crossed over his chest. 'Yes, it is.'

'Did you force your wife to write a letter and then lock it away? To use later.Against your wife. To keep her in line after she admitted her affair.'

Guy's face was like thunder.

'I put it to you that you got into an argument with your wife when she told you she was leaving you for another man. You forced her to write a letter to her lover. She wouldn't tell you who it was. So you kept it locked away. Then you strangled her and disposed of her body. Some weeks later, you remembered about the letter and decided to post it so that it looked like your wife was still alive.'

Guy was spitting feathers and wriggling around in his chair. 'I did no such thing!'

'I also put it to you that you threw your wife's mobile phone away as you were leaving Little Twichen on the Saturday she went missing.'

'I might have done that,' he confessed sheepishly.'But I did not kill my wife. I didn't want her to leave me. I wanted her to stay. Why would I kill her? I couldn't do that. Besides, I wouldn't deprive my sons of their mother. Never.'

'Well, where is she then, Mr Boden?' DI Daniels snapped.

'I don't know! I did not kill my wife.' Guy Boden repeated adamantly.

With no evidence to support his theory that Guy Boden had killed his wife, DI Daniels had no alternative but to release him.

CHAPTER 61

BILLIE

It was over a week before Lucy saw Billie again following their weekend away in North Wales. He had booked them into the best suite at The Riverside and arranged a manicure and pedicure, followed by a facial, topped off with a full body massage at Riverside Beauty.

'I thought I would spoil you, babe,' he said, flashing her one of his sexy smiles, knowing he had pissed her off.

'What the hell is going on? Why didn't you answer my calls?' she demanded. 'You're so unpredictable. I don't know where you are half the time.'

'Hey, come on, Luce. Relax. Everything's gonna be fine. I'll take care of you. I've just been busy, that's all.'

Lucy was squirming inside. 'I'm just saying that you need to be honest with me, that's all.' She didn't touch her drink and wanted to walk away but knew that she couldn't. She craved Billie like a drug. She played back the events at the beach and wondered whether their romantic weekend away had been another guise for one of his business deals, using her as a cover.

'I thought you liked all the excitement of being with me. Let's just enjoy a nice quiet meal together and have an early night. Tomorrow, you can spend the day being pampered. My way of saying sorry. I've even arranged a light lunch with some bubbles for you. I've got some business to attend to and then I'll be back in time for the evening meal. After that, you can decide what you want to do.'

Lucy looked at him across the table in the smart restaurant overlooking the river.

'Decide what I want to do?' she repeated, confused.

'Yeah. Whether you want to stay with me or call it a day...'

Lucy was stunned. Her heart was in her mouth and she couldn't think straight. In that instant, she wanted to scream at him that she wanted to stay, but deep down she knew that she had to break away. He was bad news. But she couldn't. She was in love with him, totally infatuated, and would do anything for him.

'Of course I want to stay with you!' she pleaded.

'Good. That's that sorted then. Look, babe, that credit card. I'll need it back.' He looked at her with a sardonic look on his face. 'Things aren't going too well at the moment.'

Lucy picked up her bag, fished out the card from her purse, and handed it back.

'You're earning a good wage now. You can afford to pay for your own treatments.' Billie's message was loud and clear.

CHAPTER 62

MISS MOORCRAFT

A Highways van laden with bright orange traffic cones, road signs, traffic lights, barriers, and other paraphernalia, pulled up outside Bert Humble's old home, which was looking sad and unkempt. It was a good job Bert wasn't around because he would have given the workmen short shrift for blocking his entrance. Fortunately for them, the house was still waiting for Probate to be granted, so they had free reign to park outside without being balled out by Bert.

Oblivious to the back story behind 5 Laburnum Lane, the Council workmen set about the laborious task of blocking off the road, so that they could start work laying the services.

The Meadowbank site was progressing well and the smart, modern houses beyond the metal fence gave prospective owners a chance to see where their new homes were going to be situated. It looked as if the site had always been there and it was surprising how new houses suddenly fit into the landscape.

Life goes on and although Bert was opposed to the new development, Miss Moorcroft thought he would probably have quite enjoyed getting to know his new neighbours. She had made a list of all the people she had heard saying that they were either interested in buying a house there, or had put a deposit down. She even had a plan that she had sneaked out of the meeting to discuss the development some months before. In her spidery handwriting, she had written the names of those she had heard were hoping to move in. On one of the corner plots, she had written Kate and Zelda's names with a flourish. It was the first time she had felt up to doing anything since Bert died. She had hardly ventured out other than to nip to Tidder's for some essentials, like milk and sticky labels, or pop into Ludlow once in a while to buy cat food from Pets2Go on the Industrial Estate. She had even stopped her weekly trips to the library because secretly, it had been part of her ruse to try and wheedle her way into Bert Humble's affections, bringing back a stash of books for him to read.

Bert's death had hit her hard and she often wondered what could have been between them, but now she would never know. As the nights were drawing in, she was dreading the long, dark, cold winter evenings that lay ahead. She hated the cold weather and dreaded the loneliness which stretched before her like a long, dark, dank tunnel. She made a mental note to stock up on sherry on her next visit into town; she had even taken to dropping the empties into the recycling container near Pets2Go. With the rising cost of living and electricity prices going through the roof, it was going to be a long, harsh winter for a lot of families. She was fortunate. She didn't have a mortgage to worry about. She had finished paying for the rickety old cottage years ago. She resolved to wrap up well and only lit the fire when it was absolutely necessary. Besides, a nip of sherry would keep her warm, she reflected, trying to justify the expense of buying her favourite tipple.

Hearing Kitty meowing loudly reminded her that it was time to feed the cats. Easing out of the chair, she turned to go out into the kitchen but slipped on a magazine she had left lying on the floor. Flying headlong into the heavy wooden sideboard, she went down like a sack of potatoes and felt dazed by the heavy impact. She tried to get up, but her ankle was in agony. She lay there for what seemed like hours and wished she had put the damned light on instead of penny-pinching and sitting in the half-dark room. As she lay on the cold, hard floor unable to move and bleeding from a head wound, she wondered how she was going to feed Kitty and Katty, who were meowing so loudly she could hardly hear herself think.

CHAPTER 63

LUCY

'Alex, have you seen this e-mail about the industrial unit off Station Road?' she said, striding into his office, not caring whether he was busy or not. As it happened, he was checking the football scores on his phone.

'Lucy! How are you? Nice break away?'

She couldn't work out whether he was being sarcastic or not and didn't really care. 'I'm going to get in touch with the solicitors. There must be some mistake.'

'Wait. Let's not get the lawyers involved at this stage. Besides, didn't I ask you to talk to Billie about it? There must be some misunderstanding, that's all. Billie will sort it. He's probably got cash flow problems, that's all. Don't worry about it.' He was calm and aloof. 'Anyway, we need to talk.'

'You're telling me,' she said, glaring at him stonily.

'What do you mean?'

'Oh, come on. You and Billie are as thick as thieves and you've both involved me in whatever it is you're mixed up in.'

'What do you mean?' he asked, a serious look on his face.

'Billie and I might be an item but I'm not happy about my name being on the Lease for the warehouse. I don't want to get caught up in whatever it is you're cooking up between you. You didn't say anything about it being in my name! Now I'm being hounded by the Landlord for late rent payments.'

Alex's face suddenly clouded over. 'I don't know what you're talking about. I don't know anything about that. Billie has a reputation for being a wheeler-dealer. Everybody knows that. Ever since he was that kid in school who stole chocolate bars from his parents' shop and sold them in the playground, it was obvious to everyone which direction his life would take. Billie and I go back a long way, we're old acquaintances. We put business each other's way. But that's it. I'm sorry about your name being on the Lease. I wasn't aware of that. Billie must have organised it. Didn't you agree to sign it?'

A shiver ran down Lucy's spine. 'Christ,' she whispered, the colour draining from her face. 'He asked me to sign something but told me it was to do with the bonus he'd given me as the deposit for the flat.'

Alex broke into her thoughts. 'Look, why don't you head over to Meadowbank. Have a quiet afternoon.' He looked at her sympathetically.

'Yeah,' she said flatly getting up to leave. 'I'll make my way there.'

'Are you sure you're okay?'

'Yeah, fine. Thanks.'

***

Phase one of Meadowbank was cleverly camouflaged by smart new wooden fencing designed to show off the twenty-five bright, shiny new houses. Anyone viewing the show home would not see the heavy machinery, mounds of earth, and piles of building materials on the other side, where phases two and three were ongoing.

The show home was immaculately presented and the moment Lucy walked in, she wanted to live there. The designers were very astute, cleverly portraying a luxurious and modern feel while making it homely and attractive. The carcass of a house had been transformed into a sumptuous home.

Each New England-style house had an integral garage with access from inside the house, three good-sized bedrooms, and a decent-sized back garden. The composite cladding on the upper half of each house was a beautiful shade of duck egg blue. A glass Juliet balcony adorned the double doors in the master suite, offering superb views over the Shropshire hills beyond.

Some houses, in particular the corner plots, had larger gardens and while others had better views, it was down to Lucy to convince prospective buyers that each house was as special as the next. The houses with not such great views were priced the same as those with sweeping views, so it was a case of the early bird catching the worm.

As Lucy wandered around the show home wearing blue paper protective coverings over her shoes, she admired the designers' choice of colours and beautiful textures, down to the fluffy white towels in the main bathroom, broken up with pops of colour in the form of tasteful retro paintings on the walls or a bright turquoise bathmat, which pulled everything together, from the detail on the elegant tiles to the dark grey flooring.

Browsing through her list of potential buyers, she realised that she had a viewing in a few minutes. A young family were hoping to make Meadowbank their first home together. Mrs Bursford, her two boys, and her partner, Zelda. She should have been excited for them but she was angry and distracted. She was pissed off with the way Billie had tricked her into putting her name on the Lease for the warehouse. He had defaulted on the monthly rent so she was receiving nasty debt collector's letters about huge amounts of money owing. She couldn't believe how naïve she had been and was worried sick.

Making herself a quick, reviving cup of coffee in the small kitchen, which was a make-shift, temporary ensemble in the show home garage, which doubled up as the Marketing Suite, she checked her appearance in the mirror and planted a smile on her face. It didn't reach her eyes, but it was the best she could do.

CHAPTER 64

KATE AND MISS MOORCRAFT

K ate called through Miss Moorcroft's letterbox when she didn't answer the door.

'Hello! It's me, Kate. Helena, are you in there?' She had called in to drop in some crochet patterns she had promised Miss Moorcroft, who had told her that she needed something to help fill her long evenings. Some of the teachers at the school were keen crocheters and were happy to share their designs.

'Miss Moorcroft! Are you in there?' she called. She thought it was odd because she had told Miss Moorcroft she would be calling by. She knew the lonely spinster was looking forward to some company. She had taken Bert's death very badly. She also knew that she was fretting over Marsha. As they both were.

Kate stuffed the patterns through the letterbox in exasperation and walked away. Perhaps Helena had got her days mixed up, she thought. As she was walking away, she decided to call her.

After several rings, she was about to end the call when a very faint voice answered, which Kate could just make out.

'Helena. It's Kate. Are you all right?'

'No, dear. I've had a fall and can't get up. It's very cold.'

Kate thought on her feet. 'Is the back door open?'

'Yes,' came the faint reply.

'Stay still. I'll be round straight away.'

As soon as she saw the old spinster prostrate on the floor, she knew it was serious.

'I'll call an ambulance. Then I'll get you a blanket and some nice hot tea.'

'Oh dear,' Miss Moorcroft groaned. What about feeding the cats?'

After several hours of waiting around in corridors on a wheelchair at Hereford General Hospital, a young man finally came along to wheel Miss Moorcroft along some corridors to the Fracture Clinic. A young nurse had very kindly given her a cheese sandwich and a cup of tea. The old lady watched people coming and going. Some were wearing ear pods, listening to something on their phones, and others were wheeling patients in beds or chairs from one department to another. Visitors burst through swing doors earnestly looking for directions.

The staff appeared to be incredibly busy and Miss Moorcroft wondered why they kept getting called away. The whole place seemed very chaotic. She had little choice but to sit and watch the world go by until whoever was tending to her returned, or invariably, a different member of staff came and asked her a raft of questions that she had already answered, several times before. She found it all very confusing.

Finally, her ankle had been encased in plaster of Paris and she was ready to be discharged. But that led to another mind-numbingly long wait, while the staff tried to contact Kate Bursford. She was the only person Miss Moorcroft could think of who would help her. Marsha would have gladly fetched her, she thought with sadness. The interminable waiting around was exhausting, and all she wanted to do was get back to her cats and a glass of sherry in front of the fire.

Kate Bursford received the call from Hereford Hospital just as she was sorting the boys out after coming back from visiting her parents. 'Yes, of course. Tell her I'll be there as soon as I can. Robbie! Chase!' she shouted up the stairs. 'We have to go out.' As she called out for the second time, 'Robbie! Chase! Come on!' she shouted again, darting around turning off lights and grabbing her car keys and handbag.

'Alexa, off! Come along, boys. We have to go and collect Miss Moorcroft from hospital.'

'Why?' they asked in unison, suddenly materialising in the kitchen, their hair all dishevelled and Chase's tee shirt ripped at the neckline.

'Never mind why. Just go and get your coats and we'll call for a Mc-Donald's on the way. But only if you're quick! And I thought I told you, Robbie. Be careful with your brother.' Robbie completely ignored the admonishment from his mother. 'Yeah! McDonald's. Hooray!' and they scampered off to get their coats.

'Mummy we're not friends with that weird old cat lady,' Robbie said, strapping himself into his car seat.

'Robbie. That's not very nice. Miss Moorcroft doesn't have anybody else who can help her. We're just being kind neighbours,' she told him, strapping his younger brother into the car seat next to him.

By the time she reached the hospital, having kept her promise to the boys and calling into a McDonald's drive-thru, which they ate in the back of the car, she eventually found a space in the visitors' car park. By the time she had worked out how to use the incredibly complicated parking fee system and herded the boys together after they had run off to play hide and seek between the other cars, she was exhausted. All she had to do now was negotiate the never-ending labyrinth of corridors to locate Miss Moorcroft. Very soon, she began to feel as though she was in one of those dreams where you never get to where you're going because the route keeps changing. Obstacles are constantly being thrown in your path, like a staircase that suddenly ends with a sheer drop or an elevator door that opens with a brick wall behind it.

Hurrying along and stopping a nurse and a porter along the way for directions, she eventually found Miss Moorcroft sitting in a wheelchair with a hospital blanket draped over her knees. Her right ankle was encased in a plaster cast and she had a bandage around her head which had little tufts of grey hair poking out at odd angles. She looked like a casualty from a war zone.

'Ah, Kate. There you are,' she said wearily, hearing the clip-clop of Kate's shoes hurrying towards her.

'Come on', Kate said gently, kneeling beside her, 'Let's get you home.'

Miss Moorcroft looked as though she would disintegrate into a thousand pieces if you blew on her.

'You had better come and stay with us tonight,' Kate told her gently.

Miss Moorcroft didn't even respond. She looked worn out.

By the time Kate got back to The Granary, it was way past the boys' bedtime, but thankfully, because it was school holidays, it didn't really matter.

'What about my cats?' Miss Moorcroft asked, once she was settled comfortably with a nice cup of tea.

'I fed them earlier. When you went off in the ambulance. I put plenty of food down for them. I'll pop round first thing and feed them again.'

'Well, I'll be going home tomorrow, so I can feed them myself. I'm really tired, Kate. If you don't mind giving me a hand, I think I'll turn in.'

Kate helped her up. She had made up a bed for her in the snug. It would be impossible to get Helena up the stairs, and the sofa bed was, by all accounts, very comfortable. She and Nigel had had friends to stay once. A long time ago.

'I can't thank you enough, dear,' Miss Moorcroft said, sitting on the edge of the bed. 'You've been so kind to me.'

'Oh, it's no bother. Now, if you need anything in the night, just ring that bell.' Kate had put some paracetamol, a glass of water, and a small china bell she had found at the back of a cupboard, an unwanted gift from way back, on a small side table next to the bed.

After she had settled Miss Moorcroft into bed, she went back out into the kitchen and poured herself a large glass of wine. Flopping down onto the sofa in the open-plan kitchen, she scrolled to recent calls on her phone and hit Zelda's number.

'Hey, Zeld. How are you?'

'Okay, thanks. You?'

'Oh, not bad. I've not long got back from Hereford Hospital.'

'Oh? Is everything alright?' She heard the concern in Zelda's voice.

'Yes, we're all fine. Miss Moorcroft had a nasty fall at home. She's broken her ankle and gashed her head open. An ambulance took her to hospital this morning. I couldn't go with her because I've got the boys. Anyway, she didn't have anybody who could bring her home so she called me. I'm keeping an eye on her. She looks very frail.'

'Oh, that's so kind of you.'

'It's the least I could do. I've gotten quite fond of her recently. I think she gets lonely. She misses Marsha as much as I do.'

'Yes, I'm sure she does. Is there any news?'

'No. At least I haven't heard anything. I'll keep you posted. Anyway, I just wanted to hear your voice. I'm going to clear a few things away and get ready for bed.' An intimacy crept into her voice.

'Wish I were there with you. In bed...' Zelda's voice was low and husky.

'Me too. It won't be long now. What's the news on your house?'

'Oh, nothing much. A couple of viewings but no offers.'

'Ah, well. Fingers crossed.'

As Kate flopped into bed exhausted, she couldn't wait for the time when she would have Zelda's warmth next to her all the time.

CHAPTER 65

KATE AND ZELDA

Kate had put her and Zelda's favourite playlist on and was busy rustling up a salmon risotto. They hadn't seen each other for a while because Kate had been busy looking after Miss Moorcroft. She had eventually persuaded Helena to have a lady from Country Cousins to stay with her for a week. Just until she got used to getting around on crutches.

'Searching, searching for my baby,' she sang along to Robert Plant and Alison Krauss's, "Searching for My Love", sipping her wine as she slowly stirred the risotto, which smelled delicious. She was chopping some fresh parsley when she heard Zelda's key in the door. The boys were all tucked up in bed, so they had the evening to themselves.

'Hey! Love the new hairstyle. It suits you.'

'Thanks.' Zelda responded shaking her head around as if to show off the sexy new cut.

'Let's get you a glass of wine. I'll tell you all about what's been going on. Red or white?'

'Red, thanks.'

Kate poured the wine and handed it across. 'I wanted to ask you something.'

Zelda looked at her and took a sip of her drink. 'Go on, she said tentatively.'

'Will you marry me?' Kate's eyes were sparkling and she was expecting an instant response.

Zelda held her glass mid-sip. 'Marry you?' she repeated.

Kate was smiling nervously. 'Yes! Will you marry me? I'll get down on one knee if you want. I haven't bought a ring because I wanted you to choose one that you liked. I thought we could go away for the weekend....'

'Whoa. Kate. Stop.' Zelda placed her glass on the island worktop and shook her head. 'I'm sorry. It's a bit too full on. Can we just slow things down a bit?' she said, looking directly at her, unwavering, a stoney look in her eyes.

Kate looked at her intently, the smile quickly sliding from her face. 'What do you mean?' Her voice was thick with concern.

Zelda's face clouded over and she became very serious. 'I don't want to live the rest of my life looking over my shoulder. I've been doing some digging around. Billie Tidmarsh is bad news. You didn't tell me he's got a criminal record.'

'I didn't know. I've been to the police and told them everything I know,' Kate cajoled, trying to salvage the situation.

'He's been done for GBH. Did you know?'

Kate looked very sheepish.

'Kate? What are you not telling me?'

'He hit me. Once or twice. Nothing much. Just a slap.'

'Christ! It's unacceptable to hit anybody. Unless it's in self-defence. I mean, come on...and why didn't you tell me?

'I, er, I don't know.' Kate looked as though she was going to cry, and she looked down at her hands. They were shaking. 'I'd forgotten all about it. Buried it. Deep down inside.'

Zelda took her friend in her arms. 'God, Kate. I wish you'd told me.'

A minute or so passed and neither of them spoke. They just held each other close.

Finally, it was Zelda who spoke. 'Look. You have got to let me in, Kate. Not sharing things with me. It's not what I want from a relationship. I want honesty and openness. Trust. The whole nine yards. I've got to go away for a while. A work-related thing. They've been bugging me for ages. The Senior Lecturer at the University wants me to present my paper. To a university in the States.'

Kate pulled away. 'But you never told me about that!'

'I only found out about it myself today.'

A frostiness developed between the two and instead of staying the night, as they had planned, Zelda went back home to her house in Ludlow.

CHAPTER 66

THE WAREHOUSE

Lucy still had a key to the warehouse on Station Road and decided to have a mooch around. She was suspicious about it being used to store antiques. She also had a feeling that Billie was not being honest with her. She wanted to see if she could find out what was going on.

Parking far enough away so that her car wasn't spotted, she walked to the unit, which was halfway along a narrow cut-through into the town. The place felt creepy. She noticed some empty wine bottles in the alleyway as she neared the entrance. She unlocked the door and slipped inside. It was still crammed full of tat and smelled musty and dank. The boxes of books, ceramics, knick-knacks, old chairs, sofas, and standard lamps looked in pretty much the same place as when she had first been to the warehouse with Alex. The junk looked like a mixture of the contents of an old lady's house and dross that people had thrown out in the Seventies. The one small window was thick with grime and the horrible stench was making the back of her throat and nose prickle. The cold concrete floor was dirty and the whole place looked rundown.

At the furthest end, she saw what looked like two old shipping containers, which she hadn't noticed before. She made her way over to them and along the way, behind a wall of old furniture, she noticed an orange cable trailing across the floor. When she followed it, behind the furniture, there was a makeshift kitchen. A kettle, an old fridge, a cupboard with remnants of food in it. There was an acrid smell that she couldn't distinguish straight away. Then she discovered a container of milk had been left out on the makeshift worktop with the lid off.

Back out in the body of the warehouse, she noticed boxes of clothes and old shoes. They were jumbled up and looked as though they had been rummaged through in a hurry. There were several rows of them. Children's clothes too, some small shoes and even some toys.

Suddenly, the sound of footsteps made her jump. Her heart quickened and her breathing became shallow. Quickly scanning the area to see if she could see anywhere to hide, in her peripheral vision she noticed an old oak barrell. It wasn't ideal but it would have to do. She ducked down behind it and waited. The footsteps stopped. Her breathing became hard to control. Her legs turned to jelly and she felt sick to her stomach. The footsteps were getting closer and closer. Then they stopped again. Her head was pounding and she could hear the blood rushing around inside her head as if she was underwater. She could smell expensive aftershave and thought her heart was going to explode, it was beating so fast. She held her breath. Then she looked up and saw a shadow.

'Who the hell are you?!' she asked, surprised to see a man wearing a rather fetching Fedora hat.

'My name's Lloyd. Lloyd Peterson. I'm trying to find out what happened to Marsha Boden.'

Lucy stepped out from behind the barrel and felt a huge rush of relief.

'What are you doing here?' Lloyd asked her.

'The same as you. Digging around trying to find out what goes on here.' She was relieved to have Lloyd's company and instantly, felt at ease with him.

'I'm Lucy, by the way. I work for Ashcroft's and I'm based in Little Twichen a few days a week up at the new development. I knew of Mrs Boden. Through a friend of mine, Kate Bursford. Her husband died recently.'

'Yes. I remember,' Lloyd said looking furtively around. 'There was talk of him committing suicide, wasn't there?'

Lucy nodded. 'Yes, that's right. It was all very sad. They have two young boys.'

'I heard that Mrs Bursford had taken up with another woman. But anyway, what has that got to do with Marsha's disappearance? Do you think the two are connected?'

Lucy looked pensive. 'I don't know. I hadn't really thought about it. But what I do know is that this warehouse is used for something other than storing antiques. Have you seen all those boxes of clothes and shoes out there?'

'Yes, I saw them. Marsha mentioned something to me about some guy called Billie Tidmarsh. She used to do his books for him and then one day he fired her. Told her that he didn't need her anymore. Just like that. She told me that she was curious about the source of his income streams. There were a lot of them, apparently. He's the fellow behind that new housing development, isn't he?'

Lucy felt herself blush. 'Yes, he is.' She decided not to say anything more at that point. At least until she knew that she could trust Fedora man. And then she had to ask, 'How did you know Marsha Boden?'

It was Lloyd's turn to blush. 'We were going to move in together. The day she disappeared, as a matter of fact. I can't work out what happened. She contacted me in the morning and said she was collecting a few things together.' He looked down at his feet, clad in working boots, and then his voice wavered. 'I never saw her again.'

'I'm so sorry...' Lucy didn't know what else to say. After a few awkward moments, she said, 'Why don't we have a good poke around, while it's quiet?' After hearing Fedora man speak so fondly about Marsha, she suddenly felt stoked, eager to see if she could find out what was really going on in the warehouse. Which might, or might not, she reflected, lead them to discovering the whereabouts of Mrs Boden.

'Good idea,' Lloyd said, and they set off together, not knowing what they were looking for, but desperate to find some clues.

'Do you think these clothes are handed out to people? Poor people. Perhaps even people who have travelled to the UK from war-torn places. People seeking refuge?' Lloyd Peterson's thought process kept rolling as he spoke. 'Christ!' he exclaimed.

'What?' Lucy asked, wondering if he had heard somebody coming and suddenly feeling on edge again.

'You don't think...' he said, taking in the boxes of dishevilled clothing.

'What?' Lucy asked again, not knowing where he was going with this.

'People trafficking.'

The two of them stood in stunned silence as they both tried to process the enormity of what he had just said. Lucy felt sick to her stomach. If Billie was involved in any way whatsoever with such a despicable act, she would never forgive him.

'What do you think the shipping containers are used for? Lucy asked, looking at Fedora man, who, for an older man, was very handsome.

'Let's take a look. My view is that, if we are on the right track, the poor folks are brought here and then distributed elsewhere.'

Lucy flinched inwardly at his choice of words. As if people were a commodity, which, if their findings proved correct, is exactly what they were. A commodity with a high street value, Lucy surmised. Otherwise, why else would Billie be involved? He only ever did things to make money. He was obsessed with it.

As they made their way to the two large metal containers at the back of the warehouse, they kept their wits about them, conscious that somebody could arrive at any moment.

After a few minutes of walking around both containers, they discovered that they were securely locked.

Lucy's face registered a confused look. 'I wonder what these are used for?' She looked bamboozled.

'Anyone who objects to being sent somewhere they don't want to go. Or being separated from their family. Might be locked inside...'

Lucy's face went ashen. 'That's awful,' she murmered.

Suddenly, headlights lit up the dingy warehouse.

'Quick! Let's get out of here!' she shouted.

They ran to the side door where they had entered earlier. Then stopped. And waited. They were both breathing heavily and scanning all around them. A horrible stench of mustiness hit them both, as if they had stumbled into an ancient church. There was a wall of books behind them, some on old bookcases and others in towers of boxes. They looked at each other, not sure what to do. The lights had been killed and nobody approached the warehouse. It was a false alarm.

'I wonder what's behind here?' Lloyd said, dragging a stack of boxes to one side. They both peered behind and were shocked at what they saw. Standing between rows of makeshift beds, it looked like a squalid dormitory.

'Jeez, it stinks in here,' Lucy exclaimed.

'I've seen enough. Let's get out of here,' Lloyd instructed. Lucy's hands were shaking when she locked the door. 'I'm guessing you followed me?' she said in hushed tones.

'Yes', Lloyd answered quietly, following her lead. 'I saw you go inside and slipped in behind you. Marsha told me about an old warehouse, so I thought I would try and find it. As luck would have it, I saw you go inside just as I arrived. I didn't even know this was what I was looking for, but it obviously is the place that she had concerns about. Shall we meet up at that housing development tomorrow? So that we can talk more. Try and piece together what happened?'

'That's a good idea. How does eleven o'clock sound?'

'Perfect, I'll see you there. Now, where are you parked?' Lloyd asked, 'I'll walk you back to your car.'

'Oh, there's no need. I'll be fine. But thanks anyway. I'll see you tomorrow.'

They both went in different directions and Lucy hurried off, eager to get as far away from the warehouse as quickly as she could. It gave her the heebie jeebies. As she half ran, half walked towards the Tesco car park, she felt as though she had met an ally. A friend. Somebody else who cared about Mrs Boden and who wanted to find out what happened to her. She decided that she liked Mr Peterson. As soon as he had told her that he and Mrs Boden were close, it felt disrespectful to call him Fedora man.

CHAPTER 67

KATE

Kate had finished giving the morning assembly and headed back to her office, collecting the mail from her pigeonhole on the way. It was usually flyers about upcoming events at the school, parent-teacher evenings, or charity-raising events. Ukraine had been the focus of most fundraisers recently. Absent-mindedly she wondered what today's post had in store for her. Settling down in the leather chair behind her desk, her eye was drawn to a hand-written envelope marked 'Personal'. She recognised the handwriting immediately. Taking a sip of the strong coffee she had collected from the staff room on her way through, she ripped the top of the envelope deftly open and read the contents.

'Dear Kate, I have accepted a sabbatical in the States. It's for three months. I don't want a long distance relationship. I think we need a break. Forgive me. Zelda

PS I sent this letter to you at school so that you could take time to digest the contents before seeing the boys.'

'Mrs Bursford? Mrs Bursford? Are you alright?' Jane, the school secretary was standing at the doorway telling Kate that her nine-fifteen appointment had arrived. The first of a string of young mums from the village looking for work as a Teacher's Assistant.

'Give me a minute, Jane. I need to read the CVs again. Can you get me another coffee?'

The ever-efficient Jane collected the empty mug from Kate's desk and closed the door quietly behind her.

So that was it. Zelda hadn't addressed the issue of the hefty deposit they had put down on the plot at Meadowbank, or the bits and pieces she had left dotted around The Granary. It was too much for Kate to deal with now; she had some interviews to conduct, and, as if Zelda's letter wasn't enough for one day, that afternoon she had to attend the inquest into her late husband's death. It never rains but it pours, she thought paradoxically.

CHAPTER 68

LLOYD PETERSON

Lloyd turned up at the show home at Meadowbank at precisely eleven o'clock. When Jed jumped up to speak to him, Lucy intervened. 'I'll take this one, Jed, thanks. If you wouldn't mind putting the kettle on?' She could see that her colleague was miffed.

'Good morning,' she said, smiling at Lloyd as he wiped his boots on the coconut mat. 'Filthy day, isn't it?'

'Yes, it's terrible. Cold as well as wet.' He smiled back at her and Lucy saw the warmth in his eyes. 'So, which plot are you interested in?' she asked. They were both standing in front of a coloured chart of the site which was hanging on the wall. Lloyd went along with the façade, asking questions about the different-sized houses and then Lucy said, 'Why don't we take a look around the show home first, and I'll take your details when we get back.'

As soon as they were inside the show home, Lloyd asked her whether she was okay.

'I think Billie Tidmarsh is definitely involved in something illegal,' she began tentatively. 'Billie told me about Bryan, who used to work at Boden's, who is now a driver making deliveries for him, but of what and to where I don't know. He was very vague. As he is with most things. But I don't know if he has anything to do with Marsha's disappearance. My guess is that Billie is using Bryan to protect him. It's what he does. Surrounds himself with fall guys.' She turned and sighed, casting her eyes down.

Lloyd rubbed his chin. 'So, what you're saying is... you think Billie Tidmarsh could be involved with Marsha's disappearance? Do you think she found out about the people trafficking?'

'I don't know. Possibly. You mentioned something last night about Marsha finding out about various income streams that Billie had. I was involved with Billie for a while. I still am, actually...'

Lloyd's head snapped up. 'What?!' he asked incredulously, his face like thunder.

'Oh, don't worry. I'm only keeping him on the side until I have pieced things together. You know what they say about friends and enemies. As soon as we have any evidence against him, I will go to the police. He's a slippery character, though. Always one step ahead.'

Lloyd listened and his face softened when he realised that Lucy was on his side after all and actively helping him to try and find out what happened to Marsha.

'Thanks for last night. And today. It's so good to talk to somebody. I've been going crazy. I'll do anything to find Marsha, safe and well.'

Lucy smiled at Lloyd. 'Well, let's keep at it then,' she said seriously. 'We have to be realistic, though...' her voice trailed off.

'I know. I realise that the longer she's missing, the less chance we have of finding her. But...' Lloyd's eyes welled up. 'I can't bear to think about that,' he said sadly.

CHAPTER 69

KATE

The Coroner recorded an open verdict at the inquest into Nigel Bursford's death. The toxicology report had found high levels of alcohol and barbiturates in his bloodstream, but the Coroner was not convinced that it was suicide. In his summing up, he said that it could have been a terrible accident.

Kate had found the whole experience harrowing, and the open verdict had confirmed her suspicions that Nigel might not have killed himself. She had felt guilty about his suicide, and blaming somebody else seemed the obvious way out to ease her suffering, especially somebody as nasty as Billie Tidmarsh. She knew there was something going on between the two of them. Something shady. But at least she had told the police everything.

She was grateful to her parents for accompanying her to the inquest, and would not have been able to get through the ordeal without them. A neighbour was looking after the boys for her, now that Marsha was no longer on hand. Feeling utterly drained, she headed home in a daze. First the letter from Zelda, then the interviews, and finally the inquest. She could have done without any of them, let alone all three of them on the same day. But at least the day was almost over. She pushed the image of her dead husband out of her mind for the umpteenth time that day. She just wanted to get home to her boys.

As soon as she stepped in through the door of The Granary, she knew something was wrong. She noticed the door of the snug was open, but distinctly remembered closing it that morning. She wondered fleetingly if Nigel's ghost had come back to haunt her. Dropping her handbag onto one of the barstools at the island, she flicked on the overhead lights.

'Boys! Are you here?' she called out. Then she saw a shadow in the doorway of the snug.

'Hello, Kate. Long time no see.' She would have recognised that voice anywhere.

'How the hell did you get in here?!' she spat vehemently.

'Now, now, that's the last question you should be asking me. What you should be asking me is, 'What do you want?'

She wondered if this was really happening or if it had been such a long day that her mind was playing tricks on her.

'What do you want?' she asked through clenched teeth, her voice loaded with anger.

'Calm down,' the intruder instructed her with an intimidating look, 'I just wanted to make sure that we're on the same page, that's all. Nigel was getting sloppy; the booze had addled his brain. He told me that he was going to spill the beans and tell you everything. I just wanted to make sure that if he did, you are going to do the sensible thing and keep your mouth shut. After all, what good would it do now, now that he's dead?'

'You evil bastard!' she spat at him. 'I don't know what you're talking about. Nigel never discussed anything...' she stopped halfway through her sentence. She didn't want Billie Tidmarsh to know that her marriage had floundered.

'Now, now, Katie. You need to watch that mouth of yours.' He moved closer, so close she could smell his distinctive aftershave. 'I hear you've been talking to the police, he said menacingly.'

Kate's blood ran cold. 'How did you get in here?' she demanded, fear rippling through her.

'Nigel often used to invite me over for a drink. But it was always when you were out. At your parent-teacher evenings or yoga classes. I got to know quite a bit about you, Kate, through that loose-lipped husband of yours. And you know how he liked a drink. It didn't take much to take one of the keys hanging up in the kitchen...'

'Did you have anything to do with Nigel's death?' Kate asked, glaring at him.

Billie looked at her straight in the eye. 'Of course not. Why would I want Nigel dead? I needed him.'

'Yoo-hoo! Kate! We're back!'

Kate's knees almost gave way with relief. She didn't like the way Billie was looking at her. It was the same stoney glare he used to have. Just before he punched her.

'Billie? What on earth are you doing here? Kate?' Mrs Tidmarsh looked at them both, a confused look on her face.

'Billie was just returning something of Nigel's,' Kate said quickly, thinking of something to say.

'Hello Mum', Billie said coolly. 'I was just on my way to the development,' he lied, stepping forward to greet her. 'How are you?' he asked and leaned in to kiss his mother's cheek, the perfect, adoring son. Mrs Tidmarsh beamed at him.

'Thank you so much, Mrs Tidmarsh,' Kate gushed, gathering the boys protectively towards her, keeping them as close as she could. 'I'm sorry it's so late.'

'Oh, not at all, dear. It was a pleasure. They've been fed and watered and Mr Tidmarsh showed them how to make a catapult.'

'What do you say to Mrs Tidmarsh, boys?'

'Thank you Mrs Tidmarsh and for the yummy cake,' they sang out in unison.

'Go and watch TV for a bit and I'll be through in a minute,' Kate whispered to them. They scampered off and did as they were told.

'You look very pale, dear. Are you alright? What's going on, Billie?' Mrs Tidmarsh asked sternly.

'It's nothing, Mum. I think we're done here, Kate.' Billie shot her a glance.

Kate stared at him, and then turned to address Mrs Tidmarsh.

'An open verdict was recorded on Nigel's death.' Kate's insides were churning. 'Now, if you'll both excuse me, I have two boys, who no longer have a father, to get ready for bed.' She herded them both out of the front door and locked it firmly behind them, leaning against it to regain her composure. She needed to see her boys first, then she would call the police. And, first thing in the morning, she would get a locksmith to change the locks.

Robbie came to find her when he heard the front door close. 'Mummy, I miss Daddy,' he told her, hugging her thigh.

She knelt down and took him into her arms, 'I do too, Robbie. I do too.'

'And where's Auntie Zelda?'

Kate bit back the tears and hugged her eldest. 'Go and get your pyjamas on and I'll read you the best bedtime story ever.'

'Yeah!' he shouted, scampering off.

CHAPTER 70

MISS MOORCROFT AND KATE

A grey mist was rising over the fields tucked into the nape of the Shropshire hills behind Little Twichen. The sun warmed the earth from a bright, clear sky on a beautiful, Autumn Day.

Miss Moorcroft was slowly adapting to life back home after her fall. She hated using the Zimmer frame that the hospital insisted she take home with her, and couldn't wait to be rid of it. She was from an era of post-war Britain when you squared your shoulders and got on with it. No whining or showing any signs of weakness. 'Keep calm and carry on' was instilled into her. As a Land Army girl working in the fields harvesting crops to keep the country going during wartime, a broken ankle and a gashed head were small fry.

The worst thing about the Zimmer frame was having to negotiate her way through the narrow doorways of her rickety old cottage, and up and down the uneven, well-worn steps. Everything seemed to take twice as long and even feeding Kitty, Katty, and the other strays, took forever, as she ambled back and forth in the kitchen, like a slow-motion pinball machine. She ricocheted from one side to the other, as she forgot to get a knife from the drawer to scrape every last morsel of cat food from the pouches, and kept having to retrace her steps. Eventually, she got the job done, but then had to sit down to catch her breath.

When she looked up and out through the kitchen window, she noticed a dog running across the fields in the distance near Dovecote Manor. It looked just like Marsha Boden's dog. She was desperate to get her binoculars, but by the time she had shuffled to the other end of the kitchen to get them, the dog had gone. She sat down to catch her breath again and wondered if she was seeing things.

There was a tap at the front door and Kate's voice called out, 'Hello! It's only me.' She appeared in the doorway of the drab kitchen looking as elegant as ever. 'Hey, are you alright? You look a bit pale,' she observed, peeling off her camel-coloured winter coat. 'You haven't been overdoing things, have you?'

Miss Moorcroft smiled. 'No, I have not,' she responded in her plummy voice. 'I've just fed the cats, dear, that's all. Just feeling a bit tired. Nothing to worry about. But I thought I just saw Marsha's dog. In the field, up by Dovecote Manor.'

'Are you sure,' Kate asked, seeing that Helena was clearly perplexed by the sighting.

'Well, it looked like Jasper. But I couldn't get my binoculars out in time, so I can't be certain.'

Kate stared out through the kitchen window for a few moments, but the dog didn't reappear. 'I'm sure there's an explanation.'

'Kate, dear' she began tentatively. 'What do you think happened to Marsha? I mean...'

Kate sat down on one of the hard wooden chairs next to Miss Moorcroft.

'I don't know. I lay awake at night, trying to piece everything together. It's a complete mystery. I think Marsha might have stumbled across something when she worked for Billie Tidmarsh. She did some bookkeeping for him, but then he suddenly told her he didn't need her anymore. If you ask me, she got close to finding something out and he didn't like it.

'Well, I spoke to Ann Jones the other day, and she didn't have a good word to say about Billie Tidmarsh. Reckons he's rotten through and through.' Miss Moorcroft looked as though she had sucked on a lemon. 'Anyway, dear. How did it all go yesterday? I was thinking of you.'

'The Coroner recorded an open verdict. Which kind of makes me feel better. I was torturing myself because I thought Nigel had killed himself because I was leaving him for Zelda. But as it turns out, it could just have been a terrible accident.'

Miss Moorcroft took hold of Kate's hand. 'Well, whatever happened, you mustn't blame yourself. You've got those boys to think about.'

Kate smiled and nodded. 'Yes, you're right.'

'Listen.'I would like to repay your kindness...'

'Helena, there's absolutely no need whatsoever,' Kate interjected getting up and filling the old kettle from the ancient tap. 'I'm just being a good neighbour and friend. Really, there's no need.'

'Well, that's as may be but I've been thinking. You and the boys need to get some fun back into your lives after, well, after everything that's happened.' Kate had told Miss Moorcroft about Zelda going to the States, and how the relationship was now over.

'So, I was thinking. I haven't booked it yet because I wanted to check the dates with you. I was going to book a carriage on the Santa Express train in Bridgnorth. Apparently, there are reindeer, elves, and all sorts. Christmas lights and...'

'Oh, Helena! That's a great idea,' Kate cut in. 'The boys would love it. I can't think of anything nicer to do with them this year, you know...being their first Christmas without...' Her eyes welled up. Miss Moorcroft stood up and stepped shakily away from her Zimmer frame. She wrapped her bony arms around Kate in a loose embrace. Kate reciprocated, enveloping her friend in a warm, perfumed hug.

'Well, that's settled then, dear,' Miss Moorcroft pronounced as she lowered herself slowly back down onto the chair.

'On one condition,' Kate instructed, looking at her sternly.

Helena looked confused, her rheumy eyes looking up at the beautiful woman before her.

'Only if you agree to come too. After all, you lost somebody special this year too. Life can get very lonely at times.'

Miss Moorcroft nodded slowly, her thoughts turning to Bert. 'Oh, I couldn't. Really. Besides, it's for children. Not old biddies like me.'

'You'll enjoy it!' Kate enthused.

Miss Moorcroft instantly regretted her foolish idea. What the hell was she thinking?

Kate put a cup of strong tea on the table in front of her, together with a plateful of custard cream biscuits. 'Now, tuck in and I don't want to hear another word. The boys would love it if you joined us,' she lied.

CHAPTER 71

KATE

Kate stopped on the corner of Mill Street to admire Wisteria Cottage, with its beautiful pie-crust thatch and traditional straw pheasant on the ridge. Tearing herself away and walking along Laburnum Lane, past Bert Humble's old house and into the new housing development at Meadowbank.

Lucy smiled when she saw her approaching.

'Morning Lucy. How are you?' Kate asked, genuinely concerned. 'Gosh, you look awful. Is everything okay?'

Lucy was clearly distressed and fought back tears. 'It's a long story. Mr Peterson and I did some digging around at that warehouse in Ludlow. Did you know that he and Marsha were thinking of moving in together?'

'No! She never told me!' Kate tried to process the information.

'Anyway,' Lucy continued, 'It seems that Billie has been people trafficking. We told the police what we had found and Billie was arrested. I've been implicated.' She looked like she had the weight of the world on her shoulders and looked incredibly sad.

'Oh, God, Lucy. That's awful. But good news about Billie, though. Let's hope they keep him locked up for a long time,' she said.

Tears ran down Lucy's face and she hid herself behind both hands as she sobbed openly. 'I've been such an idiot. I was completely taken in by him,' she said, wiping her blotchy face with a tissue.

'Hey. You're not the first,' Kate said softly. 'You had a lucky escape. Believe me,' she said solemnly, remembering how Billie used to hit her. 'People trafficking. That's despicable. It's inexcusable. You're off the hook, though?' Kate asked, clearly mortified that Billie had implicated Lucy in his seedy underworld.

'Not yet. The police want to take a formal statement. I honestly thought Billie and I had a future together. Christ, how could I have got him so wrong? Now that I know what he's capable of, it makes me feel sick to my stomach that I let him get close to me.'

As the two women were trying to process all the information, Ann Jones came marching up the path towards them to the marketing suite.

They looked at each other and stopped talking.

'Ladies,' she announced, addressing them both. 'Sorry to interrupt but Tom and I are thinking about moving here. You know. Now he's retiring.'

'You're not interrupting, Mrs. Jones,' Lucy said, composing herself as best she could. 'Kate and I were just talking about Billie Tidmarsh. The police have arrested him for people trafficking.'

'Well, I never! I always knew he was an evil pig!'

Kate and Lucy exchanged glances at Mrs Jones's strong choice of words.

'I can't believe that two lovely ladies like yourselves would get mixed up with somebody like that. Have they found any connection between him and Marsha Boden yet?' she asked, peering at them both over the top of her glasses. She didn't wait for an answer but ploughed on. 'Bryan told me, confidentially, that he'd seen something in that warehouse. Something that would connect Billie Tidmarsh to her ... disappearance. I bumped into him the other day. He was about to confide in me when his phone rang. Then I had to go and I think he'd changed his mind by then. But he knew something. I could tell. I think he was afraid to tell me.'

Ann could see that Lucy was clearly in shock and the poor girl had obviously had strong feelings for the conniving conman. She realised that she had stumbled upon the young girl pouring her heart out and her friend was trying to console her. Poor girl, she thought, getting mixed up with a pig like him. 'Look, I'll leave you to it. I can come back another time,' she said matter-of-factly.'There's no rush.'

Jed, Lucy's colleague, arrived right on cue.

'Perfect timing, Jed,' Lucy gushed. 'Can you see to Mrs Jones, please?'

'Yes, of course.'

Ann was delighted.

'What are we waiting for?' Kate whispered to Lucy with an urgency in her voice.'You've got a key, haven't you? Come on!'

Lucy grabbed her bag.

'Oh, I nearly forgot. Zelda and I won't be going ahead with the purchase of the corner plot. She broke up with me.'

'Oh, I'm sorry to hear that,' Lucy responded, feeling sorry for Kate, especially after everything that she had been through. 'Thanks for letting me know though,' she said, compassionately.'You do know that the deposit is non-refundable?'

'Oh, no. I didn't actually.' Kate was clearly shocked by the news. 'But I think we've got more important things to think about, don't you? Let's go and see what we can find to incriminate that heartless bastard.'

Lucy smiled wanly and looked as if her entire world had come tumbling down around her.

CHAPTER 72

LUCY AND KATE

Kate and Lucy were scared stiff but hell-bent on trying to find some evidence that would connect Billie Tidmarsh to Marsha Boden's disappearance, as alluded to them by Mrs Jones. Neither of them could believe that he was capable of murder but clearly, they had to keep an open mind.

'I've only got an hour or so,' Kate informed Lucy. 'I've dropped the boys off with Mum and Dad but I'll have to get them back in time for bed. We've got school tomorrow.'

'Keep an eye out for anybody watching,' Lucy whispered as they approached the alleyway leading to the warehouse.

The two women slipped inside and waited. Silence. It was eerie and Lucy got the heebie jeebies again once she was inside. The dank smell was still there and the place looked as though it had been ransacked. The yellow light from a street lamp outside wasn't enough. They both put the torches on their phones on once they had ascertained that they were alone, and set to work.

'This is going to take forever,' Kate exclaimed.

Lucy was more focused. 'Come on. We've got to find something to incriminate him. After all that he's done to us.'

Kate nodded and wandered around. She couldn't believe that Billie Tidmarsh, a man she had once loved, could be involved in something so awful. He clearly had no conscience. As she returned to help Lucy, she stubbed her toe on something. Looking down, she noticed it was one of those big, heavy family Bibles. She picked it up and laid it on an old desk. It was quite heavy. Opening it up, she was intrigued to read the flysheet to discover which family it had once belonged to. She was shocked when she looked inside.

'Lucy! Quick. Look what I've found.'

Lucy stopped what she was doing and joined her. As Kate shone her torch on the open book, Lucy saw that a deep square had been cut out of the pages. Nestled inside was a collection of rings. Some of them looked expensive. There were diamonds, sapphires, emeralds, and ruby stones all sparkling in the torchlight. 'They must be worth a fortune,' Kate exclaimed, lifting them out for a closer look.

'But that's not why we're here, Kate,' Lucy admonished. 'Come on! Let's try and find this...whatever it was that Mrs Jones reckons Bryan saw.'

Kate was distracted, busy looking through the rings.

'Kate!' Lucy hissed.

Miffed at having to stop browsing through the beautiful jewellery, Kate was drawn to the rings. Who would have put them here and why? A family feud perhaps? She was intrigued and couldn't stop wondering what they were doing here, hidden so well.

Lucy carried on flicking through the pages of some books, shaking them vigorously and then discarding them untidily in a pile on the floor. It would help if she knew what she was looking for

'Lucy.' Kate was standing in front of her, deathly white.

'What?' she asked, the irritation in her voice clear.

Kate had two rings in the palm of her hand and was holding them out for Lucy to see. She picked them up with a confused look on her face.

'Read the inscriptions on the inside,' Kate instructed.

The colour drained from Lucy's face when she read them.

Kate had to sit down. She felt physically sick.

CHAPTER 73

GUY BODEN

Bonfire night was barely over when Christmas carols started blaring annoyingly out of radios across the nation. Even the street musicians in Ludlow had started early this year. A saxophonist, who had positioned himself outside The Buttercross, played 'Once in Royal David's City,' which drifted melancholily through the streets of the medieval town.

Guy Boden was dreading the festive season this year. It was seven months since his wife had disappeared. He knew that the first Christmas without her would be difficult. He wished he could close his front door on Christmas Eve and not open it again until the second of January, and get the New Year underway without all the fuss.

People still died over the festive season and sometimes, if there was a particularly cold snap, business got extra busy. Macabre thoughts rattled through his mind as he hoped for a bitterly cold spell. That way, he could keep himself busy and get through this difficult time.

'What are your plans for Christmas?' Ann asked.

'I haven't thought about it yet. The boys have asked me over. I wish I could get on a cruise ship and sail away to some distant island, returning when it's all over and done with.'

'I'm sorry. It's going to be tough for you and the boys but the staff here too. We all miss her.' She sounded a little trite.

Guy looked at her.

'Honestly. We were like one big happy family. You know that. Although I wasn't particularly close to Marsha, you know, because of...'

'Yes, I got that, but I hadn't realised how much her disappearance had affected everybody.'

***

When somebody dies, a funeral is held. Sometimes a memorial service takes place at a later date to celebrate their lives. The family has closure. When a person goes missing, there is no funeral, no celebration of their life, and no closure. The not-knowing can eat away at the family. Some cope with it and bravely soldier on, hoping, always hoping, that their loved one will turn up one day. Safe and sound. Others can't, and it destroys them.

The law in England and Wales states that '*the fact that a person has been missing for seven or more years (and there is no reason to believe that person is alive) is evidence that the person is dead*'.

Guy Boden had read up about it. Even though it was just over seven months since his wife had disappeared, not seven years, he thought it best to understand what would happen, legally, if she never came back.

CHAPTER 74

LUCY AND KATE

D I Daniels was surprised and slightly irritated when Lucy and Kate presented him with the evidence they had found at the warehouse. Surprised because his team hadn't found the rings and irritated because they had entered a crime scene, and found something that his had team missed.

'You're certain these belonged to Marsha Boden?' he asked, clearly concerned, having placed the rings carefully into an evidence bag.

'Definitely,' Kate said solemnly. Marsha's wedding anniversary was 29th July and she and Guy would have been married for over thirty years.

DI Daniels was examining the rings through the plastic and reading the inscriptions, which were the same on both rings. One was a plain gold band and the other was a diamond solitaire. Engraved was: 'G&M – 29.07.1989. Together forever.' Although the inscriptions were faded, they were still visible.

'And where did you find them?'

'They were hidden in a Bible which was tucked under a shelf behind the boxes of books, near the entrance to the makeshift dorm. I caught my foot on it as I walked past,' Kate told him.

'So, does this prove that Billie Tidmarsh killed Marsha Boden?' Lucy asked, clearly very perturbed.

'No. It does not. First of all, we will have to examine the rings and show them to Mr Boden to confirm that they belonged to his wife. Then we will take DNA samples and we will take it from there. But things are not looking good for Billie Tidmarsh. Bryan Jamison could be an accomplice or a suspect in his own right. He told us that he had seen a note on the table in the kitchen when he had called in for coffee with Mrs Boden on the day that she disappeared. He told us that he had read it, and that Mr. and Mrs. Boden were clearly having marital problems, and that Mr. Boden was keen to make amends. We could find no evidence of that note. I don't suppose you ladies found it, did you?'

Lucy and Kate both shook their heads. No. We didn't find anything. Except the rings.'

'Yes. That's interesting. Now, ladies. You entered a crime scene without permission. You know that's a serious offence?'

'We had no idea,' Lucy responded timidly. 'We just wanted to help. I had a key, through my job at Ashcroft's, and I, we,' she looked across at Kate, 'Wanted to find something to prove that I had nothing to do with any of Billie's dodgy business deals. I had no idea that he put the Lease in my name. You have to believe me,' she pleaded.

Kate spoke up for her friend. 'Honestly, Lucy is completely innocent. You have to believe her.'

'Well, leave these things with me and I'll be in touch. But I will need a formal statement from you both. Particularly you, Miss Holden.'

CHAPTER 75

LUCY

'Now. Tell us everything you know about William Tidmarsh. For the record, this interview is being recorded. First, please state your full name and occupation.'

'Lucy Holden, Sales Negotiator with Ashcroft Estate Agents.'

'And what is your relationship to Mr Tidmarsh?'

Lucy found herself blushing in front of the austere man in front of her, who had introduced himself as Detective Inspector Clive Daniels, and the younger officer sitting next to him. 'Billie was my boyfriend.'

'And how long were you going out with him?'

'About four months.'

'And you used to go out with Bryan Jamison. Before. Is that correct?'

'Yes,' she replied, blushing again. She wondered fleetingly whether her and Bryan's rampant sex sessions had been mentioned during one of Bryan's interviews. She hoped not.

'So. Please. In your own words. What do you know about Mr Tidmarsh's business enterprises?'

The solicitor that Lucy's father had advised that she take along with her, leant in and whispered something in her ear.

'He told me that he was a property developer. I know that he owns the company, Green Circle Housing Group. The developer behind the

Meadowbank site in Little Twichen. He was always vague about his where-abouts. He never told me anything about his businesses.'

'You went to Dubai with him. Is that correct?'

'Yes. It was for a long weekend. It was soon after I started going out with him.'

'And did Mr Tidmarsh have any business dealings while he was there?'

Lucy thought carefully before answering. 'Well. He told me he had 'done the deal of the century' with some guy he had played golf with. I had to wait for him. It was that place on the creek.' She thought momentarily. 'The Dubai Creek Golf and Yacht Club.'

'Right. We have reason to believe that the man he met with was a phar-maceutical rep, and was supplying him with prescription drugs and other medical equipment.'

Lucy was astonished and frowned as she processed the information.

'He used Rohypnol to calm the people down that he was trafficking. We discovered that he put it in their food and drink. It made them very sleepy, and compliant.'

'Oh, God,' Lucy croaked. 'That's awful.' Suddenly the penny dropped. That day out on the coastal path.

'Billie Tidmarsh was just a small cog in a much bigger wheel. He trans-ported the people, who came in on boats to the small coves around the North Wales coastline, from there into Birmingham. On the way, he would take them to the warehouse in Ludlow, and then get Bryan to deliver them to various destinations in the city where they were left to fend for themselves. He was always careful never to show his face at the warehouse. Always got others to do his dirty work for him. Which brings me to you, Miss Holden.'

Lucy looked like a rabbit caught in headlights.

'What was your name doing on the Lease for that warehouse?'

'Billie tricked me into signing it. He told me it was something to do with the bonus he had given me...' Her solicitor leant in and stopped her. She blushed, realising that she was incriminating herself.

'What bonus would that be?' DI Daniels asked.

'It was all above board,' Lucy explained, having spoken quietly to her solicitor. 'It was a bonus for selling so many houses off-plan. I used it as the deposit for the flat that I bought.'

'And the flat is in your name and you have a mortgage?'

'Yes, yes, I do. It's mine. I've worked hard for it,' she insisted adamantly.

'Did you help Billie Tidmarsh with the activities connected to the warehouse?'

'No! I most certainly did not. I had nothing to do with any of it.' Lucy turned to her solicitor with a look of complete horror on her face. 'You've got to believe me. That's why I went back to try and find some evidence to connect Billie to Marsha Boden's disappearance.'

'And what did you discover when you went to the warehouse?'

'While I was there, Mr Peterson followed me in, so we looked around together.'

'Yes, Mr Peterson came in to speak with us about it. Go on.'

'Well, he, er, we deduced that it looked like Billie was people trafficking.'

'We had already worked that out because we had had the warehouse under surveillance for some time. Luckily for you, we had completed our search there. But it is still a crime scene.'

Lucy went pale. She hadn't even thought about the warehouse being a possible crime scene. She shook herself mentally, trying to recall that night she and Mr Peterson had been there. 'So, we tried to find out what went on inside the shipping containers. But they were both locked. Very securely, from what I remember. Then we thought somebody was coming, but it was a false alarm. That was when we discovered a...' she tried to think of the right word to describe what they had found. 'A dormitory. Beds in rows in a room. At the side, behind a wall of boxes.'

DI Daniels watched the young woman in front of him very carefully before asking his next question. 'So. You had no idea that Billie Tidmarsh was involved in organ trafficking?'

Lucy's jaw dropped. 'Oh, my God! No! I had no idea! Jeezus Christ!' she exclaimed, looking all around her as if unable to process what she had just been told. She looked at DI Daniels. 'That's awful! Of course, I had no idea. What do you take me for?' She went very quiet. Then she looked up and said, 'He's a bloody animal.'

DI Daniels clearly agreed with her.'Do you have anything else to add?'

'No. Other than I had absolutely no idea what Billie was doing. I would never have got involved with him in the first place if I had known what a nasty piece of work he is.'

DI Daniels sighed. 'But the fact that you provided some key evidence against Mr Tidmarsh either supports your case or it could suggest that you were involved and you planted those rings in the warehouse.

'No! No! I was helping Kate try to find out what had happened to Mrs Boden. And Fedora man, I mean, Mr Peterson. I would never have got mixed up with anything like that! What do you take me for?! You've got to believe me!'

DI Daniels shuffled some papers. Fortunately for you, Miss Holden, I believe you. But you will be called to give evidence when the case goes to court.'

Lucy looked at him angrily, a stoney look on her face. 'It will be my pleasure, officer. I will do everything I can to help you.'

CHAPTER 76

MISS MOORCRAFT AND KATE

'Hello! It's only me.' Kate let herself in with the key Miss Moorcroft had given her following her accident. She couldn't wait to tell Helena the news about Billie Tidmarsh being arrested. And her two other pieces of news.

'No need to shout, dear,' Miss Moorcroft said gruffly without taking her eyes off the TV. Gardeners' World was on and Alan Titchmarsh was extolling the virtues of planting tulip bulbs 'for an explosion of colour in the Spring'. She was sitting with her leg propped up on an old threadbare footstool.

Kate smiled and went through to the kitchen to unpack the items she had picked up at Tidder's on the way over. She loaded up a tray with some custard creams, two Schooner glasses, and the new bottle of sherry.

'What's all this?' Miss Moorcroft asked, her arms folded across her chest, clearly irritated that Kate was interrupting her afternoon's viewing.

'We have a celebration!' Kate announced, peeling the plastic coating from the top of the bottle and pouring two glasses to the brim.

Miss Moorcroft pressed the mute button on the remote and her eyes lit up when she saw the generous measures of sherry being poured.

'What exactly are we celebrating?'

'New beginnings,' Kate said cryptically.

'Oh. To new beginnings it is then.' Miss Moorcroft gulped the warming sherry down, almost emptying the glass.

'What do you mean?' she asked, her face clouding over, realising what Kate had just said. 'What new beginnings?'

'Well,' Kate said, scooting Kitty along so she could sit down on the armchair opposite. 'I've decided to move. You know, what with everything that's happened.' Her eyes took on a faraway look.

'What? You're not leaving Little Twichen?' Miss Moorcroft asked, clearly perplexed.

'No! Wisteria Cottage has come up for sale,' Kate continued. 'I've always liked it. It has a lovely garden which goes right down to the river. The boys will love it. I've spoken with a friend of mine, Lucy, who works at the estate agents and she's going to help me sell The Granary. There are too many ghosts there and I need to move on. We should be in by Christmas, if all goes well. And, there's something else.' Kate sounded triumphant. 'Billie Tidmarsh has been arrested. He was caught Human Trafficking with the intention of Organ Harvesting. Lucy told me.' Kate decided not to tell Miss Moorcroft about her and Lucy's discovery at the warehouse.

Miss Moorcroft gingerly lowered her encased leg from the footstool and sat bolt upright. 'Good heavens. That's dreadful. Have they said that he had anything to do with Marsha's disappearance?'

'Well,' she said tentatively, 'If he's capable of harvesting organs, he's capable of anything.' A shiver ran down Kate's spine. She had a horrible feeling that Billie was involved with Marsha's disappearance. But she wasn't going to share her thoughts with Helena.

'Oh, dear. I hope nothing awful has happened to Marsha.' Miss Moorcroft's face fell and she looked terribly sad.

Kate touched her arm. 'I think we ought to start thinking the worst at this stage. Don't you?'

They sat in silence for a few moments. Then Miss Moorcroft said, 'I thought you were moving away for a moment there. That would have been awful. I would have lost two friends then. I don't know what I would do without you.'

'Don't be silly. Why would I leave Little Twichen? The boys are settled at school and I love my job. I can't ever see myself living anywhere else. I would miss you too. I'm still just a short walk away.'

'Good for you. You deserve some happiness in your life. A fresh start will do you good. And the boys. It sounds perfect.'

'There's one more thing,' Kate ventured.

'Oh, good heavens!' Miss Moorcroft exclaimed, lifting her right hand and resting it on her chest. 'I don't know if I can take any more shocks today.'

Kate took a deep breath. 'Zelda and I have split up.'

'Oh, no. I'm sorry to hear that.' Miss Moorcroft took a sip of her sherry, ' Well, all we need now is for you to meet a nice young man. Or woman,' she added quietly under her breath. 'Be a dear, and pour me another sherry. I think I need it, don't you?' she said, a twinkle in her eye.

CHAPTER 77

THE FINAL INVESTIGATION

DI Clive Daniels was perplexed. 'We have had some interesting developments, he announced to his team, who were gathered around. 'When we raided the warehouse purported to be used for storing antiques, we discovered illegal immigrants were being housed there temporarily. Billie Tidmarsh and Bryan Jamison have been arrested. It looks like they were lower down the chain of a criminal gang running a people trafficking ring. The people being trafficked were just a commodity. They were promised safety and a brighter future. When we questioned them, most of them had used their life savings to get here.' The disgust in DI Daniels' voice was clear as he addressed his team. 'But that's not the worst of it.' It was obvious that he had difficulty in comprehending what he was about to tell his team of officers. 'We made the connection between Dr Nigel Bursford and Billie Tidmarsh, which was the illegal supply of prescription drugs. We don't have any evidence to suggest that Billie Tidmarsh was connected to the doctor's death. Indeed, he was more use to him alive than dead. Billie had to find a new supplier. Which he found in Dubai in the shape of one Rohit Kumar. A pharmaceutical rep. He was a much bigger fish than Nigel Bursford. Now, Billie had access to medical supplies.' DI Daniels broke off for effect. 'In particular, surgical supplies.'

There were some puzzled looks on faces around the room.

'Remember those shipping containers at the back of the warehouse? They were makeshift operating theatres.'

A ripple of gasps rang out.

'It was a pretty slick operation. Absolutely no pun intended. This is no joking matter. Desperate people do desperate things. We tracked down a website that one of Billie Tidmarsh's IT gurus set up. It was basically an organ wish list. He only harvested organs that were pre-ordered. And of course, paid for, in full, up front.' He paused, waiting for his team to grasp the enormity of what he was telling them. He went on. 'Dr Bursford's widow and her friend, Lucy Holden, who was Billie Tidmarsh's girlfriend, took it upon themselves to search the warehouse. Even though we had already done that.' His jaw was pulsating and he was clearly angry. 'They seemed to think that Billie might have had something to do with Marsha's disappearance and, I have to say, they found some pretty incriminating evidence.' He held up the evidence bag containing Marsha's wedding and engagement ring.

Another ripple of gasps spread around the room. 'Now, we are pretty sure that it was Guy Boden who posted the letter written by his wife to Lloyd Peterson. He denies forcing her to write it or sending it but we think he did it out of spite. He could have done it to try and prove that his wife was still alive.

'How do we know that Marsha isn't alive and she sent it herself?' Sgt. Henshaw asked.

'We don't,' DI Daniels retorted. 'But that wouldn't make any sense at all.'

Della Carlton raised her hand and asked the question. 'How do you explain the rings being found in Billie Tidmarsh's warehouse, sir?'

DI Daniels paced around the room. 'It could be that Mrs Boden found out about the people trafficking and the harvesting of organs, and was silenced before she could get that information to us. We found some of her

DNA in the small kitchen area. We're still processing all the other samples we took.'

I'll talk to Guy Boden again. I had to show him the rings to see if they belonged to his wife. Now, if you'll excuse me, I believe Mr Boden is here now.'

***

DI Daniels had telephoned Guy Boden earlier and asked him to come to the station immediately, as there had been a major development in the case.

'Can you confirm that these rings belong to your wife?' he asked.

Guy Boden was staring at the plastic evidence bag that DI Daniels handed to him. His face was ashen. He held one between his fingers through the plastic and read, 'G&M – 29.07.1989. Together forever.'

'Yes. They're Marsha's. Where did you find them?'

'In a warehouse in Ludlow. The one rented by Billie Tidmarsh. The one that your wife had concerns about.'

Tears welled up in Guy's eyes. 'She's dead, isn't she?' he gasped. He took his handkerchief from his trouser pocket and wiped his eyes.

'We can't say for certain, but there doesn't seem to be any other explanation, I'm afraid.'

The Detective Inspector watched Guy Boden closely. Then he left him with a Family Liaison Officer before heading back to the team briefing.

***

DI Daniels continued briefing his team on the findings. 'With the recent discovery of the rings at the warehouse rented by Billie Tidmarsh, it is looking likely that Marsha Boden is no longer alive. It also means that Billie Tidmarsh is our number one suspect. We know that Marsha Boden had concerns about the warehouse. We have evidence to suggest that she had been there, and we know she was curious about Billie Tidmarsh's income streams. She was also strongly opposed to the housing development.

We also suspect that Bryan Jamison had a crush on the funeral director's wife, so he could have made an advance which she shunned and things turned nasty, but we found no evidence of a struggle. He also told us that he had seen a white van in a layby down the road from Boden's on the day that Marsha disappeared. We were unable to trace that vehicle. It could be significant, or it could have been a red herring if Bryan had something to do with Marsha's disappearance.' He looked around the room at his colleagues. 'Bryan Jamison was also involved in Billie Tidmarsh's horrendous activities connected to the warehouse. He drove people to various locations as instructed. He used a motorbike when he had to deliver an organ. We found leathers with a false courier company logo on it when we searched his house. We also found a couple of cool boxes in the warehouse. We didn't attach much significance to them at the time. Unmarked cool boxes are used so as to keep attention away from the contents. Bryan was paid handsomely for his services. And for keeping his mouth shut.'

DI Daniels stopped to gather his thoughts and referred to his notes. 'We have a statement from Lucy Holden, Billie Tidmarsh's girlfriend at the time, saying how she had seen him acting suspiciously on a trip to North Wales. When we interviewed Billie Tidmarsh, he told us that the boats would arrive in a small cove and Bryan would take them to the warehouse, where they were fed and rested before being disseminated in and around Birmingham. Billie Tidmarsh and Bryan Jamison will both go on trial for their part in these activities. I must add at this point that both men deny having anything to do with the disappearance of Marsha Boden.'

'Sir,' Della Carlton chipped in. 'Do you think Kate Bursford wanted to blame somebody for her husband's death because she felt guilty and Billie Tidmarsh was an obvious target?'

'Yes. That could well be the case,' DI Daniels responded. But, as the Coroner recorded an open verdict, it could well have been a terrible accident. Alcohol and barbiturates are never a good combo.' He continued with his summing up. 'The DNA results on the rings were conclusive. It was Marsha's DNA. No other DNA was found on them.'

Damien Henshaw spoke. 'But sir, we have no evidence of a struggle and we don't have a body. Also, the rings were found in the warehouse.'

'Do you think somebody might have planted the rings there to try and frame Billie Tidmarsh? I mean. Those two women could have planted them.'

'No, I don't.' DI Daniels addressed his team. 'Those two women were just trying to find out what happened to their friend. I think that we have enough evidence to add murder to the list of convictions for Billie Tidmarsh. He got angry when Mrs Boden rumbled what he was up to. He got somebody else to do his dirty work for him. We know that he has no scruples. Anybody who can harvest organs from a fellow human being is, in my book, completely heartless. He deserves to be behind bars for a very long time. Bryan Jamison will be charged with "an accessory to murder."

There was a collective nodding of heads around the incident room.

CHAPTER 78

KATE AND MISS MOORCROFT

Father Christmas had delivered gifts for Robbie and Chase to their new home, Wisteria Cottage. They were worried he wouldn't know they had moved, but Kate had told them to write and tell him, which they had done, addressing the letters to Santa Claus, Lapland, The North Pole, The Universe. Kate had melted while watching their faces light up while unwrapping the gifts one by one. There was a delicious aroma of turkey roasting and Nat King Cole was singing about chestnuts roasting on an open fire.

Miss Moorcroft arrived dead on eleven o'clock to join them for the Christmas festivities, and in plenty of time for a pre-lunch drink. 'Helena, welcome! Come on in. I have a surprise for you,' Kate announced as she helped her friend out of her coat.

Zelda came through to the hallway when she heard the doorbell.

'Auntie Zelda!' the boys yelled when Zelda appeared from the kitchen, right on cue.

'Come here, you two.' She pulled them to her and savoured their closeness.

'Oh, what a surprise!' Miss Moorcroft said jauntily, a twinkle in her eye.

'Boys, why don't you go through and play with your new toys?' Kate suggested. They needed no encouragement and scampered off, whooping and hollering as they went.

'Well. You are a dark horse, Kate. You didn't tell me you and Zelda had patched things up.'

The two women put an arm around each other's waists and smiled.

'I don't think I comprehended just what a difficult time Kate had been through. And, after being apart for three months, I realised I had made a terrible mistake,' Zelda said, turning to her partner, who gazed at her with an admiring look.

'It's been a bumpy ride. But me and the boys managed. Robbie is settling down again. I think we are all learning how to cope after what happened.'

'Now that Billie Tidmarsh is behind bars, and we no longer have to look over our shoulders all the time, I feel so much better about things. Now, it's my turn to surprise you both.'

'Miss Moorcroft, can I get you a drink' Zelda asked.

'Oh, please. Call me Helayna. And yes. I would love a glass of sherry. Thank you.'

'Do you drink champagne?' Zelda ventured.

'Oh. Only if I'm celebrating something. Which, to be honest, I don't do very often at all. In fact, I can't remember the last time I had a glass of champagne. It's been so long.'

Kate was perched on one of the kitchen bar stools, looking a little bemused.

'Well, in that case,' Zelda continued, 'I think we definitely have something to celebrate!'

Kate's attention was focused on the beautiful young woman in front of her, who was reaching into her jacket pocket for something.

'Kate,' she began tentatively, getting down on one knee, holding out a small white box with a diamond ring nestled inside. 'Will you marry me?'

Kate covered her mouth with both hands in surprise. Eventually, she managed to respond. 'Yes! Yes! Of course, I will!'

Zelda took the ring from the box and placed it gently onto Kate's third ring finger, where her wedding ring from Nigel used to sit.

They kissed briefly and then Miss Moorcroft hugged Kate, congratulating her. 'Wonderful news.'

Zelda popped open some champagne and poured three flutes before handing them around.

'Oh, Kate. I'm so happy for you. A new home. A new life. Here's to you both.' She raised her glass in the air and took a sip of the champagne.

Kate hugged Miss Moorcroft and kissed her on the cheek. 'You've been a good friend to me.'

Miss Moorcroft brushed the compliment aside. 'Nonsense. I don't know what I would have done without you. Especially after my accident. You were wonderful.'

The three women congregated on the sofas at the far end of the modern room and chatted for a while before the boys came bounding back in.

'Ah. I've got something for you both', Miss Moorcroft announced, delving into her wicker basket. She pulled out two presents with a flourish and handed one to each child. Smiling across at Kate, who had bought them with money that she had insisted on giving her, she watched as the boys unwrapped their gifts. Kitty's head suddenly popped up out of the basket like a jack-in-the-box, she watched in bewilderment, yawned, and then disappeared again under the flap.

Zelda smiled. 'Happy Christmas everybody! I wanted to make our first Christmas together special.'

'Well, you've certainly done that!' Miss Moorcroft said, laughing heartily as Kate admired the sparkly ring on her finger.

At around five o'clock, after a stupendous lunch, far too much sherry, and too many mince pies, Miss Moorcroft made a move to leave.

'I'll walk you back,' Kate said, helping Miss Moorcroft on with her coat. She waited while she tied on her headscarf then handed her her Kitty in a basket.

'You'll do no such thing,' Miss Moorcroft admonished. 'I'm quite capable of getting myself home.' She kicked her left leg out in front of her. She was wearing some very cosy-looking fur-lined ankle boots. 'Look. Good as new, now!'

Kate laughed. Miss Moorcroft gave Zelda a perfunctory hug and called through to the boys who were so busy playing, that they just yelled out, 'Bye!' Then she hugged Kate. A big bear-hug of an embrace. She had never felt so loved in her entire life.

Chapter 79

Marsha Boden

Seven Months Earlier

Somebody visited Marsha Boden on the morning of her disappearance. They waited in an unmarked white van in a layby just down the road from Boden's until the coast was clear. Then, they drove into the courtyard, knocked on Marsha's door, and was invited in. As they went inside, they were careful to hang the dark hooded jacket they were wearing in the hallway before going into the kitchen. They were wearing jeans.

Marsha was agitated and seemed preoccupied. When she had her back to them, they went up behind her and put a chloroform-soaked rag over her mouth. She slumped into the perpetrator's arms, who then strangled every last breath out of her with the scarf she was wearing, and stuffed the rag into her mouth.

They had parked the van near the back door and laid a sheet of tarpaulin out. They carefully laid Marsha's body onto it, then dragged her to the back door. They lowered the lift from the back of the van and rolled the body onto it, raised the motorised step, and pushed her into the back of the van. They were careful to wear gloves.

Jasper suddenly appeared and started barking. The killer kicked the dog to shut it up, then went back inside, swept the floor, and made sure everything was as they had found it, careful to retrieve the dark hooded jacket.

Jasper started barking again and they tried to entice the dog inside when they realised that he might follow the van. They grabbed some dog treats they found on a shelf in the hallway and threw them onto the floor near the dog's basket. But the dog was having none of it. Jasper stood, rooted to the spot, barking loudly. The perpetrator kicked him a second time so hard, he yelped and slunk in through the back door. In their haste to get away, they didn't shut the door properly.

Jasper scratched at the door and escaped and was seen at Dovecote Manor. He had run away to try and find Marsha or alert Lloyd. Miss Moorcroft had spotted the dog and mentioned her sighting to the police but by that time, Marsha was already dead.

The killer took the body back to the butcher's yard and lowered it from the back of the van. They dragged it to the walk-in freezer where they stashed it behind some animal carcasses. Tom Jones was away visiting family in Wales all week.

Ann told the staff in the shop that nobody was to go into the freezer because the lock was faulty. She was arranging for it to be repaired. She put a notice on the door and gave them strict instructions to use the other freezer. She then paid a visit to Lucy at the marketing suite in Meadowbank to enquire about one of the plots. Her interest was more to do with the day the concrete footings were being poured than with the house itself. Jed, Lucy's colleague, proved invaluable and gave her regular updates.

Once she found out that it was to be first thing on a Monday morning, under the cover of darkness, while her husband was still away, she dragged Marsha's body out to the van. Then she drove to the perimeter of the development, lowered Marsha's body from the van, and dragged it through the fencing. Some kids had broken through, leaving a gap. She dragged the body, wrapped in tarpaulin, to the corner plot. She had put a shovel on board, securing it with rope. Then she jumped down into the footings and started to dig. It didn't take long to dig a Marsha-sized hole. The woman was the size of a mouse. Happy with her work, she climbed out, pushed the body into the earth, giving it one last shove with her foot, then earnestly, she began shovelling earth from a nearby pile of topsoil onto the body. The brown tarpaulin was a perfect camouflage. She made sure she covered it well. Checking her handy work, she flattened the area with the back of her shovel. When she climbed out again, she leant over and made sure she destroyed her boot prints. She knew that concrete would be poured over her crime in a few hours' time.

The police never followed up the receipt from The Silver Pear that Ann purported to have had, the day that Marsha Boden went missing. It was easy to slip Tom's old family Bible containing Marsha's rings into the warehouse. Bryan had been distracted the day she popped in to see how he was doing. He was busy texting on his phone. After that, all she had to do was hint at something being in the warehouse, the day she visited the Marketing Suite. Jed had been so much more helpful than Lucy. She had been careful to tear out the flysheet from the Bible and burnt it, together with the note that she had found on the kitchen table.

She had always despised Mrs Boden, with her beautiful smile, kind heart and, worst of all, the love of Guy Boden. Ann Jones had no idea that the day she chose to murder her, was the day that she had planned to leave her husband for Lloyd Peterson. But at least now, she had Guy all to herself. Just as she had always wanted.

As the development progressed, Ann went ahead with the purchase of the house on the corner plot at Meadowbank. The one where she had buried Marsha all those months before. It was one of the best plots on the estate, she thought.

Guy visited her more and more often since things had calmed down over Marsha's disappearance, and Billie Tidmarsh's subsequent trial for her murder.

One evening in the summer, after Ann had settled in, they were sitting out in the garden. It was a beautiful evening and the birds were in full song.

'Marsha would have loved it here,' Guy said, a faraway look in his eyes.

It was all Ann could do to stop her smile from turning into a full-blown grin as she took his hand in hers.

'Yes, I'm sure she would. Although I don't think she would have approved of all these new houses, do you?'

EPILOGUE

Lloyd Peterson was distraught when the police told him what they had found. Heartbroken, he tortured himself every single day. If only he had driven over to collect Marsha first thing on that Saturday morning when she went missing. He would never forgive himself.

***

Miss Moorcroft had been deeply affected by Bert Humble's untimely death, Marsha's disappearance, and the tragic news of the discovery of her friend's rings. She could hardly believe it.

For the past God knows how many years, she had sat alone in her cottage with a microwavable turkey dinner on her lap in front of the TV, with only Her Majesty the Queen for company at three o'clock sharp, every single Christmas Day, without fail. This year, there would be no speech from Her Majesty Queen Elizabeth II. Instead, her son and heir, King Charles would keep up the tradition. And so it was that Miss Moorcroft had broken with her tradition, and accepted Kate's kind offer of Christmas lunch with her and her family, which she had thoroughly enjoyed. Without even realising it, she had been very glad of the company.

***

Kate Bursford had had a tough year, losing her husband and fearing for her and the boys' safety from retribution by Billie Tidmarsh. After his arrest, she was able to convince Zelda that they were no longer in danger. She had a new life to look forward to with Zelda and her two boys, who were getting taller every day.

***

Lucy Holden was thriving at Ashcroft's and had been promoted to Senior Sales Negotiator. She had been invited out to Dubai by her friend Sapphire, who had relocated there and opened her own Real Estate business.

Occasionally, she met her Fedora man for coffee at The Swan.

***

Billie Tidmarsh was serving a life sentence for people trafficking, organ harvesting, and murder. He rigorously denied the murder of Marsha Boden. He kept saying that he had been framed, but his claim fell on deaf ears.

***

Jasper pined for Marsha and was never the same after the day that she disappeared.

***

Ann Jones decided not to move to Wales with her husband but to stay in Little Twichen. She continued to work at Boden's. The discrepancy she had found in the office was due to her registering the death of the one-hun-dred-and-two-year-old lady from the care home, the one that Bryan had driven to the cemetery, in the wrong county. Guy had eventually spotted it. She continued to cream off money from the Golden Leaves plans.

***

Guy Boden hated going out for Christmas lunch. Marsha had always prepared a traditional roast turkey dinner with all the trimmings, while Christmas music blared out all over the house, and the boys ran amok with whatever new toy was in vogue that particular year. He remembered one year he had queued for hours outside ToysRus for Buzz Lightyear after the release of Toy Story, but when he finally got inside, the shelves had been picked clean. Eventually, after driving hundreds of miles, he had managed to track one down, which, inevitably, caused a near riot on Christmas morning.

***

The year 2022 had, in her late Majesty's words, been truly annus horribilis. There would be no Christmas frivolities for Guy. He had lost his wife but because there was nobody, he had no closure. He would have been a tormented soul if it were not for the love of a good woman. Ann Jones had been a brick. Despite his business dwindling and struggling, she had stood by him. They were going to move in together. Her husband had sold the business and moved back home to his beloved Wales.

Rumours surfaced from time to time around Little Twichen about Marsha's disappearance, with everybody having their own theory about what had happened. Some say that the police should have exhumed more bodies in the local cemetery because that's where her husband had buried her. Even though Billie Tidmarsh had been jailed for her murder, some still believed that it was her husband who killed her.

Marsha Boden's body lay undiscovered, buried deep beneath the earth, in the shadow of the Shropshire hills. A blackbird, sitting on the branch of a nearby tree, broke into a beautiful, melodious song. A chorus of other garden birds joined in, warbling, cheeping, and chirping. The church clock chimed out on the hour, every hour, as Little Twichen watched over her.

ACKNOWLEDGEMENTS

I would like to thank Lauren Ilbury at RomaReads Publishing for believing in me and for making my dream come true. I will be forever grateful. She has also been a wonderfully supportive editor and I could not have wished for a better foray into the world of traditional publishing. I would like to thank Helga Jensen, my great author friend, for her guidance, support, and encouragement. Martin Garlick, thank you for allowing me to pester you while away on holiday for your medical knowledge, and thanks to Carrie Garlick for her insight into policing procedures when a person goes missing. I would like to thank my friends, too numerous to mention, for their kindness and for listening. You all said that you knew the day would come when I would publish a novel. Well, my friends, this is that day! I would also like to thank my husband, Adrian, for his unwavering patience and support. To my beautiful daughter, Rachel, to whom I have dedicated this book, which I hope will be the first of many. You always believed in me and when I doubted myself, you were there, metaphorically waving a finger at me to dispel any self-doubt. Thank you from the bottom of my heart, and for being the best daughter that any mother could ever wish for. Finally, and most importantly, thank you to you, my readers without whom this work would not be possible. I hope you enjoyed this book and if you did, don't forget to leave a review! Thank you.